D0423380

# A STRANGER THING

Also by Martin Leicht and Isla Neal

*Mothership*

BOOK TWO OF THE EVER-
EXPANDING UNIVERSE

# A Stranger Thing

MARTIN
LEICHT
& ISLA
NEAL

SIMON & SCHUSTER BFYR

New York  London  Toronto  Sydney  New Delhi

An imprint of Simon & Schuster Children's Publishing Division
1230 Avenue of the Americas, New York, New York 10020

This book is a work of fiction. Any references to historical events, real people, or real places are used fictitiously. Other names, characters, places, and events are products of the author's imagination, and any resemblance to actual events or places or persons, living or dead, is entirely coincidental.

SIMON & SCHUSTER BFYR is a trademark of Simon & Schuster, Inc.
For information about special discounts for bulk purchases, please contact
Simon & Schuster Special Sales at 1-866-506-1949 or
business@simonandschuster.com.
The Simon & Schuster Speakers Bureau can bring authors to your live event. For
more information or to book an event, contact the Simon & Schuster Speakers
Bureau at 1-866-248-3049 or visit our website at www.simonspeakers.com.
Jacket design by Lizzy Bromley
Interior design by Hilary Zarycky
The text for this book is set in Electra.
Manufactured in the United States of America
2 4 6 8 10 9 7 5 3 1
Library of Congress Cataloging-in-Publication Data
Leicht, Martin.
A stranger thing / Martin Leicht and Isla Neal. — First edition.
pages cm. — (The ever-expanding universe ; [2])
Summary: "Elvie Nara is sequestered away by the Almiri after her baby is
born and it is not what was expected"—Provided by publisher.
ISBN 978-1-4424-2963-5 (hardback) — ISBN 978-1-4424-2965-9 (eBook)
[1. Human-alien encounters—Fiction. 2. Babies—Fiction. 3. War—Fiction.
4. Antarctica—Fiction. 5. Science fiction.] I. Neal, Isla. II. Title.
PZ7.L53283Str 2013
[Fic]—dc23
2013025253

*To Ryan and Jenn*
*and Alexander,*
*their new little stranger*
—I. N.

*To my sister, Felicia,*
*who has always been a little stranger*
—M. L.

*What a strange thing is man? and what a stranger*
*Is woman!*

—Lord Byron, "Don Juan," canto 9

# Chapter One

# IN WHICH OUR HEROINE IS LICKED BY A BEAR

"Everything's okay, Elvs. Seriously, like, no worries."

Easy enough for Cole to say—he didn't just push a *person the size of a watermelon* out of his private parts. Nor does he currently find himself under the piercing gaze of several suddenly constipated-looking Alien McHotHotts.

Now, I know I was preoccupied and everything, but I am *certain* that there were only five people in the room as I grunted, strained, and (let's be perfectly frank here) farted the Goober out of my womb and into the world. Besides me, there was Cole (my baby daddy), Dad (my dad), Ducky (world's best bestie), and one smokin' Almiri doctor. And baby makes six. Or so I thought. Now I realize that several others were either waiting in the wings the entire time, or standing elsewhere out of sight. And now that my little bundle of joy is lying in my arms, they have all stepped forward, each one looking grimmer than the last.

"It's female?" one of the dudes asks the doc gravely.

The doctor nods, stunned. And everybody in the room—even my own father—is staring at me and my newborn like we just snuck a jumbo-size combo meal past the ticket guy into the movie theater.

"I'm confused," Ducky says, scratching his head. "I thought Almiri were always male."

"I was under a similar impression, Donald," my father says beside him. "Fascinating."

Maybe "fascinating" isn't the word *I* would use, but yeah, I'm a little perplexed myself. From everything Cole's told me about his race (or species, or whatever you want to call an extraterrestrial group that traveled to Earth thousands of years ago to use human women as hosts for their offspring), I took it as fact that the Almiri only have one gender—a gender that requires a dongle. And yet . . . looking down at the gooey infant in my arms, it's hard to argue that she most definitely has a full array of girl parts.

"Take it," one of the Almiri snaps. "And secure the host and the father for questioning."

No sooner are the words out of his mouth than all of the Almiri burst into a flurry of panicky action. One of the fellows standing in my peripheral vision rushes forward and snatches the Baby-Formerly-Known-as-Goober away from me before I can even react.

"Hey!" I shout, reaching clumsily to grab my baby back, but the thief is already moving toward the exit. Another Almiri falls into step behind him.

"What do you think you're doing?" I hear Cole demand.

*"Ibrida,"* the baby-napper says . . . to which Cole (who, I should mention, can barely speak English most days, let alone whatever language *that* was) responds with a completely blank stare. "It's a mule," the guy says—as though that clarifies anything. His voice is even but strained. "Did you know about this?"

"Know about what?" Cole asks. "What are you talking about?"

"What's going—ahhh!" I turn at the sudden sharp pain and see the doctor remove the syringe from my arm. "No, please, I . . . ," I begin, but words are failing me. *They have my baby. They took my baby.*

I turn my head—which, holy *crap*, just got forty pounds heavier on my neck—to see if I can catch another glimpse of my daughter. Instead, I see only the second Almiri, who turns to Cole with a disgusted look on his face. "You just can't help finding shit to step in, can you, Archer?"

"I don't even . . . Hey, come back here with my kid!"

That's when whatever night-night cocktail the doc has fed me begins to set in, so the Almiri at the door blocking Cole's path and clasping him by the arms, trying to immobilize him, goes kinda fuzzy. Little swirlies dance in my field of vision, mixing in with the sight of Cole head-butting his restrainer—but *that* can't be right, I think. The guy was his friend just moments ago, when they arrested the Jin'Kai heavies who chased us here in the first place. I'm pretty sure the head-buttee crashes to the floor, but there's three more of him who take his place. And then I *know* the happy mommy juice is really starting to get to me, because I see two more Almiri move in beside Dad and

Ducky, and calmly but forcibly escort them out of the room. And that shit just doesn't make any sense.

"It's all right, Elvie!" I hear Cole call, his voice growing fainter. "Don't worry about anything! I'm here!"

The rest is all purple unicorns and gold stars singing show tunes, until everything goes black.

The first thing I wonder, as I come to, is whether or not the handcuffs shackling me to the hospital bed will be covered by my health insurance. My *second* thought, obviously, is what the flip am I doing handcuffed to a hospital bed? And where in the hell am I? This certainly doesn't look like a recovery room at Lankenau Medical Center.

The haze quickly lifts, and I shuffle through a few blurry memories, mostly overheard snippets of conversation.

". . . did we have any indication . . . ?"

". . . Archer doesn't seem to have a clue . . ."

". . . never met a bigger numbskull . . ."

". . . wreck was not salvageable . . ."

". . . decrypted full records from the ship . . ."

". . . last time this happened . . ."

". . . what Byron has to say when we get there . . ."

". . . have you seen my lip balm . . . ?"

None of which is helping me solve Elvie Nara and the Case of the Mystery Room. There are no monitors, nursebots, or any other medical gear keeping track of vitals or anything like that. As far as I can tell, the room consists of four white walls, a door, and a bed.

And me, of course.

"Hello?" I call out. There is no response for, like, a while, and I start to worry that I'm in some sort of soundproof room, or that maybe I'm just hallucinating the whole weird scene. Creepy dead silence, that's all I get. But right when I'm really about to panic, the door slides open and in walks the same doctor from the delivery room, carrying a slender lap-pad and a scowl.

"Hey, are you my OB/GYN?" He scrolls through something on his lap-pad and does not respond. "What's with the cuffs?" I try again. "You guys afraid that I'll Hulk out on you?" I'm trying to play it light, hoping my gay spirits will take the edge off the fact that they're treating me like a Jin'Kai POW, instead of, you know, their old pal Elvie. But the doc doesn't seem to want to play along. "How long have I been here?" By the way my stomach's growling I'm guessing it's been at least a day, if not longer.

At last the doc looks up. "You're feeling normal? No discomfort or odd sensations?"

"I'm hungry." Understatement of the millennium. "Where is every—"

"I'll see about getting you some food. In the meantime, Alan here is going to take you upstairs for a little while."

Before I can ask if Alan is the doc's imaginary six-foot white rabbit, the dude comes walking through the door.

Most of the Almiri are young-looking, but this guy's stiff demeanor makes him look even younger, like he's fresh out of the Almiri Acadamy for Impregnating Unsuspecting Earth Girls. He's bland as toast, too. Standard-issue haircut, no scars or wacky tattoos to help place him in a lineup. As Ducky might put it, if Alan were on *Star Trek*, he'd be wearing a red shirt and an expiration date.

Alan glances at me. "Uh, what am I supposed to do, wheel her?" he asks.

"She can walk," the doc replies. "We can undo the cuffs for now, I think."

The doc strolls over and jabs a code into the handcuffs, quickly ridding me of my shackles. I rub my wrists like they're terribly sore, but it's mainly just an effort to garner a smidgen of sympathy.

My captors do not seem to notice.

"Hey, guys?" I say as they help me to my feet. "Two questions for you. First, where's my baby? And second, could I get something to wear besides this gown? My butt's, like, flapping in the wind."

"There's a robe in the closet," the doc replies. And with that, he walks out the door, leaving me alone with Alan.

"He didn't answer my first question," I say. "That was kind of the important one."

"Come on," Alan says, clearly anxious to be rid of me. "Byron's waiting."

I sit quietly in the middle of the room where Alan has deposited me, tugging nervously at the trim of my not-quite-long-enough terrycloth robe. It solves the butt-on-display-to-the-world problem I was having, but I'm still flaunting enough leg to make a burlesque dancer blush. If I was feeling particularly whimsical, I might enjoy conjuring the image of the Almiri prancing around in these robes that, at best, are going to cover them to mid-thigh.

I can hear several voices coming through the adjoining side door keep rising and falling—some sort of group powwow. The volume occasionally reaches a decibel that indicates that nobody inside is feeling very polite.

Alan didn't leave anyone to guard me while I wait. Well, I should say, he didn't leave any *person*. I am currently surrounded by a literal menagerie of assorted animals. And we're not just talking goldfish and kittens and parakeets, your typical household pets. Oh no. There are two large flamingos crowding me on the faux leather chair that's busy sticking to my thighs. Seated across from me on the ornate stone desk are the three smallest monkeys I've ever seen, fighting over a banana that's bigger than they are. Behind me, two foxes and a badger are wrestling with one another, and a peacock fans its feathers in a defensive stance as it tries to convince the meerkat to look elsewhere for a playmate.

And then, of course, there's the bear.

It's probably not a real big one, by bear standards, but honestly, when you're sitting three feet away from a bear—any bear—it seems like the most gigundous thing in the entire universe. This particular *Ursus whateverus* has been blocking the main doorway, licking its own cinnamon fur, for the past ten minutes, oblivious to anything else in the room.

I look away (because everyone knows it's rude to stare at animals that can eat you) and find myself studying an oddly familiar oil painting hanging over the mantel of the fireplace. I know I've seen the thing before somewhere, but I can't place it. Old-school mustachioed dude with a chin dimple, sporting a seriously ugly orange-and-green headscarf.

Lots of terrible thoughts are running through my mind at the moment, and only a few of them are bear-related. Obviously, my Almiri hosts are not quite as benevolent as they once appeared. The fact that my baby turned out to be a girl must either have them confused, scared, or both. They've done something with the baby, something with Cole, something with my dad and Ducky. And they're clearly planning something for *me*. A sane person would sit quietly and pray to come out of this whole situation in one piece.

I have never been accused of being a particularly sane person.

I rise to my feet with thoughts of bursting into the side room, all bravado and bluster, and shouting that I'm tired of being shoved around by different factions of extraterrestrials who think they're entitled to mess with my reproductive organs, and that I'm sick of waiting in this zoo, and if they're going to interrogate me or torture me or whatever, could they please just get it over with already? But I don't get that far, because that's when Cinnamon finally realizes I'm in the room. He flops forward onto all fours with a harrumph and plods toward me.

"Okay, okay!" I shout. My mind is racing. Which are the sorts of bears you're supposed to try to scare off, and which are the ones you're supposed to play dead with? Shit. "I'm sitting," I tell it, more gently. And I plop back down on the chair. "See how well I'm sitting? Like nobody's business. So heel. Or mush. Or . . . go away."

Cinnamon does not go away. He shuffles over to me, and I realize with a great amount of uneasiness that even on all fours he's looking *down* on me. He starts nuzzling my shoulder, and his head is so huge that he practically pushes me off the chair into a pile of something one of the birds has left behind. His fur is rough and scratchy, prickling my neck. Less "teddy bear" and more "roadhouse creeper." I want to grab the thing's jumbo noggin and shove him away, but I have this overwhelming desire to keep all my limbs attached to my body, so I just grip the edge of the seat until my fingers turn white, and try to look nonchalant. Like I get nuzzled by bears all the time.

"I'm just sitting," I mutter. Cinnamon continues to get his nuzzle on. The giant furball is now licking my neck and the side of my face, long leathery slurps that leave trails of sticky bear saliva on my skin. "Not going to let a big-ass bear licking half my face off get in the way of a good sit," I squeak out in between slurps. "Why don't you try sitting too?"

The door to the side room opens up, and the muffled voices from within are suddenly clear.

"You cannot expect us to go along with this," comes a strident voice. It's angry. Pissed, even. "It goes against every protocol!"

Then I hear another voice, calmer and steadier than the rest.

"I've made my decision, gentlemen." I look past the furball assaulting my personal space to see a tall, slender figure in a red jacket standing with his back to me in the doorway. "I do not make it lightly, nor should you take it as a point of debate."

That's when another angry voice chimes in. "The Council will never stand for such a blatant disregard for procedure!"

The figure in the doorway shifts casually. "The Council

will have their say, of course. But so long as I'm the commander of this station, I will make the call."

"But—"

"Thank you, gentlemen, that will be all for now," the man in the doorway interrupts. "Alan, please see that the arrangements are being made. There's a good lad." And with that, he turns and steps inside to join me, closing the door behind him. And the moment he enters the room, he owns it.

Byron.

That's what the Almiri call him. Their leader. I've seen him before, of course—on the communication view screen back on the *Echidna*, when we were trying to avoid being blown to smithereens. But I've seen him elsewhere, too. *East of Eden. Giant. Rebel Without a Cause.* No matter what the leader of this group of parasitic alien life-forms chooses to call himself, I will always think of him as James Dean, my mother's favorite 1950s flat-pic dreamboat.

"Drusilla!" he booms to the gargantuan mound of fluff that's currently using my face as a tasting menu. "Get down off of Elvie, please. That's a good girl." And just like that, the licking stops. Drusilla backs away from me, giving me one last sneeze as a parting gift before retreating to her master.

I've got to say the guy looks pretty good for a dude who's supposedly been dead for 120 years. He pets Drusilla on the head as he makes his way over to his desk. He's followed by two dogs, a black-and-white long-haired Newfoundland and a large husky. Drusilla grumbles at the dogs as they pass, and the husky scurries away, tail between its legs. The Newfoundland, though, despite weighing approximately as much as one bear poop, defiantly nips at Drusilla before wandering right up to me and putting his head in my lap.

"Boatswain likes you," Byron says as he flops down in his big swivel chair. "That's a good sign. Poor Thunder here"—he rubs the timid husky under the chin—"has always been a little shier with new people. Haven't you, girl?"

I scratch Boatswain behind the ear, because it seems like the most normal thing I can do. Bears, peacocks, *James Dean talking to me about his pets*—those are the things that I'm not quite ready to process yet. "Dogs seem to have a thing for me," I say, kneading the bed of Boatswain's floppy ears a little harder, until he lets out a satisfied whine.

"Amazing creatures, aren't they?" Byron replies, putting his feet up on the desk. He looks very much like he did when he was James Dean in *Rebel Without a Cause*, perhaps a bit older but not by much. He's even wearing a red windbreaker and some antique-looking jeans, which should seem ridiculous and sad, but somehow he pulls it off effortlessly. Utterly assured of himself, cool, and in charge of the whole room without even trying—that's James Dean, all right. *"The poor dog,"* he goes on, leaning back in his chair with his eyes closed, as though reciting words he's said many times before. *"In life the firmest friend, the first to welcome, foremost to defend."*

"Uh," I say. "Yeah. Sure."

Byron's eyes pop open, and he smiles warmly. "It's nice to meet you at last, Elvie Nara." He seems awfully friendly for someone who's kidnapped me and taken my newborn child. "I've heard only good things."

I nod and clear my throat. "Look," I start, as much of an edge to my voice as I dare use with a guy who has a pet bear, "you're a very busy alien, I'm sure." His smile shifts sideways a little, amused. "So I'm not going to waste your time with the totally appropriate amount of indignation that I should feel right now."

"That's awfully understanding of you."

I fold my arms across my chest, ignoring Boatswain's whines for more scratching. "Why don't you just cut to the chase and tell me what the hell is going on?"

Byron's eyes brighten, like I just complimented his haircut. I cannot detect even an ounce of the cruelty that someone like, say, Dr. Marsden had when he had me at gunpoint back on the *Echidna*. By contrast, this Byron guy doesn't seem to find the whole situation all that serious. Like hospital bed abductions are as common as artificial grass.

"Elvie, everything's going to be fine, don't worry. You haven't done anything wrong. Your baby is in perfect health, and your father and friend are safe and in our care."

It's his casual tone that's more disconcerting to me than anything else. I was kind of expecting a villainous speech. Boatswain starts licking the sweat from my palm. As interrogations go, I have to admit, this is all pretty chill. Everything, as Byron says, seems to be going fine.

"What was all that shouting about? Me?"

Byron waves me off dismissively. "Don't worry about all that. Some of the lads have their knickers in a bunch over this whole Ares mess."

"Ares?" I ask, confused. "The Ares Project?" The Ares Project is the multitrillion-dollar government program whose purpose is the wide-scale terraforming of the surface of Mars for human habitation, the first such attempt of its kind. The idea that the Almiri are behind it in some way probably shouldn't shock me as much as it does—since I'm well aware of how technologically advanced they are, and how they've made a habit of getting their hands into every major scientific break-through of the past several thousand years. It's more of the fact that Byron's dropping the information so nonchalantly that has me baffled. After all, aren't I some sort of prisoner here?

"A bit of an issue with some cyberterrorism, nothing that should slow matters down terribly, but enough of a breach that some folks are nervous." Byron leans forward in his chair. "Cole told me how keen you were on being a part of the proj-ect someday. You don't know how happy that would make—"

"Cole," I say. "What have you done with Cole?"

Byron's face turns slightly more serious, but it's undercut by his tickling one of the miniature monkeys with his index finger. Seriously, the thing is the size of a Ping-Pong ball.

"Cole has broken our cardinal law," he says simply, "and will have to be dealt with accordingly."

I can feel the color leave my face. "What do you mean, 'dealt with'?"

"Don't worry. It's not—"

"Don't *worry*?" I screech out. He might as well tell me not to blink. "Don't WORRY?" Drusilla lurches to her feet at my sudden outcry, like there's some threat she needs to deal with, but one low growl from Boatswain and she backs off. "Please don't hurt him." My voice is shaky, and I am *this close* to crying, but I use every ounce of strength to hold it together. Boatswain drops his head into my lap.

Again, Byron's pretty chillaxed about the whole scene. "Ah," he says calmly. "The drama of young love." And he closes his eyes once more. *"I tell thee, minstrel, I must weep, or else this heavy heart will burst; for it hath been by sorrow nursed, and ached in sleepless silence."* He opens his eyes once more and gives me a bittersweet smile.

"Cole told me all about your Code, or whatever," I say, petting Boatswain with both hands in an effort to calm myself. "I know that what he did was bad. I mean, I know *you guys* think it was bad." Cole was not supposed to sleep with me. The Almiri have superstrict rules about which human ladies are meant to be knocked up and how frequently an Almiri can do the deed, in order to avoid overpopulation and the eventual destruction of both our species, since Almiri pregnancies lead to sterility in their human hosts. Cole was originally sent to Ardmore, PA, to knock up übercheerleader-mega-skank Britta McVicker, but he disobeyed orders because, as he put it, he "fell for me."

Also, he's sort of a chromer.

"But it wasn't his fault," I go on. "I, like, totally seduced him. He tried to resist, but . . . what's going to happen to him?" I whisper around the lump forming in my throat.

"You've learned quite a bit about us the past few weeks, Elvie," Byron says. And perhaps I'm misreading things, but there seems to be some sympathy in his voice. "And seeing that this is the case, I hope that you can appreciate the reason for the Code, and why our adherence to it is so important. I can't overemphasize what a big deal it is." The monkey lets out a miniature cheep of insistence until Byron returns to tickling him. "Like, humongous big."

"But Cole didn't *mean*—"

Byron cuts me off. "I've tried to shield Cole from repercussions with regards to your situation, as best I could. It was no easy task, mind you. The fact that Cole violated protocol and had relations with a second host—someone who clearly had not been vetted for hosting—was not only foolish but dangerous. For both our species." He clears his throat. "However, in light of the heroism Cole displayed on the *Echidna*, I felt compelled to petition for some degree of leniency for the boy. It was not the most popular sentiment, I can assure you, but I was able to arrange a sort of . . . tenuous probation for young Mr. Archer. Which might have been the end of it, were it not for his unfortunate behavior at the hospital. At this point, my hands are tied. One simply does not head-butt a superior and walk away, even under the cheeriest of circumstances."

So Cole *did* head-butt that dude. At least I wasn't hallucinating.

Byron shakes his head in a mannered gesture of regret. "He will be punished, Elvie, but I swear on my life, he will not be harmed."

"Oh, well, if you swear on your *life*," I reply. Still, I am relieved by the news. But . . . "That doesn't explain why you've taken me or my dad. Or Ducky. And where is my baby girl?" I shove Boatswain away, suddenly very frustrated. The dog whines piteously.

Byron stands up, and Boatswain and Thunder snap to attention and move into flanking position beside him as he walks to the front of the desk. He sits on the edge and looks down on me, much like a hip teacher from a bad sitcom about to dole out "serious life lessons." Byron temples his fingers in front of his mouth and considers me with an intense gaze.

"Elvie, do you know how incredible your baby is?" he begins. "I mean, all babies are incredible. Life, I mean, wow, right? Whether it's human or Almiri or, I dunno, whales . . . it's just a miracle. But *your* baby . . . she's even more special."

"Because she's a chick," I say.

"Because she's a chick," he confirms. "Almiri do not have baby girls." He reaches across his desk for a round red tin and pops open the top. "Biscuit?"

I seem to have lost my appetite. "So, my daughter's, like, a miracle squared?"

Byron sets the tin on the desk and rests one hand on each of the heads of his two dogs. It's a measured and self-conscious pose. I can totally picture him practicing in front of the mirror for dramatic situations just like this. Then he lapses into that annoying closed-eye reciting thing again. *"What a whirlwind is her head, and what a whirlpool full of depth and danger is all the rest about her."* He opens his eyes again. "No," he says, and the ice that's suddenly in his voice startles me a bit. "Not a miracle. On the contrary, the child is a great danger."

"A danger?" I ask, baffled. "To who?"

"All of us," Byron says. And just as quickly he snaps back into levity. "Seriously, you should try one of these biscuits." He plucks one from the tin. "They're delish."

I'm not even sure I manage to shake my head. *Danger-ous?* How can one baby girl be a danger to anyone, let alone a guy who's well over a hundred years old and has two Academy Award nominations on his résumé?

"What's an *ibrida*?" I ask. Byron chokes on his biscuit, trying his best to hide a double take.

"Where'd you hear that word?" he asks pointedly.

"At the hospital, when your goons decided to go all batshit crazy on me."

Byron tries to smile casually. "That's not really important at the moment," he says, and it's the first time I don't buy the acting job. His eyes shift to the biscuit tin for a split second, before he looks back up at me. "I know you are somewhat aware of the history of the Almiri, Elvie, but let me explain it to you a little more fully, so that you'll understand." He nudges Thunder's nose away from the biscuit tin. "We came to the Earth nearly five thousand years ago. Humans were one of six viable host species in the entire galaxy, and they were remarkable creatures. We sought to make them more remarkable. You are familiar, to some extent, with Greek mythology?"

"Sure," I say, bracing myself for yet another history lesson. The Almiri seem to love them. "Zeus, Athena, all that crap."

"Exactly," Byron says. "Those were us."

"Excuse me?" I say, eyebrows up. "Sorry, but not for one second do I believe that you guys are *gods*."

"No, of course not," Byron replies. "You misunderstood my meaning." Beside him, Boatswain manages to sneak a biscuit from the tin unnoticed, but I decide to let this go unmentioned. "When we first arrived on Earth, we couldn't blend in as we do now, so of course our appearance was strange to humans. They had stories of deities already in their society, and whenever anyone happened to spy one of us, they simply slotted us into those appointed roles. Burning bushes, talking clouds, showers of gold, these were ways for them to describe what was beyond their understanding. Thunder, no. You *just* ate." Thunder glares at Boatswain, who's licking the crumbs stealthily off his doggy gums. "Soon," Byron continues, oblivious, "we Almiri had our first children, and they appeared to be human. Their abilities, however, made them stand out."

"Lemme guess," I interject. I'm wondering when this is going to lead to a smidgen of information about my baby. About my dad and Ducky. About Cole. "Achilles, Hercules, Perseus . . ."

"They were the first Earthborn Almiri," Byron confirms. *"Thy Godlike crime was to be kind, to render with thy precepts less the sum of human wretchedness, and strengthen Man with his own mind."* He's doing that closed-eye thing again. Boatswain sneaks another cookie. I clear my throat, and Byron's eyes fly open. "Where was I? Oh yes. Over time, successive generations appeared as human, and it became easier and easier to simply disappear into human society."

"This is all fascinating, really," I lie. "But can we skip along? You were explaining how my baby was going to bring about the apocalypse."

Byron smiles again and starts pacing around the room. The dogs follow obediently at his heels, with the husky staying as far from the bear as possible. On the wall next to the oil painting of the dude in the headscarf is one of Boatswain, though the picture appears to be very, very old, and the pooch couldn't be more than six. Byron considers it for a moment in silence, then turns back to me.

"Elvie, we have always been a very small, discreet society. We took to heart the mistakes of our ancestors, and were careful to never endanger mankind with reckless propagation. Basically, we tried not to be dicks about it. And along the way, we've pushed the humans toward advances that would have taken eons for them to come up with on their own. I mean, take jazzercise."

"My apocalypse baby," I remind him.

"We need human females to breed, Elvie. We have no alternative. Without you there would be no Almiri. Human female, Almiri baby. That's the way it's always been. Then suddenly you come along, and young Mr. Archer . . . and somehow your child is not Almiri."

"What do you mean she's not an Almiri?" I say. "Sure, she's an anomaly, I get that. But she's Cole's kid. I'm not some wanton slut-bag, if that's what you're imply—"

"The child is *not* Almiri," Byron repeats. "The child—your child, Archer's child—is somehow something else. An 'anomaly,' as you put it. But not a benign one. If left unchecked, this anomaly could be the end of the Almiri . . . and of humans, too."

An icy ball is beginning to form in my stomach. "What are you going to do to my baby?" I ask slowly.

Byron examines me curiously, as if he's honest-to-goodness confused, before realization breaks across his face. "Oh, poor child, what monsters we must seem right now! As I said, nothing that is happening is your fault, nor your child's. We will not harm either of you, I promise."

"So, then what? We're free to go?"

He looks at me sadly. And maybe I'm just overreading his

superdramatic facial expressions, but I swear I see something there. Something that tells me it pains him, deeply and personally, to say what he's about to. "The situation is not your fault, but it is still the situation at hand. I'm afraid we're going to have to . . . contain the threat."

I shift uneasily in my chair. "And here I thought the only threat was the Jin'Kai."

Byron reaches for the tin again, then thinks better of it. Suddenly he seems to be avoiding my gaze. "Keeping you out of their hands is paramount as well. You and your child will be sent to a secure facility. For the time being. Until we can straighten this whole mess out."

"What about Dad? Ducky?" I ask, rising to my feet. Drusilla rises as well, but this time I don't back down. Being bear food is suddenly the *least* freaky thing I'm facing.

"We wouldn't want to risk your father and friend falling into Jin'Kai hands either. So they will accompany you." He's trying to make this sound like some sort of temporary vacation or something, but I'm getting the strong vibe that wherever he's sending us, it's not going to be pleasant.

"So where is this Almiri Alcatraz you're shipping me off to?" I ask. "Outer space again?"

"I think you've had enough adventures out there for a while, don't you?" he says, jovial once more. "No, you'll be stationed at a secret facility near Cape Crozier."

It's not a place on the planet most people would probably know. But I happen to have a deceased mother with a passion for travel and a detailed book of maps.

"*ANTARCTICA?*" I screech. What. Da. Fuh.

"The camp is home to a number of Almiri. A sort of . . . 'time-out' zone for brothers who have broken the Code."

I drop my head so that my chin is practically digging into my chest, but my glower shoots directly into Byron's pretty eyes.

"And you really think the safest place you could put me is in the middle of the frozen tundra with a whole bunch of superbuff aliens who *you already know can't keep it in their pants?*" I ask in disbelief.

"Come now, Elvie." Byron scrunches up his face and gives me a quick headshake, as if I have a filthy mind for even thinking what I'm thinking. He walks back over to his desk and hits a button on his intercom. A voice crackles in response.

"*Yes?*"

"We're just about finished in here," Byron replies. He takes his hand off the intercom.

"Elvie, I realize that right now I must seem like a terrible villain—well, let's be honest—an asshole. I'm sure I can't blame you for thinking as much. Hopefully, someday sooner than later, you will understand that I have no choice. For the time being, Cape Crozier is our only option, however imperfect."

The main door slides open, and my new buddy Alan is on the other side. Byron leans in to me and whispers so that Alan can't hear. "Just remember that I won't stop trying to help you, dearheart." I flinch at the sound of the pet name that I've only ever heard my father call me.

Just how much does this guy actually know about us, anyway?

"Are the preparations made?" Byron asks Alan.

Alan, already at attention in the doorway, stiffens at his commander's voice. "Nearly, sir, another hour at most," he says.

"Please lead Miss Nara to the holding area, until then," Byron says. "And for God's sake, get the girl some clothes."

I walk down the long, sterile corridor with Alan beside me, my slippers sliding across the slick linoleum floor. The rooms along the corridor do not have normal doors. Rather, the doors are thick, heavy, and mechanized, like the kind you might find in a factory, or a cargo ship.

Or a prison.

"How long are you going to 'hold' me here before I get started on that all-expenses-paid trip to the Earth's rectum?" I ask Alan.

"Not long, Miss," Alan says, and I can't tell if he's being polite or condescending.

Each door has a small, circular window about the size of a dinner plate. As we pass by one such window, I think I catch a shadow standing at the door, peering out at me, but in a flash the shadow disappears.

"Hey, what's that?" I wonder, pausing. I try to look inside, but whatever was just there has disappeared. Alan takes my arm and gives it a slight tug, and my feet slide away from the door.

"This way, Miss," Alan says.

I pull against Alan's grip to crane my neck and look inside. I make out a tall, willowy figure and a very familiar-looking long blond ponytail.

"But—"

"*This* way, now."

If I didn't know any better, I'd swear that the Almiri were keeping my arch-nemesis, Britta McVicker, under lock and key.

But no, I think. That wouldn't make any sense.

We come to the final door along the corridor, and Alan slides a card over the side sensor. Immediately the locking mechanism springs to life and the door slides open. The inside of the room is even more drab than the one I woke up in. It's gray, with nothing but a couch built into two sides of the wall. Like a karaoke room without the karaoke.

I step inside, and without another word, Alan closes the door behind me. My options are pretty much stand or sit, so after a few moments of pacing, I decide to sit.

I'm not sure how long I'm sitting there—five minutes? ten?—when I hear the door sensor beep and the locking mechanism disengage. The door slides open, and in steps Byron, carrying something in his arms.

"I thought you might want a little company," he says. I look down at the bundle he's balancing so delicately in the crook of his elbow.

He is cradling my baby.

The Goober is tiny and pink and wrinkly, cooing softly as Byron bobs her gently up and down.

"We've made arrangements for your journey," he tells me as he nears with my daughter. "You'll leave on the *Fountain*. It will only take a few hours to get to the continent, although from there I'm afraid you'll have to travel by dogsled. Technology is great, but it can't trump Mother Nature.

Still, it's a relatively easy journey, at least to the base."

But I'm hardly listening. In the instant he hands me the Goober, the whole world seems to drop away.

I am a mother.

This wrinkled pink raisin is my daughter.

She finally opens her eyes, and blinks up at me, and that's when I start to cry. Huge, blubbering sobs. Worse than when Christian was killed off in season three of *Martian Law*.

Byron takes in the scene quietly. Almost as if he were ashamed. I can only hope.

"I never did ask," he asks softly. "What are you going to name her?"

I rub my daughter's left cheek, where, curiously, her constellation of freckles seems ten times lighter than the last time I saw her. "Olivia," I say through my sobs. I hold her close, feeling the rise and fall of her perfect, tiny breaths. "After my mother. Her name is Olivia."

# Chapter Two

# IN WHICH DUCKY BARFS FOR HOURS

Grown men—even ones who, like my father, have difficult jobs to which they wear a suit and tie every day, and know how to use big words like "hypnagogic" in a sentence, and have even, perhaps, raised children of their own—might be forgiven for breaking down and weeping at the sight of their brand-new grandbaby, cradled in a daughter's arms. You might even *expect* that such an event would cause tears—giddiness, even. Perhaps the grandfather in question might go so far as to tuck his legs up underneath him in his chair and clap his hands together like a kindergartner who's imbibed too much orange drink.

My father is currently doing all of these things. But it is not because of little baby Olivia. Oh, he likes her fine. He said she's "adorable," even, and "a miracle," and he did spend a good amount of time cuddling with her when we first got on the mag rail.

But the thing that's actually making my father squeal like a preteen who just got Hansel Wintergarden's autograph is, in fact, our means of transport.

"You'd never even suspect how fast we were moving if you didn't know it!" he gushes, pressing his nose against the window. "It's smoother than the SleekTransit mag line, by far. Such a marvel of engineering. Wouldn't you agree, Donald?"

Next to my father, Ducky has turned a shade of pea-soup green that is such an exact match to the train's upholstery that I could have sworn the designers used his face as a color swatch. "Yeah," he moans. "A marvel." The Duck, clearly, was not built for high-speed travel.

Neither, apparently, is little Olivia, who is enjoying the ride about as much as having knitting needles crammed into her ears. She's wailing a piercing wail, and doing the baby equivalent of the Electric Slide up and down my chest.

"I think we're going to be docking with the space elevator soon," my dad gushes on. "Oh, wait until you see it, Elvie. Did I already mention it's a marvel? A *marvel*! And to call it the *Fountain*? Ha, let it not be said these Almiri gents lack for sense of humor."

"I think you're forgetting that this marvelous space elevator is taking us to a prison in Antarctica," I mutter, bobbing Olivia in a futile attempt to get her to quiet down. Seriously, the girl might not be an Almiri like her father, but she sure has superhuman pipes.

Dad must be able to tell that I'm feeling especially low at the moment, because he puts a hand on my shoulder. I stifle a tear that's threatening to break loose from the corner of my eye and smile a tight smile at him. He smiles back, and I wait for his words of comforting fatherly wisdom that will get me through this whole ordeal.

"Did I mention that the *Fountain* is the world's first completely free-navigating space elevator?" he says earnestly. "There's no Earthbound anchor needed at all!"

"Flipping fantastic," I say, turning away from my view of Ducky—who, at the mere mention of more travel, has begun hiccupping noxiously. "But, seriously, Dad, what's our escape plan? How are we getting out of here?" I know my father, and if Mr. Harry Nara doesn't have fifteen exit strategies in his pocket at this very moment, then I'll be a monkey's uncle. Or mother, at least. I shift the screeching Olivia away from my eardrums. Her wailing is reaching a decibel I thought only tweaked dolphins were capable of, which is not superconducive to the whole "crafting a master escape plan" thing. I try to run through a list of ideas—diversion? sabotage? fan dancing?—but my head is so fuzzy from Olivia's squealing that I'm practically useless.

"Dearheart . . . ," Dad says at last, offering me a kindly smile.

"I know you like me to figure these things out for myself, Dad," I reply, shifting Olivia's position again. If anything, she only gets louder. "But just at this moment I could really use some hel—"

My father lifts the baby from my arms. And, without another word, he nestles Olivia's tiny, slightly misshapen infant head securely in the crook of his left elbow. He shifts her up a few dozen centimeters, so they are nearly nose-to-nose. And then . . .

My father starts singing.

*"I love you, a bushel and a peck.*
*A bushel and a peck, and a hug around the neck.*
*A hug around the neck, and a barrel and a heap . . ."*

"Uh, Dad?" I say. This is for serious the weirdest escape plan I have ever seen. "You care to fill me in on what you're—"

"*Shhhh.*" Ducky cuts me off with a sweaty green hand on my arm. "I think it's working."

"What's work—" I start, before, duh, *lightbulb.*

My baby has stopped crying. With me she was all screams and flailing, but two seconds with my dad and she's calm as a cucumber. She's even *cooing.*

"How did you . . . ?"

But Dad only has eyes for the baby. "'*Cause I love you,*" he finishes, "*a bushel and a peck. You bet your pretty neck I do.*" He brushes a hand across her forehead, smoothing out her fuzzy baby hair. "Sleep tight, baby Olivia," he tells her. And sure enough—my mouth drops open—my little girl is asleep.

Funny how a person can look about nine thousand times cuter when she's not screaming bloody murder.

I raise my eyebrows at my dad, who rocks Olivia gently in his arms.

"Just like riding a bicycle," he replies with a genial smile. He looks up at me. "That song used to be your favorite."

At that moment, the train car door slides open, and in

walks Alan, a.k.a. the World's Most Forgettable Man. Alan's been nothing but a bundle of yawns this whole trip, just "Yes, ma'am"s and "No, sir"s, with hardly anything in between. Seriously, the guy practically has "Expendable" tattooed on his forehead.

"Alas! Alack! It's Alan!" I say, hoping for some sort of reaction.

"Yes, ma'am," he says, all formal-like. "It's almost time — "

Dad shoots upright in his chair, clutching the still-dozing Olivia. "Time to dock with the elevator, yes! I could tell by the shift in the frequency of the train's vibration. Elvie, just you *wait*. The whole thing will blow your mind, I promise."

"Golly gee," I mutter. "Why didn't I think to get myself shipped off to prison years ago?"

Alan tosses each of us a silvery-gray jumpsuit. There's even a bitty silvery papoose for Olivia.

"What are these for?" I ask. "Are we going to need to free-float to the station? 'Cause I've had some experience in zero-grav."

"The thermals are for when we arrive in Antarctica," he replies. "It's cold there." From anyone else, that would have sounded snarky, sarcastic, or just an attempt at deadpan humor. But God love 'im, Alan is one-hundred-percent not kidding.

"We're almost ready to transfer," he goes on. "You have five minutes." And with that, he leaves.

"Better get a move on!" Dad says, more overcome with excitement than I've seen him since the New England Crossword Puzzle Championships (where, he'd have you know, he placed thirty-seventh). He hands Olivia back to me so he can put on his thermal suit, but of course, the instant he does so, she wakes up and begins wailing again.

"It's so nice to be loved," I mutter, bouncing the baby in my arms in my best imitation of my Super Dad. But Olivia's having none of it. *"I love you,"* I squeak out, *"a bushel and a peck . . ."* I am growing more and more frantic with each second of Olivia's piercing distress signal. And it's not helping things any that Ducky's sitting on the other side of the train car with his fingers jammed in his ears, the pain written clearly across his face. "Is it my singing or Olivia's screaming?" I ask him.

He pulls a finger from his ear just long enough to answer. "Can't it be both?"

My father, of course, already has his arms and legs jammed into his thermal suit. "Don't worry, Dearheart," he tells me. "You'll get it. Being a parent takes practice." And with a quick peck to my forehead, he races down the hall as he zips his suit up down the middle. "Hurry up, now!" he calls back to us. I swear I can hear him tittering with glee.

I glance down at the screaming infant wedged between my left arm and my boob, and then at the two thermal suits in my lap. Across from me sits Ducky. He doesn't seem to be in much of a rush either. I take advantage of a moment when Olivia's gulping for air, and there's an actual second of silence between us in the train car.

"Ducky?" I say softly.

He looks up.

"I'm really sorry," I tell him. "About . . . everything." How I managed to drag the best friend in the universe into this whole mess is beyond me, but here he sits. Dragged.

Ducky shakes his head. "Not your fault," he replies simply. And somehow the fact that he seems to really mean it makes me feel even worse. But before I can kick up my apology another notch, he reaches across and plucks the baby thermal suit from my knees. "Here, let me help," he says. "You look like you could use it." Ducky's face, I should mention, is still green as a jar of Manzanilla olives.

"You think she's always going to cry this much?" I ask Ducky as we stuff the screeching baby's chubby legs into the infant thermal pouch. Ducky's not a baby expert or anything, but he seems to know more than I do. Maybe because while I spent the past nine months actively avoiding any useful baby knowledge, Ducky actually read, like, half a baby book.

"She's hungry," Ducky tells me. "She probably hasn't eaten all day."

"Oh God," I say. And my eyes go huge. Because, duh, Ducky's right—babies need to eat. Like, almost always. But it has suddenly occurred to me *what* she needs to eat. I may have been avoiding baby knowledge, but even I'm not such a chromer that I'm unaware of an infant's natural food preference. "You think that's why she's been so squirmy?" Ducky shrugs. "Shit." I'm really beginning to wish I took On Your Own class first semester, before, you know, our school exploded. But . . . well, how hard can it be? I look down at Olivia, still wiggling and screaming in my arms. Her little head is like a rag doll's, doing its darnedest to flop around on her neck. I hug her closer. Moms have been breast-feeding for years, right? It's probably, like, in my genes to know what to do.

"Here goes nothing," I declare.

And so, while Ducky feigns an unnatural interest in the lining of the thermal suit in his hands, I quickly snap open the top four buttons of my shirt with my right hand, balance Olivia with my left, and try my best to work some slick shifting-bra maneuvers. This shit is definitely *not* in my genes, though, because by the time I've exposed enough skin to the baby for her to nosh on, my shirt is practically tied in a knot at my armpit. Worse, Olivia seems completely uninterested.

"Come on, Livvie, chow time," I coo. I thought babies were supposed to go gaga for this stuff, but *my* kid just keeps crying and wiggling in my arms. "Come *on*," I say, trying to swoop her head at a better angle toward the boob, like a reverse "Here comes the airplane." "You're *hungry*. You need to eat." She wails and flails some more. "Olivia, seriously, we have to dock in a couple minutes and . . . *oh*."

The child has found my boob.

"She did it!" I tell Ducky, who is now staring at a stain on the ceiling of the train car like it's a Rorschach test he's being quizzed on. "She's totally eating. I'm feeding my baby. I'm like a mom, Ducky, seriously. Can you bel—"

Olivia undocks and starts screaming again. And no matter how much I nudge her in the right direction, she's completely uninterested. "What's going on?" I ask, definitely way past the end of my tether. I can't calm my baby down, and I can't feed her either. Total mom fail. "I thought babies were, like, booby *fiends*."

Ducky lets out an enormous sigh. "You're probably not producing any milk because it's been several days and you didn't start feeding right away when she was born," he says, still staring at that spot on the ceiling. "The book said that would happen."

Ducky's not looking at me, but I give him my "I'm going to pinch you in a sensitive area" death stare anyway. "Why didn't you tell me that *before* I rearranged my whole ensemble?" I ask.

Ducky just shrugs, picking up my thermal suit and doing a fairly half-assed job of blindly covering my décolletage as Alan appears again in the doorway to summon us.

"We're coming, we're coming," I say, before the guy even has a chance to chastise us.

The steady hum of the train rises in pitch a good half tone as we all walk, single file, out the door and down the length of the train to the center docking car. My dad was right, the ride is smooth, but the wailing infant with the crazy octopus limbs is making it difficult for me to keep my balance anyway.

"Hey, uh, Mister Almiri Guy?" Ducky says as we walk. He's already forgotten Alan's name—and the Duck can list *from memory* every Spider-Man villain in reverse-alphabetical order. "Elvie here needs something for the baby." And I gotta give the guy props, because despite the fact that he is clearly about to lose his lunch, he's still trying to make sure that Olivia gets hers. "She's hungry."

"Yes, sir, but what do you suggest I do about it?" Alan answers. And do I detect a little bit of annoyance in his tone? Look who just found a personality.

"Well, you guys must have been feeding her something for the past couple days," Ducky answers. "Whatever it was, we need some more of it."

"I suggest your friend lets nature run its course," Alan says in reply.

"Well, first of all," Ducky says, going all "Revenge of the Bestie" on the dude's ass. "I don't think you understand that expression, like, at *all*. And secondly . . ." I'm not gonna lie—Ducky's take-no-crap attitude is kind of impressive right now. Who knew he had it in him? I clutch Olivia's butt tighter and hustle to keep up, glad for the moment that Ducky has taken to the role of Male Protector. "Either you find something for this poor kid to eat pronto, or I'm gonna shove one of these thermal suits right up your—"

"Hey."

The voice stops Ducky in his tracks. Me too. I look up, and sure enough, there's Cole, flanked by two Almiri guards, wearing the same gray thermal jumpsuit we've all been outfitted with. He looks none the worse for wear, except he's sporting cuffs. I guess the Almiri didn't figure Dad and Ducky and I posed the same sort of threat to escape as one of their own commandos.

"Cole!" I squeal. Yes, actually *squeal*, like a little girl. And I don't even feel one titch embarrassed about it either. I rush to him, shouldering the guards aside, and hit him hard with one massive I-was-so-worried-you-were-dead lip-lock. "You're okay," I breathe.

He smiles, his face so close that his breath makes my skin tingle. "Better now," he replies.

I tilt Olivia so that she's facing him. She's still screaming and kicking, but she's never seemed so beautiful. "Meet Olivia," I tell him.

He bends down ever so slightly. "Hello there, Olivia," he greets her.

She is mesmerized by the sound of Cole's voice. Like, absolutely mesmerized. She goes stone silent, eyes wide, and stares at him.

"Remind me to keep you around," I tell Cole—right before Olivia lets out a tiny baby fart and begins wailing again.

Well, it was nice while it lasted.

Cole turns to Ducky beside me. "Hey, Duck Man." He offers him a clumsy high-ten, but Ducky only stares at him. I can't tell if he's being rude or annoyed or just motion-sick again—his face has moved from pea soup to limeade—and I guess Cole can't figure it out either, because he steps toward my father instead, not two meters away. As he approaches, Cole extends his hand. Well, actually, both hands, because of the cuffs and all.

"Mr. Nara, I'm Cole, we met at the hospital," Cole says. I roll my eyes, but Dad has the good grace to just smile knowingly and take his hand in a good, sturdy "dad shake."

"Yes, son, the birth of one's first alien grandchild is a memory that lasts," Dad says. Cole laughs nervously.

"So your friends are kind of douchetards," Ducky pipes up finally, nudging his head toward our Almiri guards.

Cole sneaks a look at Alan, who doesn't appear all that amused. Or annoyed. He simply seems to not want to be anywhere near us. "Yeah," Cole agrees. "They get that a lot."

Cole turns back to me then, but he doesn't say anything, he just kind of blushes and looks at the floor. I guess he's a little ashamed that he's gotten us all into this mess, I mean, having the Almiri keep tabs on me after we got back from the *Echidna* and tracking the end of my pregnancy. But he thought he was protecting me, and I can't really fault the dumb ox for that.

"Elvie . . . ," he says, trailing off. I take a step forward and dip down slightly so that I can look him in the eye.

"It's okay, Cole," I say. "It's not your fault. I'm just glad you're all right. That we're all together."

"I can see your nipple," he replies.

A space elevator, for the record, is just like a regular elevator, except that—similar to those of the Willy Wonka variety—this one's not stuck inside a building. According to Dad, our resident expert on such matters, the elevator component moves down on a long loop of reinforced cable, harnessing the Earth's own gravitational pull to generate the power it needs to lift us back up, up, up into space to a satellite station, which will then navigate the orbit around the planet down to Antarctica, where we will take the elevator back down and transfer to the high-speed mag rail on the other end.

Out the window to our right swoops the elevator car, speeding along like, well, a speeding train. We all watch, silent (except for the occasional wail from Olivia and the occasional nauseous burp from Ducky), as the train's and the elevator's speeds begin to match up. And then, suddenly, this crazy speeding bullet from outer space has actually *docked* with our car. That's when Alan ushers us over into the elevator. Honestly, I want it to feel like a more momentous experience— this moving from our past world to the futuristic spacecraft that will shuttle us to our doom—but the ride is (yes, Dad) so smooth that I'll be damned if it doesn't feel just like walking from business class to the snack car.

Once we're all aboard, the door *whooshes* shut and the elevator detaches from the train. Suddenly we're shooting up into the sky, using the built-up kinetic energy from the trip down.

"So," Dad explains, "from here we'll deboard at the satellite station, which will take us counterclockwise around the Earth on about a twelve-hour"—Dad looks to Alan for confirmation, who merely grunts—"yes, about a twelve-hour journey, until we're above Cape Crozier. Then we'll dock with *another* mag-rail train, and we're home free." I frown. "Or, er," my dad corrects, "in prison."

"It sure is a long way down," Ducky says, looking out the window the way a condemned prisoner might look at the guillotine.

"It is at that, Donald," Dad says. "But you shouldn't worry. These cable cars hardly ever fail."

"*Hardly* ever?" Ducky asks. His face is changing colors faster than a chameleon on a speed bender.

"These cables are very sturdy," Dad replies, "and most of the electricity on board is generated by the motion along it. So malfunctions and explosions are rare."

"*Explosions?*" Ducky is a quivering ball of lunchroom-quality mac 'n' cheez.

"You're getting scared out of proportion with the risk," Dad says, frustrated by Ducky's seeming lack of pragmatism. "It's not as if we're going to need to jump out the window or anything. Besides, there are evacuation procedures. I can go over them with you if you'd like." Dad points to one of the walls, which has a bright red panel with the word EMERGENCY in big block letters. Underneath the panel is a lever. "That would be where you'll find all the equipment you would need for a safe evacuation."

"What's in it?" Ducky asks, hardly sounding reassured.

"Well, some sort of parachute device, I would imagine," Dad muses. "I don't know how they grade for high altitudes. Perhaps something that could survive atmospheric reentry? I've read about some metallic mesh fabrics that NASA has been working with . . ."

"We could always just fly down on capes," I say, trying to lighten the mood.

Ducky gives me a long cold stare. "Elvie, that's not even a little funny," he tells me.

When Ducky and I had just graduated from fourth grade, Dad planned a day trip with us where he *said* he was taking us to the amusement park on the boardwalk down the shore. Instead (and really, in retrospect, this should have come as no surprise), Dad had signed us all up for a daylong training seminar on emergency evacuation scenarios. The only "event" that Dad could convince Ducky to participate in—and again, I stress that we were both *nine*—was the building jump, and that was only because they used gliding capes, which Dad managed to convince Ducky would make him look like a superhero. The capes, which made us all look like flying squirrels more than anything, were, in theory, meant to help an evacuee of a troubled high-rise ride the wind currents safely all the way down to the ground. The capes used sensors imbedded in the nylon fabric to automatically adjust tensile strength, creating the appropriate lift and drag as you "flew," so they were supposed to be foolproof. They did not, it turned out, end up being Ducky-proof. Poor old Duck managed to flail around for a few seconds before sailing right past the safety net and dropping like a stone to the concrete below, breaking his ulna in the process. After that the seminar center instituted a minimum age limit to participate, and Ducky's folks didn't let Dad plan any more trips until we were in high school.

"Don't worry, Donald," my Dad reassures Ducky. "I doubt you'd survive using a gliding cape from this high up."

Dad sure knows how to make a guy feel better.

We make it to the satellite station without any mishaps or adventures, besides some world-class ralphing by Ducky, who finally can't contain it any longer. No one seems to have much to say, shockingly enough. Even baby Olivia has cried herself back to sleep. I stare out the window at the blackness and the stars. I can see the Earth, kilometers below. A blue-green orb. And even though I've seen almost this exact same view so many times before, when I was circling the planet on the *Echidna*, this time it feels a lot different. Like, even though I'm about to go right back down, in another very real way, I've left the planet forever.

Antarctica. The Bottom of the Earth. They might as well cut this elevator cable and send us all floating out into the void.

All that's left is to settle in for our half-day orbit toward the South Pole. And Ducky, apparently, has decided to use the entire twelve hours to puke on stuff.

"Ducky, these were my best sneaks," I say, stepping out of the vomit that he just deposited at my feet.

"Sorry," Ducky whimpers, wiping his mouth. His hands

are trembling, and he's turned an even whiter shade of pale, if that's possible. Guess he puked all the green out of his face. He really does look pathetic, crouched on the floor. "I'll get you some new ones."

"You reckoning on there being a Foot Locker in Antarctica?" I say.

Ducky lets out a low moan. I take a few steps back, just in case, but reach out my baby-free arm and rub his back in little circles. Cole keeps actively looking in any direction other than Ducky's. Seems like my Almiri baby-daddy has a pretty loose gag reflex.

"I think your motion sickness may be psychosomatic, Donald," Dad says, in what I can only assume is an attempt to be helpful. "After all, these transports are incredibly smooth. There should be no distress put on the inner ear, even one as sensitive as yours."

"Maybe I should find a . . . ," Ducky begins, before pausing to retch on my left foot—completing the matching set. ". . . good hypnotist while we're in Antarctica," he finishes. "But I'd bet that it's more the rocketing through the atmosphere than my mind that's doing it, Mr. Nara."

"There are no rockets on the *Fountain*, Donald," Dad replies, missing the point as only a science nerd can. "That's the most spectacular thing about it. We've harnessed the power of the Earth's gravitational pull to create near-perpetual motion without the use of conventional rockets or fuel. The theory is revolutionary, really."

Ducky's rebuttal splatters all over the floor, which at least temporarily quiets Dad. Even Alan and the other guards have moved away from us in disgust. I look over at them with a contemptuous glare.

"Could you, like, get us a towel or something?" I ask. Alan, the tension almost visibly building in his neck muscles, doesn't bother to respond to me, but motions to his buddies, who wander off down the corridor with him.

I leave Dad to tend to Ducky and walk over to the window with Olivia. The last thing I want is for this madhouse puke-fest to wake her from the first real nap she's decided to take all day. "Don't worry," I whisper into her ear as I lean up against the window. The glass is cool, comforting. "I'll find you something to eat soon, I promise." She nestles her little mini-melon head farther into the crook of my neck, and I rub the ridges on the back of her head with my thumb, studying her perfect microscopic features.

Maybe I really could get used to this whole mom thing.

It's funny, I think, because last time I was on a spaceship, I spent as much time as I could up on the observation deck staring at the view of the Earth, mesmerized by the hugeness of it all. Now that seems to pale in comparison to the teeny human being curled up on my shoulder.

Olivia has hair already, dark brown like mine, and fine as feathers. It's short and straight, but you can already tell the girl will be sporting a cowlick when she gets older, right at the crown. She has big eyes—blue-green like her daddy at the moment, although who knows if they'll change. Her eyelashes are perfect, like a porcelain doll's, and her bitty nose isn't too stubby and isn't too pointy. She's got my thick eyebrows, with the sharp arch, and the distinct Nara chin. Her fingers—one, two, three, ten of them—are perhaps the cutest things in existence. You wouldn't think they'd be able to fit all the right pieces into such a tiny package—knuckles and knees and earlobes and wrists—but there they all are.

The most curious thing about her, though, is her left cheek, where the "starkiss" has now vanished completely. I rub my thumb over the spot gently. Smooth skin, soft peach fuzz. No freckles.

"May I?" comes a voice from behind me. I turn, and there's Cole. He shrugs dopily at me and holds out his arms, his hands still bound in front of him.

I smile. "Of course," I tell him. "Just don't poke her with those cuffs."

"Look at those fingernails," he whispers as he takes Olivia gently into his arms. He's staring down at her in awe. And maybe it's cheese-tastic, but watching the two of them—my baby and her daddy, together in front of me—I feel a bit like the Grinch after he figured out the true meaning of Christmas. Yep, definitely some elephantiasis of the heart happening in my chest right now. "Everything about her is just *so small*," Cole goes on. "She's like a . . ." He searches for the right word.

"Marvel of engineering?" I tease, and Cole laughs. "Not the Almiri bundle of joy you expected, is she?" I say, peering over his shoulder at our little girl.

"Nope," he says. And he turns to grin at me. That dopey Cole Archer grin. "She's better, Elvs. She's *ours*."

"You cornball," I reply, but I'm tearing up, so I turn away toward the window.

We stand there for a moment, just the three of us. And it's

nice, actually, staring at the Earth below. I catch a reflection in the window—Ducky, with my Dad standing over him, patting him on the back. Ducky's looking at me, his expression making it clear that he is absolutely wrecked. I guess bringing up half your body weight in vomit has that effect on a person. But when our eyes lock for a split second in the window—when he sees I've caught him watching me and Cole—his gaze darts away quickly, leaving me with a confusing twinge in my chest.

"You know, I half expected to see Britta here," I say to Cole, by way of refocusing my brain.

Cole doesn't look up from gazing at his daughter, but the look on his face is one that might be described as "befuddled." "Britta?" he says, all . . . well, befuddled. "Why would she be here?"

I shrug. "I could have sworn I saw her back at Almiri Headquarters, in one of those holding areas, like where they put me."

Cole shakes his head at that. "Must've been someone else," he replies. "They sent Britta home, like, a week before this little chica was born."

"They sent her home?" I ask, totally not convinced. "Just like that?"

"That's what they told me," Cole replies. "They didn't let me see her . . . or she didn't want to see me. I dunno."

For no rational reason, my neck goes stiff. "You tried to see her?"

"Well, yeah," Cole says sheepishly. "I just . . . I guess I just wanted to see how she was. It's probably good that I didn't talk to her." He shifts his grip on Olivia, making sure his cuffs don't rub her exposed skin. "I'd just make things ten times worse, like a total dumbass."

"That's true," I agree, and already I feel the muscles in my neck relaxing. "You are a dumbass."

That came out slightly less supportive than I meant it to.

"Anyway," Cole says, rocking our baby slowly. "They told me they terminated the pregnancy. So that's one less Jin'Kai invader to worry about, I suppose."

My stomach does a little nauseous flip-flop, knowing just how close I came to being in Britta's shoes. While I get to stand here, watching Cole and Olivia bond father-daughter style right before me, *her* mini-Cole was swapped out by the Jin'Kai for one of their genetically manipulated fetuses/parasites. I wonder just how much it must weigh on Cole, the fact that his unborn child with Britta was a casualty of this weird breeding turf war. And I wonder what it must be like for Britta, to have had not one but two different alien things growing inside you, and then, suddenly, not.

I lean a little closer into Cole and press my thumb into Olivia's palm, her warm, tight grip helping to push the thoughts from my mind. 'Cause, let's face it, I have a lot more to worry about right now than whether or not I'll have to share a bunk in Antarctica with my high school arch-nemesis.

"What's going to happen to us down there, Cole?" I ask softly. I wish the view out the window really was the one from the observation deck on the *Echidna*. If only I had bitchy Britta McVicker to be worried about, instead of this helpless infant. "How are we going to get out of this mess? I don't even have the *start* of a plan."

But when I turn to look again at Cole, he's wearing that same life-is-my-oyster expression on his face he always has. Even the thought of banishment, it seems, can't faze this guy. "Who needs a plan?" he says seriously. "I've got my two ladies." He hitches up Olivia, kisses me on the cheek. "We're a family now, Elvs. That's all that matters. We don't have anything else to worry about."

That's a beautiful sentiment and all, and I really wish I could wrap myself up in it like a blanket, and be as warm and content in the whole idea as Cole, but . . . well, that's not *all* that matters, is it? Sorry, but *somebody* has to be the voice of reason here. "We've actually got a *lot* to worry about," I tell him. "Like food."

"Food?" Cole asks.

"Olivia hasn't eaten all day. We have to find something for her soon, or—"

And that, of course, is the instant Olivia wakes up, wailing again.

"*Shit*," I snap. I pull her from Cole's arms and do my best to calm her down, the way my dad did. But the girl for *serious* hates my singing.

"I can help," Cole tells me, wrestling something out of his pocket. "I know a couple things about babies. You just got to distract them." And he produces two long bright blue tubes of some sort of gel, which he proceeds to jiggle in Olivia's face. "There you go, widdle Wivvie. You like that, don't you?"

She *does* like it, actually. Olivia's mesmerized by Cole's distraction, having been brought down from Code Red to a mere gurgle in two seconds flat.

"Nice job," I tell him, surprised. "You know, you really

have a knack for this whole parenting thi—" I stop short, as suddenly the words on the side of one of Cole's tubes focus in my vision. "*Cole.*"

"What?" he says as I snatch the tubes out of his hand. "What'd I do?"

I push the tubes in front of his eyes and read him the label. "Infant Pablum Formula."

Cole just shrugs. "Yeah," he says. "Byron snuck them into my pocket after they cuffed me. He said they were for the baby. Good thing, too, huh? 'Cause they really came in handy."

I roll my eyes as I rip off the top corner of the foil. "I'm thinking Byron probably meant for us to *feed* her with them," I tell Cole as I lift the tube to Olivia's lips, giving it a little squeeze. She suckles hungrily, her lips smacking with the effort. I let out a breath of relief, and it feels like I've been holding it all day.

"Huh," Cole responds, watching. "You're probably right. Although my way worked too."

"God, you're a doofus," I tell him. But I can't help but laugh. My baby is eating. It's the best thing that's happened in a very crappy day.

Cole kisses my cheek once more. "I love you, Elvs," he tells me.

"I love you, too," I say back. Because I can tell he needs me to.

And, you know, because it's true.

"Look at us!" he shouts suddenly. "Officially making it happen. You and me?" His grin grows wider. "Hottest couple in Antarctica, hands down."

"I don't know," I say, laughing. Man, that goofy grin of his is contagious. "I've heard they've got some pretty hot penguins down there."

"We'll be okay, Elvs," Cole assures me as I squeeze the bottom of the gel tube to get as much food to my baby as possible. "They're not going to hurt us, I promise. These are the good guys."

"I'm not so sure about that anymore," I reply.

I look up when he bumps his shoulder into mine affectionately. "Come on, babe," he says, flashing those prize-winning pearly whites at me. "Trust me. Everything's going to be just fine."

Famous last words, I think, as Olivia—with timing worthy of a professional comedienne—yacks a little blue spit-up onto her daddy's gray jumpsuit.

Yeah, I think. Me and the kid are going to get along just fine.

# Chapter Three

# WHEREIN, AGAINST ALL ODDS, OUR LITTLE BAND OF MISFITS AVOIDS MAKING A SINGLE VANILLA ICE REFERENCE . . . EXCEPT THIS ONE

So I realize the following thought isn't going to help my application for the MacArthur Genius Grant any, but it bears relaying anyway:

Antarctica is cold.

Like, balls cold.

The Almiri don't seem to be feeling it, obvi. Alan and the rest of them have their thermals unzipped and their heads uncovered. Heck, their cheeks aren't even rosy. Cole, now that he's finally been uncuffed, has his thermal tied around his neck, and despite the fact that he's wearing nothing more than a T-shirt underneath, his arms show no sign of goose-pimpling.

Meanwhile, I can't hear myself think over the chattering of my own teeth. I've got my thermal zipped up to my chin and my hood pulled down tightly, but every centimeter of skin that's exposed to the air burns with cold. I snuggle Olivia tightly against my chest. She's well-protected in her little papoose, but I think the shock of the cold has taken some of the fight out of her lungs. Silver linings, and all that.

Alan and his cohorts shuttle us off the train and down a flight of stairs toward the small depot that sits at the end of the mag-rail line that must serve as the staging area for the transfer of goods and prisoners headed to the Cape Crozier facility. It's not much more than a station house and a long, low-lying extension that I'm assuming is a kennel for the dogs. The stairs are icy slick, and I have to catch myself more than once on my way down, navigating the rail with one hand and balancing Olivia with the other. No fewer than three times Ducky tries to offer me his hand, but I shake him off.

"I'm okay, I swear," I say. "Just need to take it slow."

I'm on the second-to-bottom step, though, when I lose it for real, and I know—in that way you do when the ground just slips out from under you completely—that no amount of scrambling is going to stop my fall. I let out a startled yelp, because I don't have time for anything louder, but it's too late. Me and my baby are ice pancake—

"Gotcha," Cole says.

I look up at him, stunned. Sure enough, I'm lying, almost horizontally, in Cole's arms. Olivia is fine too, curled up at my chest, none the wiser for my clumsiness.

"Uh, thanks," I say.

Cole is grinning. Seeing as he was in front of me on the steps, he must have done some pretty epic ice-dancing moves to spin around quickly enough to catch me. I'm kind of sad I missed it.

"Doesn't the hero get a kiss, at least?" Cole asks.

I grin back. "Of course." I'm moving in for the kiss when I feel the tug at my side. Looking down, I see Ducky's fingers gripped tight around the side of my thermal. Clearly he was doing his best to rescue me too, but all *he* got for his efforts was a handful of pocket lint. When he sees me looking at him, he clears his throat and tugs his hand away.

"You okay, dearheart?" Dad asks from the top of the steps.

My eyes dart from Ducky to my father. "Uh, yeah," I say, although I'm still feeling a little dazed. "Just fine." I straighten up and give Cole a quick peck, which obviously disappoints him.

There are three large sleds waiting for us at the staging area. One has space free for passengers, while the other two are already packed high with huge crates and sacks. Supplies for the prison, I suppose.

I pile onto the first sled, and Cole squeezes up close beside me. "She looks cold," he says, peering down at Olivia. Which, okay, is not exactly trending news, but still, at least he's working on the whole "observant" thing. Actually, Olivia still seems too shocked by the temperature to cry. She's just rapid-baby-blinking in this way that's, like, disconcerting, to say the least. "Here," Cole continues, undoing the thermal from around his neck. "This might help." He drapes the thermal around Olivia and over my shoulders, so that it warms both of us.

"Thanks," I say, a little surprised. Here I thought Cole was going to jingle the jacket in her face to distract her from the chill. "That was good," I tell him, smiling. I give him a teasing elbow to the side. "What'd you do, read a baby book or something?"

Cole is very clearly pleased with himself. But: "She's still blinking all weird," he says. I glance down. Olivia is, in fact, still "blinking all weird," her cheeks scrunched up as her lids rapid-fire open-closed-open-closed. "What is that, like, Morse Code?" Cole continues. "You think she's trying to tell us something?"

"Her hood," Ducky says as he slides into the seat behind us. "Pull down her hood."

I oblige and tug down on the little baby lid so that it comes down to her nose. Instantly Olivia seems calmer. She lets out a satisfied baby sigh and wraps herself more comfortably into my curves. Within seconds she is asleep.

I crane my neck to look at Ducky without disturbing the baby. "How did you . . . ?" I begin.

"The light off the snowdrifts," he tells me. "Her developing eyes aren't used to such brightness." He crosses his arms over his chest and shrugs. "I read a book or something," he tells us before staring off into the distance.

And that's the last thing he says for the next two hours.

Before long we're underway, *shushing* and *whooshing* on our high-tech puppy-powered toboggan hurtling toward our gloomy destination. The sled jostles slightly as we zoom across the ice, jingle-jangling in this way that's fairly Christmas carol-y and would be lovely and romantic if not for the fact that, like, we've just been banished to imprisonment, perhaps for the rest of our lives, simply because my baby doesn't have a dongle.

So, okay, yeah, our lives may be rapidly going to hell in a dog-pulled handbasket, but at least the view is spectacular. Honestly, I didn't realize how beautiful ice could be before

I came to this place. The dogs pull us down the makeshift path—which is just a slightly more trodden patch of snow, marked with neon-painted bamboo poles—and it's just snow, snow, and more snow, as far as the eye can see. A desert of snow, really. But it's not mundane, not in the slightest. Oh no. There are ice cliffs, soaring fifty feet or more into the sky, ice formations sprinkled here and there that look like giant mushrooms poking up out of the ground, hills and valleys and, puckered beside the path, cracks in the ice. Every once in a while we pass a patch that's broken free from the rest of the ice mass, and the ice floes don't drift gently out to sea like I'd imagine, but rather crash into each other with the force of the waves below them.

Far in the distance, there is a loud *Crack-BOOM!* of thunder, followed by another. *Crack-BOOM!*

The sky is crystal clear.

A shiver crawls up my spine, less from the pervasive chill and more from the eerie thought that that roar of thunder must've traveled for miles, and yet it sounds like it's right on top of us. I guess it's easy to make yourself heard when you're surrounded by so much . . . nothing.

After an hour or so, Olivia takes up her wailing again. Full-throttle screaming that's so loud, I'm startled when I look around and *don't* see an avalanche forming. And even though I have a tiny bit of the blue gel left in my pocket, I'm afraid to use it up so soon. Who knows what food they'll have for her at the prison? So I try singing again. (Alan, at the front of the sled, starts spasming like my voice is giving him a stroke, but he can just shove it.)

*"I love you, a bushel and a peck.*
*A bushel and a peck, and a hug around the neck.*
*A hug around the neck, and . . ."*

Olivia is having none of it. She's screeching louder than ever. From the seat behind me, Dad leans his head over my shoulder. "Hold her closer," he instructs. "Closer. So she can hear your heartbeat. Good. Now try again."

I do as told, but Olivia won't stop howling. I'm growing more and more shaken. Any second *I'm* going to be the one crying. I break the song off midlyric. "What am I doing wrong?" I ask over the rush of the wind. My voice is a quiver of nerves. "Why won't she stop?"

Dad reaches out a hand, but it's not Olivia's head he pats soothingly—it's mine. "Your baby feels what you're feeling," he tells me. "You're anxious right now, worried, so she is too. The only way to calm her down is to be utterly calm yourself."

"How am I supposed to be calm when she's *screaming* at me?" I call back to him.

Even over the wind, I can hear my dad chuckle. "Welcome to parenthood," he tells me. And then, slightly more helpfully: "You've got to find your own inner peace, dearheart, and then give it to her. Channel it to her in your voice, your muscles, everything."

"Wouldn't it just be easier to get a vaccine or something?" I mutter. But I try again.

*"I love you, a bushel and a peck.*
*A bushel and a peck, and a hug around the neck."*

And okay, no, I definitely *don't* manage to channel my inner peace, but after a good twenty minutes of my terrible singing, Olivia finally tones the screaming down to a quiet sob. I think she just ran of steam, but hey, I'll take it.

"Where are all the penguins?" Cole asks suddenly, leaning so far over the sled that I might worry for his safety, if not for the fact that he is, you know, a rapidly-healing super alien.

"Emperor penguins don't surface until they mate," Dad informs us. Apparently space elevators aren't the only thing he boned up on in Useless Factoid School. "And they only mate in the dead of winter. Until then, they spend much of their time at sea."

"But it *is* the winter," Cole replies. "It's like"—he does the math, which based on the look on his face, is fairly painful—"December sixth. Unless we were drugged without realizing." He scrunches his nose. "Could we have been held for six whole months?"

"We're at the South Pole," I inform him, and goodness, all that singing must have really tuckered me out, because there is not even a trace of snarkiness in my voice. I bob Olivia at my chest and let out a sigh of pure exhaustion. "The Antarctic winter starts in, like, June."

"Wait," Cole says, like his mind has been *totally blown*. "So this is *summer*? But there's *snow* in it."

Somewhere out across the ice there is another crack of thunder. *Crack-BOOM!*

I look at Cole and smile wistfully. He smiles back. His teeth are so perfect. I hope Olivia gets his teeth and not mine. Some other things, however . . . I mean, I love the lug, I really think I do.

I just hope being a moron isn't hereditary.

It might seem weird to get so excited at the sight of a prison camp looming in the distance, but when you've been sledding along into nothingness for hours, *anything* is welcome. Even Alan lets out what I can only assume is a grunt of relief. I have a feeling the guy will be volunteering for kitchen duty pronto when he gets back. Dude does *not* like to travel.

The prison camp comes into better focus as the dogs trot closer. And not that I exactly knew what to expect when I heard we were being shipped off here, but this . . . wasn't it.

The building is a log cabin. As in, Abraham Lincoln log cabin. It's big, but not huge-big, maybe like medium-big. (At least, that's how I imagine the famed poet Robert Frost would have described it in his ever-eloquent verse, "Two Roads Converged on a Medium-Big Cabin.") And it doesn't look very prison-y. There are no bars on the windows, no visible locks on the doors. A few huskies similar to the ones currently mushing our sled are hanging out by the front entrance, but they don't look to be at all threatening. That's the vibe I get from the way they're busy sniffing each other's crotches, anyway.

"I guess they figure there's nowhere for us to try to escape to," Ducky says, piping up for the first time since the depot.

My Bestie. The cheery one.

I shrug Ducky's foul mood off and take in my surroundings slowly, cataloging every path, every window, every tiny crack in the cabin's wall. And I am absolutely positive my father is doing the same.

"Here we are," Alan announces when our driver brings the dogs to a stop. "Your new home away from home."

"Who do we call for turndown service?" I mutter, but no one pays me any mind.

We are greeted by a tall handsome fellow with a weather-beaten face, close-cropped hair, thin lips, and brooding eyes. You can tell just by looking at him that he's not much of a talker. He walks over to the sleds, limping ever-so-slightly, favoring his left leg, and rather than greeting any of us, he bends down to one knee to pet our dogs. As soon as they get a whiff of him, the pups all stop their playfighting with one another and sit back on their haunches and begin wagging their tails frantically, ears relaxed in doggy glee as they wait, anxiously but obediently, for their turn for a scratching. Clearly they're gaga for the guy.

"You Oates?" Alan hollers at him. The man nods, one sharp jerk of his head. "I got some cargo for you," Alan continues, motioning our way. I notice the distinct change in his tone when addressing Oates. With us, he's mostly formal, a little short. But with this guy Oates, there's a disdainful edge that's unmistakable.

The man Oates doesn't reply, just heads to the back of one of the sleds, where he unstraps a few boxes of who-knows-what. Meanwhile, we "cargo" stand shivering in our thermal suits, not quite sure what to do with ourselves. I mean, no one really ever told me if it's proper protocol to offer to help your new prison guard unload supplies or . . . what.

"If you wouldn't mind hurrying," Alan says, more to his watch than to the man. "I'd like to get back to the *Fountain* before that thunderstorm catches up with us."

For the first time, Oates raises his eyes in Alan's direction. I notice the leather hilt of a handgun at Oates's hip. "That's not thunder," he says. His words come out slowly but precise, with a definite British accent.

He returns to his knots, and in short order he has removed the entire load from the sled. He looks straight at us and makes one quick motion with his arm, summoning us. We fall into line, and in turn he hands a box each to Dad, Cole, and Ducky, who, being the weakest of the bunch, grunts under the strain as he takes it. Oates lifts the fourth and last crate from the sled and turns as if to hand it to me, then stops cold when he sees the cargo I've already got cooing in my arms. It's a long moment with him just staring, frozen in place. He doesn't look shocked, or angry, or annoyed. Which bothers me some, 'cause I don't like unreadable types, as a rule.

"So the child is staying?" he asks finally.

"At least until we hear back about that Vassar scholarship," I say, crossing my fingers in what I hope translates as an indignant bit of sarcasm.

Another sharp nod. "I see." And that, as far as I can tell, is the end of it. Oates grips the box easily in his hands and turns his attention to Alan, offering him the box to carry. Only Alan is already climbing back onto the sled with our other captors.

"You should come inside and rest for a spell," Oates tells him.

But Alan is busy rousing the dogs. The guy could not

be more ready to get out of here. And to be honest, I'm not too put out by the idea myself. "If it's all the same, I'd rather not," he says, his voice clearly implying that by "if it's all the same" he means "Is there an option to stick a live scorpion in my pants instead?" "There is quite a bit of"—he glances at Ducky—"*cleanup* to attend to on the *Fountain*."

Ducky whispers in my ear so I'm the only one who can hear him muttering. "Advanced alien civilization, but they never heard of Dramamine?"

Oates puts down his box and saunters, gimp-style, to the front of Alan's sled. The dogs sit perfectly still and watch him keenly—as if Oates had given them an unspoken command. "Your dogs will need to be swapped out with fresh ones for the trip back," he tells Alan. "Please, come rest inside." It is not a suggestion.

Alan clears his throat. "Your concern for the well-being of inferior creatures is duly noted," he replies coolly with just that faint hint of contempt. The remark garners a few snickers from Alan's fellow guards. "But nevertheless we shall be underway." And he doesn't wait for a response but instead turns back to the dogs.

Which is probably why he doesn't see it coming.

The punch, that is.

Before any of us know what's happened, Oates has dropped his crate and flown over the front of the sled, landing a real doozy of a haymaker to Alan's face. Alan careens off his seat, crashing butt-first into the snow. But before he or any of the other Almiri can respond, Oates leaps on top of him, his left forearm pressing down firmly on Alan's throat, and in one fluid motion, looses the pistol from his belt with his right hand and trains it directly between Alan's eyes. The pistol is old-fashioned, long and smooth, with an honest-to-God firing hammer. Like, for gunpowder and everything.

"Listen, brat," Oates says, his voice still quiet and steely calm. "You may think you know a thing or two, but from where I stand, you've been around about as long as a sneeze. Dogs are living creatures, like you and me, and so they are deserving of your respect and care." His lock on Alan must be solid, 'cause I've never seen an Almiri look so helpless before. Oates flicks the pistol in a slight upward motion for emphasis. "Wouldn't you agree?"

Alan nods weakly, letting out a squeaking noise I can only imagine is an affirmation.

"Good," Oates says.

And then he pulls the trigger.

"Pop."

I flinch backward and close my eyes, but Oates's verbal "pop" is the closest thing to a shot that we get. When I open my eyes, I see Oates standing up off Alan, his pistol by his side. Dangling by a long string from the barrel of the gun is a small, smooth wooden ball.

"A toy gun?" I ask, confused.

Oates holsters his "weapon" and turns back to the box he dropped in the snow. There is not a smidgen of recognition on his face that he has just made a dude nearly wet himself with a popgun. "A little levity helps to keep spirits light around here," is all he says as he heads toward the cabin, nodding for us to follow. "I'll send out a man to help you unharness those dogs."

Alan rises up off the ground and brushes the snow and ice from his thermal. "Don't think I won't tell Byron about this," he calls to Oates's back.

"See that you do, boy," Oates replies. He steps into the cabin without another word.

I turn to Ducky, who gives me a shrug.

"I guess, as wardens go, it could be worse," he says.

The inside of the cabin is just as dreary as the outside would suggest, if not more so. It's not much warmer, and the only light to illuminate the place seems to be coming from two old electric wall lamps. Several long wooden tables run the length of the room, scattered with framing squares, hammers, chisels, pencils, a sander, and other fairly low-tech carpentry gear. Along both walls are shelves crammed with toolboxes and other foreign-looking supplies, and a few crates litter the floor for good measure.

What I notice first and foremost, however, is the total lack of any other people.

"Is this it?" I ask, dumbfounded. Is this what the Almiri meant when they said they were taking us to a secure location? They were just going to maroon us in a log cabin with one (admittedly kinda badass) loner to guard us?

Oates sets down the box he's carrying and gestures for us to do the same.

"There was a time when the contents of this cabin would have seemed like luxury accommodations," he says, moving with that slight limp to the far end of the room.

"I guess I just imagined . . . I don't know," I continue.

Because, really, I'm not sure what I imagined. *Jailhouse Rock?* "Are you, like, the only guard here?"

Oates kneels down next to an inclined plane in the floor. On the side he pulls open a slide cover, revealing a small touchscreen console. He taps in a code, and suddenly the top of the incline slides open, revealing a staircase leading underground. A bright light emanates from below.

"There are no guards here, child," he says, rising to his feet again. "In this place we are prisoners all." And he shuffles down the stairs.

Ducky, Dad, and I all turn to Cole, as if he'll know what's going on, but Cole looks as lost as the rest of us, if not more so. You'd think if your civilization kept a big honking Phantom Zone–like prison on the underbelly of the planet, you might try to learn a thing or two about it, but not my Coley.

As Cole and Ducky start down the stairs behind Oates, Dad stops to make sure the straps on Olivia's papoose are snug—and that's when I see it. In a far corner, by the window, there is what appears to be an old, twentieth-century ham radio. It is rusty, and possibly missing a few parts, but still. It's a means of communication. I elbow my father. "Dad," I whisper.

He doesn't even look up, just shakes his head. "Yes," he says, as though he's read my mind and found it lacking, "but who would we call?" My face falls. He's right, of course.

"Then what's the plan, Dad?" I say. And can I help it if my voice comes out a little whiny? "Please just tell me what you're working on. I'm dying here."

"Dearheart," he says kindly, making eye contact at last. "There is no plan."

I'm pretty sure I was less shocked when my Dad showed me his high school graduation photo with the goatee and accordion bowtie (the '50s were brutally tragic, fashion-wise). "But you *always* have a plan," I say.

He gazes at me, as though deciding how best to present his fatherly wisdom. "You can't just shoot off into space in a trash compactor when you've got a baby to consider, Elvie," he tells me, adjusting Olivia's arm into a more comfortable position inside her papoose. "Things have changed now. For the moment I think it's wisest to lay low, play along with our captors, and figure out who our friends are."

"But . . ."

"The only plan you need to be concerned with is keeping this precious little girl alive," Dad tells me.

Well. It's hard to argue with that, now, isn't it?

As Dad starts down the steps to join the others, I take one last look out the window at the snow, then kiss my daughter on the forehead. *Keeping this precious little girl alive.* I can do that. "Here goes nothing," I whisper to her.

And I descend into my prison—a Nara without an escape plan.

Who would've dreamed it?

The first thing I notice, as I descend, is how much warmer it is than in the cabin above. Brighter, too, with modern light panels casting a pleasing glow across the space. We funnel into a long, white hallway with metallic walls and auto-slide doors. Blinking LED control panels are peppered along each side.

"A hidden bunker." Dad whistles. "Would you look at that."

"Come," Oates says. "You must be hungry. There's soup in the canteen. The others will want a look at you." And he leads us down the hall, Dad and Ducky up front. I hang back a few paces with Cole at my side. I rub Olivia's back nervously. Suddenly I wish she were awake, screaming even, just so I'd have something else to focus on.

"So there are others here," Dad says to Oates as we make our way through a set of sliding doors.

"Yes," Oates says. "Twenty-two besides myself." He shakes his head, correcting his count. "Twenty-three, excuse me. We've had an unexpected visitor drop in of late," he explains. "You folks make the count twenty-eight. Or"—he looks back at me—"twenty-seven and a half, at the least."

"And you're all prisoners?" I ask, massaging Olivia's back in little circles. "There are no guards at all?"

"We are all guardians of our own souls, Miss . . . ?"

"Elvie," I say.

"Well, Miss Elvie, if you're asking why we stay here, each man would have his own story, I suppose. But the long and short of it is that we've all a reason to be put here, and that's reason enough to stay."

*Sigh* . . . Almiri and their dang honor.

"And you're all Almiri?" I ask. "Everyone else but us humans, I mean?"

Oates doesn't answer until we reach the far door, where there is a faint sound of music. He raises his hand to the control switch but pauses to look down at Olivia, that same stoic look on his face. "Well, it's a complicated world, now, isn't it?"

Ducky shoots me a look that clearly means, "*Well, dur.*"

As soon as the door *shushes* open, the sound of more than a dozen macho voices bursts forth.

Voices *singing*.

There are a lot of ways I envisioned a group of Almiri prisoners spending their time (a few of them a little more X-rated than I care to share) . . . but this was not one of them. The room we find ourselves in, which appears to be some sort of dining area, has the same streamlined white metallic look of the hallway, only with a kitchenette along the right wall, and four long tables with built-in benches in the center. Around those tables are gathered two dozen handsome dudes, some sitting, some standing with a leg up on a bench. They are swinging giant mugs back and forth, slapping each other on the back, and singing. Even weirder, the tune they're belting can only be described as *jaunty*. If I didn't know any better, I'd guess that I had stepped into a flipping Gilbert and Sullivan operetta.

"Gentlemen," Oates calls out to the group. "Our new guests have arrived."

As if on cue, Olivia begins screaming. The warmth of the room seems to have roused her from her Arctic semicoma. At least having a crying baby will defuse the total weirdness of a meet-and-greet, right?

Wrong.

At the sound of Olivia's wailing, the entire chorus of singers stops and turns. Every last man looks at me, completely silent. Suddenly all the air has left the room. And, okay, I realize they probably don't get any women down here, but this gang looks absolutely *stupefied*.

"Bloody hell," comes a voice from the group.

Only one man has the courtesy to stand up. He is tall, broad-chested, blond, and ruddy. Although as he saunters our way I get the sense—from the disgusted sneer plastered on his face, I suppose—that maybe he's not standing out of courtesy after all.

Oates clears his throat as the man approaches, as though in warning. "Jørgen," he says quietly, almost in a growl. But whatever Oates thinks he's communicating, the man Jørgen does not listen.

"*These* are our newest additions?" Jørgen sneers. He has a hint of a Swedish accent, which would be slightly comical if not for the fact that he's currently leering at my baby like she's a bug he found in his coffee. His eyes flick up to me, and I quickly get the feeling that I'm the mama bug. "Is the Council just dumping any old trash down here now?"

"Manners, Jørgen," Oates says.

Jørgen scoffs dismissively. "Manners? I'll show you manners. Manners would be kicking these worthless mules back out into the cold where you found—"

Jørgen doesn't see the punch that Cole lands on the side of his head, but I'm sure the little cartoon birds that are circling above him can describe it to him later in detail.

"Cole!" I shriek. "What are you doing?" Olivia's wails grow even louder as a slender fellow with sandy-brown hair leaps up from the table to jerk Cole back by the arms. "Have you completely lost your mind?" I ask Cole, backing away from the scuffle to try to comfort my wailing infant.

Cole has a confused look on his face, like he can't tell if

he's proud of what he's just done, or embarrassed. The man pinning Cole's arms behind him seems a little more with it, however. "Oates?" the man asks, clearly wondering what to do about Cole, who's not even struggling against the restraint.

Still on the floor, Jørgen rubs his jaw. "What are you waiting for?" he asks Mr. Sandy Hair, spitting out a tooth. "Take him out to the kennel."

"When he does something out of line, perhaps," Oates replies. And without needing to hear another word, the sandy-haired fellow releases Cole.

"Sorry," the man whispers to Cole as he lets him go. "Just had to check with the boss." And then, shockingly, he *winks* at him.

"These are our *guests*," Oates repeats, his voice loud enough for all the Almiri to hear. He extends a hand to help Jørgen off the floor, but the Swedish Bond villain—no shocker—refuses, pushing himself dizzily to his feet, muttering and growling. "You will treat them all with respect." This, clearly, is directed at Jørgen.

"You're not in charge of anyone here, Titus, regardless of what you may think," Jørgen snarls. But even I can see that this is wishful thinking on Jørgen's part. All Oates has to do is take a single step in Jørgen's direction, and suddenly Mr. Very Obviously in Charge seems to have grown about ten centimeters taller. He looks down at Jørgen and doesn't say another word, merely fixes his eyes on him until the Swede finally crumbles.

"Welcome to Cape Crozier," Jørgen grumbles to me. He narrows his eyes at the top of Olivia's head, then raises one thick blond Swedish eyebrow. "I hope you'll both be very comfortable here."

Well.

"What the heck was *that*?" I hiss at Cole as Jørgen stumbles furiously out of the room. "Are you high?"

Ducky finally emerges from where I didn't realize he was crouched behind my dad to ask, "What's a mule, anyway?"

Cole just shrugs. "I don't know," he admits. "But it didn't sound very nice."

I puff out my cheeks, exasperated. Only my Coley would risk getting shivved on his first day in prison, and not even know *why*.

Mr. Sandy Hair claps a hand on his shoulder. "It's *not* nice," he agrees. "But enough unpleasantries." He offers Cole a glowing smile, and I stop to really take the man in for the first time. He's, like, überbeautiful. I guess that that shouldn't surprise me, but this guy's hot even by Almiri standards. He looks fairly young, though with an Almiri that could mean that he's "only" two hundred years old or so. "Rupert," the dreamboat tells Cole brightly, offering his hand. "Welcome to the roost."

"Uh, Cole," Cole replies as Rupert winks at him again.

So, our new buddy is weird, but at least friendly. Although I notice he doesn't bother to shake anybody *else's* hand.

Oates has moved on to unpacking supplies, and the rest of the Almiri prisoners have dispersed, either helping Oates or finishing up their lunch, so at first I think Rupert is the only guy out of the whole bunch who's going to talk to us. But it seems there's one more.

"Care to introduce me to our new friends, Rupe?" booms out a cheery Boy Scout voice. I glance up just in time to see a man slap Rupert on the back jovially. He's taller and broader than his friend, with a chiseled jaw and jet-black hair in a slicked-back hairdo that's so archaic, it comes complete with a spit curl. "Finally some new blood. There haven't been any new guests since I got here a hundred and forty-three years ago." When it becomes clear that Rupert only has eyes for Cole, his buddy shifts gears, stretching out his arm to Ducky and shaking his hand vigorously. "Pleased to meet you . . . ?"

"Ducky, er, Donald," Ducky replies. He's squinting at the guy, like he's accessing old databanks for some sort of info.

"Gosh, Ducky sounds just fine," the human action figure says, beaming. "It's good to meet you. I'm Clark."

And at that, for some reason, Ducky almost chokes on his own spit. He turns to me, eyes round as basketballs.

"Are you having a stroke?" I whisper.

"Well . . . hi there," Clark says, turning to me. The presence of me and the baby clearly has him ruffled, although he's dealing with it better than, say, the Swede.

"I'm Elvie," I tell him. "And this little screaming bundle of joy"—Olivia's shrieking is reaching dog-frequency pitches now—"is Olivia." Suddenly I feel flushed from the attention, the trip, everything, and I'm a bit woozy on my feet. "She's hungry," I say, as if it were an excuse.

"Of course she is," Clark replies, smiling. "It's a long trek for a baby." He reaches down and *boops* her on the nose. She keeps screaming. "Your little girl might be the first newborn to make it all the way to the South Pole."

"I'll have her plant the baby flag outside later." I rock Olivia, but she's too worked up to be calmed.

"Oates!" Clark calls over his shoulder. "What do we have

in the way of baby food?" And Oates, to his credit, immediately heads our way, still limping slightly.

"Sorry—" I start, but Oates stops me with a raised hand.

"No need to apologize, child. It's been a long day. A long several days, from what I gather."

"Try a few months," I tell him. I'm pretty sure that crying your first day of prison is a no-no, even under these totally bonkers conditions, but I'm thinking of trying it out anyway, just for kicks.

Oates puts an arm around me and shuffles me to a side door. "Gents," he calls back toward the room as we walk, "get our new mates something hot to fill their bellies, will you? I'm going to show Elvie here to a little privacy."

"Thank you," I whisper as we reach the door. I turn just long enough to see Rupert and Clark making room for Dad, Ducky, and Cole at the tables. The rest of the prisoners scooch far away from them, as though the marching band just invaded the football team's lunch table. I can tell we're gonna be *real* welcome here.

Oates sees me to an empty bunkroom, where I sit down on one of the impeccably made beds.

"I'll have them send down some food for you," Oates tells me from where he lingers in the doorway. "Jules makes a rather serviceable ratatouille."

"Thank you," I breathe. The exhaustion has practically engulfed me now. I'm so zonked that Olivia's screams are blurring into one mind-numbing siren wail. Oates doesn't reply but tips his head in a slight bow to me, then heads back toward the canteen.

I take in my new digs. Pretty spartan but definitely cozier than my hospital room back with Byron and his lot. There are seriously bunk beds, six mattresses in total. There's a couch and a table with a few chairs and a lamp. A few older lap-pads strewn on the table—probably without network access, I'd wager. And that's it.

"Okay, girl," I tell my shrieking daughter. "Let's get you to stop screaming. Um, inner calm, inner calm . . ."

> *"'Cause I love you, a bushel and a peck . . ."*
> *(Tired tired anxious tired we have no plan worried*
> *freaked out Cole just PUNCHED a dude hungry*
> *tired so so tired . . .)*
> *"You bet your pretty neck I do."*

Baby Olivia is having none of it. I sigh and try to placate her instead with the end of the last gel packet Cole gave me. I should have asked Oates for something for Olivia along with the ratatouille, although he's probably ten steps ahead of me on that one. I really am turning out to be the world's worst mother.

Olivia, unfortunately, refuses to eat the damn gel.

"I *know* you're hungry," I whine, suddenly totally under-standing the phrase "at the end of one's rope." "And you *like* gel! You practically gobbled it on the trip here! Come on, now. You have to eat *something*." Olivia swats the packet to the floor. At the sound of the splat she launches into a new series of wails, grabbing with her tiny little hands at the zip of my thermal suit. "No!" I shout as her tugs become more insistent.

"You can't have milk. My boobs don't work, remember? We just tried that. I'm past the point of producing milk, silly girl."

But *you* try reasoning with an infant.

"All right," I sigh, resigned. Maybe just going through the motions and being *near* a boob will calm this Goober down enough to actually eat the gel. I unzip my thermal top and fiddle with my shirt. "Let's hurry up, though, before someone comes with that food. You don't want your mommy to get a reputation as an exhibitionist, now, do you?" I shift Olivia into position, but like before she just squirms all over the place, her baby feet ninja-kicking in every direction.

"You are such a little spaz," I moan. "I don't know where you get that—"

"Whoa, oops! Hello there!"

I look up. Standing in the doorway is a man with an enormous bushy beard and long hair.

"What the *hell*?" I squeak, doing my best to cover my half-exposed bosom.

But the man seems not to even notice. He walks straight into the room and plops down on the bunk across from mine. "I heard there'd be new recruits today," he answers. "But I never expected a baby." He grins cheerfully, scratching his crazy-long, scraggly beard. "Man, this place is a trip, huh?"

"Dude," I say. "Seriously. What the *hell*?"

"Oh, don't mind me," the guy says casually, leaning down to peer under the bed, where he proceeds to root around for something. "I was just looking for my man Oates. Thought I heard him a minute ago. I was in the can down the hall. Was he just here?"

"I, uh . . . think he's in the kitchen."

There's something weird about this guy, and it's not just the fact that he seems completely unfazed to find a teenage girl attempting to breast-feed a baby in an Almiri prison camp.

"Hey, you didn't happen to see, like, a big book around here, did you?" he asks, his head buried underneath the bunk.

"Who *are* you?" I ask at last.

The man pulls his head out from underneath the bunk. "Who, me?" he asks.

He is the only other person in the room.

He shrugs. "I'm Bernard," he says. Which I guess is supposed to clear everything up.

"You're not an Almiri," I tell him, in one of the classic understatements of all time. Aside from his unruly beard and shoulder-length hair, the dude is . . . old. *Real* old. Like, almost as old as my dad. Add to that the spare tire he's smuggling under that ugly shawl cardigan of his, and you have the makings of a small liberal arts college professor, or maybe a biblical reenactment performer, but definitely *not* a centerfold-worthy Almiri.

"No," he says with a chortle. "I'm definitely not an Almiri. Don't have the bone structure for it. I'm what you might call an . . . ambassador of goodwill." He returns to his search. "I came here to talk to Oates. He's always been sympathetic to our cause, you know."

I raise an eyebrow. "What do you mean, you came here? You weren't sent here? You're not a prisoner?"

Bernard's on his hands and knees now, butt up in the air as he peers between the mattress and the bed frame. I've seen better sights. And even I can see from here that there is *abso-*

*lutely nothing* under that bed. I snuggle the still-squirming Olivia a little tighter to my chest, doing my best to channel my nonexistent calm to her, and tug up the front of my thermal a bit around her.

"Nah, man," Bernard tells me, head still under the bed. "I'm no prisoner. I walked here of my own free will."

"You *walked* here?" I squeak. At my chest, Olivia's face twists into anger, and she starts screeching again. "*Shhhh,* baby, *shhhhhhh,*" I say. "It's okay."

Bernard finally pops up from the floor. "Yeah, it wasn't really that big a deal to get here," he says. He scans the room, absentmindedly rubbing the back of his right hand with his left palm. "All I had to do was bum a flight to Buenos Aires on a buddy's prop jet, stow away on a tourist cruise to the coast here, then hike in from there. Only took thirteen days. It was a lovely journey. Majestic, and all that. I lost two toes to frostbite, but it was really invigorating."

"Ummmm . . ."

"*There* it is!" Bernard cries suddenly, and he walks over to a shelf on the far wall. "Right where I left it. Who would've thunk?"

He reaches up and pulls a large, bound book off the shelf. "Oates is in the kitchen, you said?" he asks.

"Uh, yeah," I say, still in a daze.

"Awesome." And he heads to the door.

"So, wait, who *are* you?" I ask. "And what cause is Oates—"

I'm stopped by the pinch at my chest. *Shit,* I think. My thermal's slipped down again, and this weird hippie has probably just gotten a full-on shot of my boobs.

But when I look down, the sight before me blots out everything else. Olivia has latched on. And she actually appears to be *eating*. All other thoughts fly right out of my head. Because, well, that should be impossible, shouldn't it?

But, somehow, it's not. I look down at my baby girl, feeding, and all at once, the anxiety drains right out of me. Watching her, knowing I'm doing something that billions of mothers have done before me, and feeling connected to my daughter for the first time in a real, primal way, I feel absolutely . . .

Calm.

Then I realize the dude is watching me. I'd be totally creeped out, but he's wearing this goofy "circle-of-life" grin that has reduced the creep factor by, oh, at least fifteen percent.

"Motherhood, man," he says. "What a trip."

Yeah, I think, smiling to myself.

What a trip.

# Chapter Four

# WHEREIN CABIN FEVER GIVES WAY TO DISCO FEVER (IF BY "DISCO FEVER" YOU MEAN "INVASION")

There are some things that suck no matter where you are. A consistency of suckitude, you might say. Washing dishes, for example, is a crap job no matter what hemisphere you're in.

Except, of course, to the dumb butt who signed you up for the chore.

"Don't worry, Elvs," Cole tells me as he strolls into the kitchen, Olivia tucked under his arm like a football. I would be annoyed except that she's actually *quiet* for a change. "This won't take more than two seconds." Cole tickles Olivia under the armpits, and she wriggles happily. "Will it, Wivvie? Tell Mommy that Daddy picked dishwashing for a weason."

I bite my cheeks as I lift Livvie out of Cole's arms, trying not to smile, but it's no use. The two of them are just too cute together, and I'm a goner.

"Any trouble with the diaper change?" I ask. Last time Cole strapped the diaper on backward, which resulted in some really unfortunate leakage on my only good shirt.

"Take a look and see for yourself," he says, grinning. "O-Co and I made you something."

I look at Cole curiously, and he reaches over to unbutton Olivia's onesie. "Cole," I say, suddenly not so smiley anymore. "Please tell me that's not what I think it is."

"You don't like it?" Cole replies casually. "It took a long time to get it just right." He hitches up Olivia's onesie a little higher, so I can clearly see the message he has scrawled across her tummy in thick black marker.

*I ♥ Momy!*

"You've been *drawing on our child*?" I ask, sorta horrified, although, depressingly, I'm not all that surprised.

"Don't worry, it'll wash off," Cole assures me. "The pen said 'undoable ink.'"

I close my eyes. "*Cole*," I breathe. "Do you mean '*indelible* ink'?"

"Maybe," he says, tickling our baby under the armpits. She's too young for giggles yet, but her eyes go wide with what can only be glee. "What's the difference?"

"'Indelible' means 'permanent,'" I tell him slowly. "And now our daughter's messier than she was before."

Cole pauses, as if to let the information sink in. But instead of sinking, it kind of slides off.

"Not to mention cuter," he says. And he sticks his nose right up to Olivia's. "Aren't you, widdle Wivvie? Aren't you so *cute*?"

"You spelled 'mommy' wrong," is all I can muster.

Cole just shrugs. "It was the only way to fit the exclamation mark. Now, you ready to crack these dishes?"

"Sure," I reply with a sigh. I resnap our daughter's onesie, mentally adding "scour Olivia's stomach" to my growing to-do list. It's been two weeks since Alan and his cronies dumped us here in the Antarctic and then high-tailed it back to home base, so you'd think I'd've gotten used to these little Cole/Olivia hijinx by now—the poorly fastened diapers, the "spinning airplane" game that almost always results in Olivia barfing on *me*. . . . I've tried to impress upon Super Fun-Time Daddy that maybe *feeding* the baby would be slightly more helpful than making her puke, but so far this hasn't seemed to click.

"Unless you wash dishes far better than you spell," I tell Cole, tucking Olivia safely into her papoose at my chest, "we're going to be here for *hours*."

"Nah," Cole argues. "I signed us up for dish duty on purpose." He taps the side of his head like he's extra proud of what's inside, then straightens back up and turns to Clark, who has just walked in carrying a stack of dirty tin dishes half as tall as he is. "Where are the soap pods?" Cole asks.

Clark drops the dishes with a clatter into the sink and then hands Cole a seriously ripped-up blue sponge and points to a box of borax on the counter. Cole stares blankly at the sponge in his hands as if it were a dead rat he's been told to brush his teeth with. "Welcome to the team, newbie," Clark says good-heartedly, then pats Cole's arm before turning and exiting the kitchen.

"Two seconds, huh?" I mutter, patting Olivia's bottom. I run my eyes over the towering stack of dishes. Plates, mugs, forks. Not to mention the seriously grimy pots and pans still on the range.

Cole has the look of a man who just found out the Easter Bunny was guilty of using performance-enhancing drugs. "Are you kidding me?" he squeaks. "No soap pods? Whoever heard of washing dishes without soap pods?"

I reach over and flip on the faucet for him. "Water, good," I say in my best Tarzan voice. I sprinkle some borax flakes into the sink. "Soap make bubbles. Scrub grease."

From across the kitchen, Bernard lets out a low whistle. He and my father signed up this morning for lunch prep. That's the thing about prison: the instant your crappy breakfast is over, it's time to start making your crappy lunch. Right now the two of them are busy reconstituting dehydrated potato flakes and forming them into tots to be fried.

"You're not in Kansas anymore, man," Bernard calls over to Cole. He laughs into his bowl of tots, like this is the funniest thing a person has ever said.

Weirdly, my dad is giggling too. "Or Ardmore, for that matter," he chimes in.

"Right on," Bernard tells him. "If you ask me, we've got it made here." He blows a wisp of his scraggly hair out of his face. "We've become slaves to technology, you know. Past time we broke free. *Be* the soap pod you want to see in the world, you know?" He and my dad exchange a meaningful nod, and then—I swear—they actually fist-bump.

Old people are so weird.

Yeah, Bernard and my dad have become something resembling friends in the last two weeks. They make for a weird duo—my father, the picture of control and reason, and Bernard, the scraggly, cardigan-wearing hippie. But I guess it makes a strange sort of sense, since they're the only two non-Almiri grown-ups here. My dad took an instant shine to Bernard, calling him "a walking reminder of an academia long since past." (Personally, I'm more inclined to agree with Ducky's description: "weird granola dude.") But if Bernard offers my dad a pleasant distraction in the form of philosophical debates while they reconstitute their spuds, then who am I to complain?

The door swings open, and in marches Ducky, hauling a gray mop and a bucket of sudsy water. He grunts as he sloshes half the floor. "Careful if you go out there. It's, like, wet." He jerks his head back to indicate the scattered pools of water he's left in his wake.

"Duck, I *told* you I'd help with that," I say as he starts in on what appears to be a fairly lackluster mopping job. Since baby Olivia isn't exactly the most useful shift buddy, there's an odd number for chore partners, so Ducky is continually getting stuck scrubbing toilets and changing sheets by himself. I've been feeling more than a little guilty about always doing chores with Cole, so today I told Duck I'd give him a hand once I was free.

Ducky doesn't look up, just continues to push murky water around with the mop. "You've got your hands full," he tells me.

"Ducky, really, it's not a problem, I don't mind. Just give me ten—"

"I said I've *got* it," he snaps.

I jerk my eyes to Cole, who's so busy frowning at a mound of soap scum, he seems not to have noticed the tension in the room.

"Okay," I say quietly. "Fine."

"Fine," Ducky replies.

I wonder what's up *his* butt. All I tried to do was help. But, like Ducky said, I *do* have my hands full, and heaven knows I don't need anything else to deal with.

"Hand me one of those sponges," I tell Cole with a sigh. And we get to washing.

I guess you could say we're settling into a sort of rhythm here at the bottom of the Earth, but it hasn't been easy. The first couple days I found it very difficult to sleep — less because of the whole two-hours-of-darkness thing, and more because of the screaming-infant thing. Anyway, it's mostly been wake up at 4:00 a.m.-ish, feed the baby, burp the baby, change the baby, fall back to sleep for thirty seconds, get woken up for breakfast, feed the baby while shoveling down my oatmeal, burp the baby, change the baby, chores, chores, baby poop, nap (not mine), more chores, more poop, and on and on until about 11:30 p.m., when I finally manage to zonk out. If I'm lucky, there's, like, twenty minutes at the end of the day where I can just unwind. Good ole Cole has been doing his best to help . . . but, again, there are more helpful things he could be doing than dangling our baby upside down, despite his claims that "she's into it." I'm hopeful that someday one of his fatherly activities with Olivia will *not* result in spit-up, so that he can see for himself that such a thing is possible.

After an all-too-long bout of moping, Cole finally seems to have gotten into the swing of dishwashing. Turns out he's not too bad at scrubbing when he puts his mind to it. He's whipping out three clean plates to every one of mine. Maybe that's another advantage the Almiri have over us simple humans—exceptional scrubbing skills.

"Look at us," Cole says, over the rush of the faucet. "Mom, dad, baby." He nods at little Olivia, head tilted back in her carrier and her mouth open ever so slightly as she settles into a really good snooze. Cole kisses me on the neck as I scour a particularly stubborn bit of grease crusted onto one of the frying pans. "This is pretty great, huh?"

I know from firsthand experience that there are worse ways to spend a morning than cleaning breakfast dishes with a hot guy and the cutest baby girl who's ever been created. Still, it's not exactly the ideal situation, either.

"What are we going to do, Cole?" I ask softly.

"Do?" he repeats, as if the notion of doing anything besides living out our lives in the frozen tundra was completely foreign to him.

"Byron made it pretty clear that this was only a temporary stop for me and Olivia." I keep my voice low, so as not to worry the others more than they probably already are. "And when they pull us out of here, who knows what . . ." I glance down at the sleeping creature on my chest. I can't even bear to imagine *anything* happening to her. "And you, *you're* here indefinitely, thanks to not being able to keep your junk in your pants. So, I say again, what are we gonna do about it?"

Slowly, Cole nods. "Yeah," he agrees. "You're right, we should have a plan." He looks up at me and smiles. "You're real smart, you know that, Elvs?"

"Well, 'smart' is a relative term," I joke, trying to bring some lightness back into the conversation. "By the way, 'relative' means something that's—hey!" I shriek, wiping the tiny bubbles off my lip. Cole laughs, hand tensed over the sudsy water like he's going to splash me again. "Careful of the baby," I warn him. "If you get suds in her eyes, I'm making *you* wash them out."

"Eh." Cole laughs, splashing me again. "O-Co could probably use a bath."

"Dude," I say. "I *told* you. O-Co is so not happening." I'm almost regretting agreeing to give my little girl the middle name Colette in her daddy's honor.

*Splash!* "Okay, fine," Cole says. He's got suds on his eyebrow. "Liv-Lette, then."

"That's it," I say, protecting Olivia's face as I shoot her daddy with one seriously epic water bomb of my own. "I'm suing for sole custody."

"*DUDE.*" Ducky's outburst is so loud, it stops Cole and me mid–splash attack. We turn to see my PIP, forlorn, staring at the soaking wet floor behind us. "I already mopped that spot."

I frown. "Sorry, Duck," I say. Truth be told, the spot doesn't look much different from the rest of the floor. Still, I feel like a shit. "Here." I reach for the mop. "Why don't you take a break?" There are about nine hundred things I'd rather do than Duck's chores, but I haven't seen my bud this close to losing it since the third grade, right before he hit Yani Bloomquist with his trombone case for heckling him about his band uniform. "I'll do the rest."

"Don't worry about it, really." Ducky jerks the mop away from me so quickly that he overturns the bucket. Filthy water everywhere.

"Ducky!" I screech, up on my toes. But it's too late—my

shoes are soaked through. I squint at him. "What's going on with you?"

He leans down to pick up the bucket, then slams it down on the ground hard. "Oh, nothing," he snaps. "Just cleaning up after your messes. As usual."

"What's *that* supposed to mean?" I shriek back. Seriously, who is this pissy freak, and what has he done with my bestie? In the corner I spy Dad and Bernard, trying to make a discreet exit out of the kitchen to avoid getting swept up in our little spat. I wish I could join them.

"Just forget it," Ducky grumbles.

"I will not just forget it, Spaz Attack. Spill."

"I thought that's what I just did."

"Ducky, seriously, dude—"

"You wanna know why I'm pissed? 'Cause I'm always getting dragged through shit because of you, Elvie," Ducky barks back. I freeze in place, my head back ten centimeters on my neck like the force from Ducky's words is physically shoving it. I don't think Ducky's ever yelled at me. *Ever.*

"Oh, like I've never had to put up with crap because of you?" I stammer back.

"When was the last time I got *you* locked up in a high-security alien prison, Elvie?"

I blink, trying to be sympathetic. "It sucks for me too, Duck," I begin softly, but he cuts me off.

"I haven't even *spoken* to my mom in almost three weeks, Elvie," he says. "She probably thinks I'm dead." I suck in my breath. With everything that's been going on, somehow Ducky's family never even popped into my head.

"I'm sorry," I say, suddenly feeling worse than I knew was possible. "I never meant . . . I wish you weren't here, really, I do."

His eyes flit to Cole beside me, who's totally *not* pretending to ignore our fight (thanks, Cole), just standing staring with his mouth open as it all unfolds before him. "Yeah," Ducky replies flatly, eyes fixed on Cole. "I got that."

"No," I say, face-palming. "That's not what I . . . Ducky, you're just upset."

"Yeah," he snaps again. "Of *course* I'm upset, Elvie. I'm like a frigging *stick figure* in a camp full of superheroes, and for what?" I try to grab the mop from him again, but he jerks it back once more. "I'm sick of being the sidekick in 'The Amazing Adventures of Elvie Nara,'" he tells me. He stares at the mop handle for a second as though unsure what to do with it, then seems to make up his mind. "You know what?" he says, tossing the mop at me. I catch it awkwardly. "Maybe I *will* let you do the floors. I'm done." He spins on his heel and marches to the door, tracking sudsy footprints as he goes.

That's it. Do I feel bad for the guy? Of course. But did I get him dragged here on purpose? Hardly. I will not be made to feel guilty.

"If you're so sick of being my sidekick," I shout after him as he reaches the door, "then go have your own adventure, dumbass!"

The door swings closed behind him, and I turn back to the sink, shoulders slumped. I lean the mop against the wall and do my best to shake off the argument as I begin to empty the clean dishes from the rack. Ducky's just tired, I tell myself. He didn't mean any of it.

But my mood isn't improved when I look at the dish rack.

"Cole!" I screech, suddenly realizing the key to my boyfriend's amazingly fast dishwashing skills. "Are you kidding me? These still have food all over them!"

"Really?" Cole asks, totally nonplussed. "I wiped them all."

"With what, your feet? Did you even use soap?"

Cole, of course, merely shrugs. "So they're a little dirty," he says. "So what? I'm not competing in the Olympics or anything."

I do my best to steady myself. No use fighting with Cole, too. "I'm pretty sure there's no Olympic dishwashing even—" I stop talking when I feel Cole's arm on my waist. I jump, startled. Thankfully, Livs continues to sleep soundly, still smacking her lips. "Cole," I say quietly.

He kisses the nape of my neck, wriggling his arm around the two of us—me and the baby both. "Hey," he says. And I can just hear the warm smile in that one word. "You want to, um"—he raises his eyebrows—"do stuff?"

So subtle, my Cole.

My skin is tingly at his touch. How long has it been since Cole and I had an actual moment together? I look down at baby Olivia. Oh yeah. A little over nine months.

"Cole," I say again. I do not turn around. "Not now, all right?"

"But . . ." He plants one on me. An epic Cole Archer kiss. It is wet and warm and wonderful.

I've got to say, the guy sure makes a compelling argument. Still . . .

"Cole." I pull away.

"You don't want to do it," he pouts.

"I'd rather just . . . talk," I tell him honestly.

Cole scrunches up his nose. "Seriously?"

Cole's hand is back on my waist. His lips are back on mine. I'm goose-pimply all over.

"See?" he says softly, in between pecks. His lips are soft and full and beautiful. "You *do* want to do stuff. I can tell."

My eyes dart open, and I catch a glance of the dirty dishes in the sink. Ducky's mop against the wall. And our baby—our *baby*—who's going to wake up not too long from now and need to be fed again. After which she will need to be changed. Again. And guess who's going to end up doing all of *that*?

"Not now, all right, Cole?"

"But—"

"I said not now!"

Cole's eyes go huge, like I just smacked him on the snout with a rolled-up newspaper. "Sorry," I mutter.

"It's okay," he says into the sink, taking up his terrible dish-washing again. "You're just tired. I get it."

I try not to be offended by the notion that the only reason not to suck face with Cole Archer is because "I'm tired." I've got other things to worry about. Like how right about now it's finally occurring to me that the one person I need to be talking about Serious Life Issues with is the same guy who just spelled "Mommy" incorrectly on our daughter's stomach in perma-nent marker.

"Elvs?" Cole calls.

But I'm already halfway out the kitchen door, almost without realizing that I'm walking. "I'm fine, just finish up without me, okay?" I shout over my shoulder.

Cole says something else as the door closes behind me, but honestly, at this moment, whatever he has to say can wait. Because if I don't get some air into my lungs, I think I might burst.

After I hand off Olivia to her doting grandfather, I make my way outside so that the pressure building up in my brain has somewhere to go. There are six dogs milling about outside their kennel when I exit the log-cabin exterior of the camp. The snow is light and dry underneath my damp shoes, and I laugh as one of the dogs starts lathering my face with a series of hard-core face-lickings. Yeah, maybe this was exactly what I needed right now.

"Pontius!" comes Oates's scolding voice behind me. "Down! Down, boy!"

As soon as the dogs hear Oates, all of them immediately snap to attention—back on their haunches, tails wagging, ears relaxed. I turn and see Oates heading our way, one enormous bag of puppy chow loaded across each shoulder.

"Miss Elvie," he greets me cordially. "I see Pontius is still keen on you." When he reaches the kennel, Oates unslings the food bags, which land with two heavy plops in the snow, and the dogs take that as their cue to go back to their regularly scheduled business. Two of the bigger huskies begin nuzzling the bags of food like if they're nice enough, the bags will give up the food of their own accord. Meanwhile, Pontius returns to his Elvie love fest.

I laugh. Nothing like doggie smooches to lift your spirits. "We've got a regular love affair going, Pontius and me," I say, leaning down to rub Pontius's muzzle. "Don't we, boy?" He's a beautiful tan husky, and other than Oates, I'm the only person that Pontius will play with. Unless you count when he stole Cole's hat right off his head and buried it behind the cabin.

"He's a good judge of character," Oates replies.

The dogs whine and whimper as Oates tears into the first bag, but as soon as he pours the kibble into the trough, the canines go to town, shoving at each other for prime food-gobbling position. Pontius allows me one last nuzzle before leaving to join them.

While the dogs chow down, I turn and stare out into the snow, which this afternoon is mostly masked by a heavy blanket of white fog. I can barely see more than a few hundred meters before the snow and the fog meld into one giant splotch of white. Out here, in the crisp air, my thoughts slow their frantic swirling and begin to settle at the surface of my brain.

"It's easy to find yourself a little stir-crazy at first," Oates says, reading me like a book. "Tensions invariably flare between even dear friends. It will pass."

"What if it doesn't?" I ask.

Oates shrugs. "Then it doesn't."

Great.

"I'm fine, really," I say. "Just some drama with Ducky and Cole."

Oates nods, the kind of polite nod that indicates that he'd rather be talking about just about anything besides my teen-age girl feelings. He turns around holding the two empty bags and moves without saying a word toward the large incinerator unit that's about thirty yards away from the cabin. He glances behind him when he's about halfway there, and I realize he means for me to follow him. I leave the chomping dogs and rush to catch up.

No one ever bothers to shovel out this stretch, and the snowdrifts are nearly a meter high, so I have to push hard to keep up. Oates, of course, cuts through the snow like it's powder. I stop a few meters behind Oates as he opens the chute to the incinerator feeder and tosses the empty bags in. Once he closes the chute, a sudden puff of black smoke shoots up into the air and quickly dissipates. Oates busies himself with something on the side of the incinerator.

"You're fortunate to have two men here who love you very dearly, Miss Elvie," Oates says.

"Love?" I practically choke on my own spit. How carefully has this guy been listening to my conversations? When did me and my buddies become the new Cape Crozier daytime soap? "Well, I don't think it's quite *that* drama—"

"Your child's father, and your own," Oates clarifies.

"Ah." Clearly *I'm* the only one with the soap opera fantasies. "Er, yeah," I say. "I guess that's true."

"The lad Donald is quite protective of you as well," Oates continues. "This is good." He looks at me, and even though his mouth stays even, his eyes smile down on me warmly. "It's good to have friends you can rely on to stay true."

"Oates, who was she?" I ask. "The woman who got you sent here." The question's been buzzing in my brain for weeks: What was she like, the mysterious woman so lovely that she could sway stoic, duty-bound Titus Oates away from the Code?

If Oates is taken aback by my brashness, he doesn't let on. "No woman, Miss," he says quietly.

"But I thought all you guys here had broken the Code and had, er . . . *relations* with an extra Earth girl or two."

"There are laws that govern us beyond the Code, child," Oates replies, an old, lingering sadness in his voice.

"So what are you here for, then?" Hell, if I'm already in this deep, I might as well keep digging. "Industrial espionage? Genocide? Were you one of the studio execs who green-lit *Sucker Punch*?"

Oates bends down and resumes fiddling with the incinerator. "I'm here," he says, "for staying true to my friends."

"Dude," I say, feeling the ice starting to break ever so slightly, "I'm stuck in this place freezing my butt off for who knows how long, and all you can give me is—"

"Freezing your butt off?" Oates interrupts, as if missing my point entirely. "You're cold?"

"Well, no," I say, realizing it's true. I'm not cold, though I should be. It's most definitely below freezing out, and when I look down, I notice that I didn't remember to zip my thermal up all the way when I came outside. "I guess I'm, I dunno, adapting to the cold, or whatever," I say. Even my toes aren't that chilly, despite the dirty mop water that's icing up under my laces.

Oates looks at me for a beat too long before he starts talking. "Adaptation is good, especially in a place like this. It means you're strong." He rises to his feet, gesturing toward the cabin, where the dogs have finished eating and are tumbling and tousling with one another. "Take the dog," he says. "Long ago, when the dog was still a wolf, he was a rogue, and lived or died by what he could catch. Then the wolf came into camp, learned to live with humans, and he changed. Adapted. Soon the wolf was a dog, and the dog helped man, and the man helped dog. The two species learned to coexist. They even came to depend on each other."

"So you're saying I should learn to fetch slippers?" I ask. I'm a little confused by this whole monologue.

Oates merely pats his leg for Pontius, who comes leaping over to greet him. "That which remains still cannot survive," he replies, scratching the husky's head.

I'm pondering Oates's Yoda-like proclamation when I'm shaken from my reverie by that same *Crack-BOOM!* noise off in the distance that I heard when we first arrived two weeks ago.

"Are you *sure* it never thunderstorms here?" I say to Oates, turning back around. "Because it seriously sounds like . . ." I trail off.

Oates isn't paying attention to me. He's staring intently past me into the blanket of white fog, in this way that feels vaguely ominous.

*Crack-BOOM!*

"Uh, Oates?" I say. "What is that—"

He puts up a hand to quiet me, and that's when I pick it up. It's not the thunder-crack that's got him spooked. There's another sound underneath it. A very quiet whirring that grows gradually louder. I do my own ominous staring-off-into-the-creepy-white-fog thing, but all my pitiful human eyes can make out is a giant heap of nada.

Until . . .

Several dark splotches begin to appear out of the fog. Five splotches, to be precise. As they get within a few hundred meters of us, I'm able to distinguish what they are: five large snowmobiles, cruising over the snow toward the camp.

"More supplies?" I ask Oates. "Why is headquarters sending more stuff so soon after we got here? And why didn't *we* get to cruise in on snowmobiles?"

"Because," Oates says solemnly. And when I look up at him, his stony face makes all of his previous stony faces look downright expressive. "We don't use snowmobiles."

"Uh . . ."

"Get behind me, child."

A fierce chill hits me in the stomach. The Jin'Kai. They've found us.

The snow instantly seems to grow a hundred times thicker than before. I feel like I'm stuck in one of those nightmares where you try to run but your legs won't work as I try to push through the snow to hide behind Oates. Not that it will do much good. There's at least four or five guys on each of the snowmobiles, and as tough as Oates is, I don't think he's going to stand much of a chance against twenty some Jin'Kai, who presumably are armed. Our only hope is if we can get back to the cabin and warn the others.

Oates must have the same idea, because he's slicing through the waist-deep snow to make a path for us away from the intruders. But instead of ducking inside the cabin, he suddenly shifts direction and heads to the dog kennel. A split second later he emerges brandishing a long pole, one of the snares he uses to corral the dogs when they're overly rambunctious. Oates darts back in front of me just as the first two snowmobiles blast into camp.

The riders are wearing black thermals with full ski masks covering their faces. Which is a little moustache-twirly-cliché, even for the Jin'Kai. Oates extends the snare out horizontally in front of him, and with a lightning-quick jump forward he manages to cross-check both of the drivers, knocking them off their vehicles before they can brake to a stop. They fall backward into the snow, forcing the other riders to bail out before the mobiles crash into the side of the cabin. The Jin'Kai roll away and crouch into attack positions, but they're a bit clumsier than I would have expected. At least, compared to Oates, that is. Dude is a straight-up ninja.

The Jin'Kai charge at him en masse, brandishing what look like batons. So apparently this ice-bound outfit thought they could capture me without the use of ray guns. Interesting. There's ten attackers encircling Oates, while the last three snowmobiles whir in behind them, but Oates doesn't seem fazed in the slightest. He bobs and weaves, avoiding each intended blow, using the momentum of his attackers against them as he whacks one in the back and trips another one up before lunging past.

And then it happens. One of the Jin'Kai douchetards spots me and makes a move toward me. But before the dude can get two paces closer to me, Oates has caught him around the neck with the snare. He yanks him down hard into the snow.

"Elvie, go!" he shouts.

For serious, that is some badass shit.

I'm busy thanking my lucky stars I somehow always seem to be sided with the buffest aliens, when Oates suddenly stumbles forward, tripping over the dude he's just downed, and I realize he's been smacked by a second Jin'Kai in the back. Despite his limp, Oates manages to spin on his attacker, landing a crunching *smack* with the butt of the pole against the dude's jaw.

I turn toward the door of the cabin, which is feeling a lot farther away than the six or so meters that it actually is. And I'm halfway there when one of the snowmobiles cuts in front of me, spraying me in the face with icy snow as it slices to a stop. My path is blocked. I raise my hands in the air—'cause, I don't know, that's what you do—and my eyes dart frantically, searching for Oates. But it's all a mess of confusion and snow and fog and *seriously loud barking*, and I can't find him anywhere.

"It's a girl!" one of the Jin'Kai shouts, leaping off his ride.

"Grab her!" a second shouts. The first guy moves toward me. Given the snowdrifts and all, the number of available evasive maneuvers in my repertoire is slim, so the dude's on me pretty quick. My only remaining move is one I haven't stooped to since fourth grade.

As the Jin'Kai grabs both my upraised arms, I knee him squarely where the sun don't shine.

His balls, I mean. The sun does not shine there.

"Oof!" my attacker shouts, dropping me with a *plop* on my butt in the snow. "You little—"

Before he can finish, a flash of tan fur comes to my rescue, tackling the Jin'Kai into the snow. As I scramble to my feet,

Pontius is snarling and shredding the dude's black thermal with his massive jaws.

I knew that doggy liked me. The other dogs have all run away, or are taking in the scene semicuriously while licking themselves in unmentionable places. Not my buddy Pontius, though.

"Pontius!" I shout, suddenly eyeing another intruder, smaller than the rest, who has snuck around from behind the snowmobile with his baton raised. "*Pontius!*" But the dog is too busy chewing on the guy underneath him to listen.

Before the would-be PETA offender can strike the brave pup, I jump on the guy's back. And to my surprise, the Jin'Kai topples over, burying us both in a drift. I wrestle the baton out of his hand without much effort and toss it away. He struggles underneath me, but I have him pinned.

"No offense," I say, panting. I wedge my knee farther into the guy's stomach and glare at his ski-masked face. "But you've got to be the lamest, weakest Jin'Kai I've ever met."

"Jin *what?*" comes the high-pitched response. I do a double take. The person whose kidney I'm currently grinding to paste is . . . a woman.

A baton blow to my noggin creates a rather unpleasant sensation, and I topple forward. I think I hear my female adversary call out "No!" as she pulls herself out from under me, but I can't say. The sky above me is spinning round and round and round. A few hands grab me underneath my arms, and I am brusquely lifted to my feet.

"Are you all right? Can you walk?" the woman barks at me. I try to focus on her masked face, but everything is still spinning.

Close by I can make out Oates, his arms tied behind his back, kneeling in the snow. Pontius is being held at bay with the very snare that Oates had been using only a moment earlier. "Can you walk?" the question comes again. In response I straighten up to my full five feet, three inches, and eye my attackers very seriously.

And vomit.

The woman turns around to Oates.

"We're here for Bernard Oglesby," she spits through her mask. "Your hostage. Is he inside the facility?"

Hostage? Bernard? I want to explain to this woman that Bernard's no hostage—unless he's the kind of hostage who *walks across the fricking tundra to give his captors a break on fuel cell money*. But I'm too busy working on this potential concussion I've got going to tell her that, and Oates—surprise surprise—says nothing at all.

The woman marches toward the cabin. "Bring him," she instructs her friends. She flicks a thumb at me. "Carry her."

I am lifted off my feet and carried by one of the intruders as we make our way inside the cabin. It's clear once we're all inside that these guys, whoever they are, aren't Jin'Kai. They're not nearly buff enough. Furthermore, they pretty much have no idea what they're doing—they're no finely tuned commando force like the one Cole and Captain Bob were a part of, that's for sure. They rummage through the cabin, knocking over shelves, before coming to the sliding door in the floor that leads to the underground facility.

"Bring me the C-4," the woman calls out to someone behind her. One of the goons hands her the small putty explosive, and she sticks it against the door.

"That won't be necessary," Oates says. She stops and raises an eyebrow. Well, I assume she raises an eyebrow. There's no way to tell with the ski mask and all. But it's certainly an eyebrow-raising moment. "There's no need for further violence," Oates goes on. "I will tell you the code provided you give me your word not to harm anyone else."

"We're not here to harm anyone," the woman replies. "So long as everyone plays nice."

Oates stares at her for a moment, before finally speaking. "Three, two, six, three, eight, two, seven."

The woman plugs the number into the control panel. There is a sharp beep, a slight delay, and then the door slides open. The woman gestures to some of her cohorts, who rush ahead down the stairs. I give Oates a look as we are shoved together down the stairs at the back of the group, but he gives no sign that he notices.

The door doesn't usually beep.

We come down into the main hallway, and strangely, the door to the canteen at the far end is closed. The hall is completely empty.

"Where is everyone?" the woman asks in a whisper. Her comrades have taken up defensive positions on either side of the hallway, looking around for any sign of movement.

"It's nearly lunchtime," Oates says calmly. "They'll be in the canteen down yonder, prepping the meal."

Another flick of her head, and the intruders make their way quietly down the hall. My heart is racing in my chest, my head still throbbing. I can't believe I've gotten myself in the middle of an interspecies attack *again*. This sort of destructive pattern is the kind of thing that girls seek therapy for.

"Once we have control of the facility, find out where Bernard is being kept," the woman orders one of the dudes walking with her. "Knowing him, he's probably leading them all in a drum circle —"

Before she can finish, it happens. The doors lining the hallway on either side of us suddenly swoosh open, all at once, and nearly every Almiri prisoner floods out. It happens so fast, and my brain is still so fuzzy, that I'm not even sure what's gone down. It's just a flurry of arms and shouting. There are nearly as many Almiri as intruders, and with the jump they have on them, they almost don't need their super strength. But super strength never hurts, and within a few moments all of the intruders have been disarmed and subdued.

Only then does the canteen door slide open, revealing Rupert on the other side.

"Thanks for the heads up, Titus," he tells Oates, grinning. "And to think, some of us thought that installing a fail-safe code was extreme."

"You treacherous Almiri pig," the woman spits at Oates, struggling against the prisoner who holds her arms pinned behind her. Oates moves past her into the canteen and turns his back to Rupert so that he can cut the binds on his wrists.

"I'm not the one attacking someone's home," Oates replies calmly. "Bring them in," he says to one of the other Almiri. "Let's see who we've got here."

When we get inside the canteen, I spot Dad and Ducky and Cole standing near one of the far tables. Cole is bouncing Olivia in her papoose. He holds out an arm for me, but I rush right to the baby, scoop her out, and snuggle her tightly.

"You're becoming quite the action heroine," Dad says.

"I think it's the company I keep." I stroke Olivia's feather-soft hair. I'm just so happy she's okay. She didn't even wake up in the scuffle.

"I'm glad you're all right too," Cole says, startling me into a mega-humongous bear hug. But I don't mind for one second accepting it. After all, I *did* almost just get ski-mobiled in half.

When I look up, Ducky's kicking his toes into the floor awkwardly, looking anywhere but at me. I finally catch his eye.

"Sorry," I mouth silently.

"Sorry," he mouths back.

We're gonna be okay, me and Duck. I let myself relax and squeeze my baby closer, taking in the scene around me.

One by one the intruders are unmasked, and I'm surprised to discover that the woman I went knee-to-stomach with outside is not the only female in the bunch. Of the twenty or so ski-masked baddies, about half are ladies. And if that weren't a tip-off that these enemies weren't Jin'Kai, their general appearance sure is. I don't want to sound catty, but runway models these guys are *not*. Between them they've got a smattering of receding hairlines, pronounced teeth, and weak chins, just to name a few physical knocks that afflict normal, non-Almiri/Jin'Kai folk.

Still, they're not all hard on the eyes. I notice Ducky's gaze lingering on one particular intruder standing not half a meter from Oates. A reed-thin, leggy redhead, probably about twenty-two or twenty-three.

"Cute," I lean over to tell Ducky. "Kind of a long face,

but you could almost call her striking. You have good taste in villains."

Within a nanosecond Ducky's face is as red as the girl's hair.

"What do you suggest we do with the mules?" I hear Jørgen sneer. And when I look over, I'm shocked to see that for once he's not glaring daggers at *me*. This time he's eyeing the ski-masked intruders. Talk about eloquent. Man, the guy really needs to expand his burn vocabulary.

"The lot will remain in the pantry until you hear otherwise from me," Oates instructs his fellow Almiri. He gives Jørgen a good long look. "You will not harm a one of them."

"You heard the man," Jørgen grumbles to the other Almiri, sounding about as thrilled as if Oates had just told him to go pluck his nose hairs out, one by one, with chopsticks. "Into the pantry!"

"Except for that one," Oates says, pointing to the female ringleader at the far end of the long room, who has yet to be unmasked. She's still struggling against her captor's grip, which is very clearly useless—but you've got to admire the lady's moxie. "And the ambassador," Oates continues. He shoots a glance around the room. "Where is he?"

Which is exactly the moment when the back door opens and Bernard enters, still in the process of zipping up his fly.

"What's going on?" Bernard asks, clearly unaware of all the excitement. "What'd I miss?"

"Bernard!" the masked woman calls out. Bernard turns at the sound of her voice and squints at her.

"Zee?" Bernard breaks into a killer grin, clearly unfazed by the new arrivals—or the two Almiri who have quickly tackled him to the ground, binding his hands in front of him. "Babe!" he shouts from the floor. "You came all the way to Antarctica for me? Man, you are a *warrior woman!*"

"Ew," I say, leaning over to exchange snark with Ducky. "*Babe?*"

Ducky's nose is wrinkled just as much as mine. "*Warrior woman?*" he says. "Who the heck *is* this chick?"

Which I guess is precisely the question Oates is wondering too, because he finally takes the opportunity to peel off the ringleader's ski mask.

Next to me, my father sucks in a sudden deep breath. "Olivia?" he says, his voice thin and wavering.

I look down at my baby. But there's absolutely nothing wrong with her, not that I can see. I turn to my dad.

"*Olivia.*" He says the name again, whispers it this time. And he's not looking at his grandchild.

He's looking at my *mother*.

# Chapter Five

# WHEREIN OUR HEROINE IS ALL, LIKE, WHOA

Um, *whoa.*

I mean, just, *whoa.*

My mother is *alive?* And she's *here?*

I repeat: WHOA.

"Miss?"

I snap to, and realize that Oates is waiting for me to respond. I guess he's been "Miss"-ing me for a while.

I tear my eyes away from Zee—er, my *mom.* "Yeah?" I say. My voice is shaky.

"In the medical closet," he informs me, "you will find gauze and antiseptic. Please fetch it quickly and meet us in the storeroom."

"But I—"

It's too late. He's already moving down the hall, Zee kicking and screaming the whole way as she and Bernard are dragged in tow by the Almiri.

I turn to my father, who amid the chaos and the confusion is looking . . . pretty calm, actually.

"Dad?" I say as I watch him watch his former wife being led away. "Are you *sure* that's Mom? 'Cause, well, not to state the obvious or anything, but I thought she was, like, dead."

He thinks on that, then nods.

"For a woman dead and cremated sixteen years ago," he replies, still staring down the hall—despite the fact that Oates and the others have already turned the corner, "she's holding up pretty well."

"But how—"

"No idea," he says, snapping his attention back to me. "I guess it's up to you to figure it out."

"But—"

"Medical closet's that way."

I easily find the gauze and antiseptic Oates asked for, and race to meet him in the storeroom. As I enter the large white space, the lights grow slightly brighter, then fade back to their original brightness, the censors that operate their intensity apparently on the fritz. A quick glance around the storage locker reveals a very weird assortment of items, ranging from sports equipment (rolled-up badminton nets, athletic mats, various balls) all the way to what appears to be a stash of theater costumes and props. Ever since we landed here, I've wondered how the Almiri manage to keep themselves occupied for decades or longer in this snowy prison without any computer access. I guess now I've found the answer. I shudder as I spy a pair of black-dyed corn-husk wigs, imagining what degree of cabin fever could ever push a group of grown men to stage a full production of *The Mikado*.

Bernard and Zee are sitting in two folding chairs in the center of the room, Oates standing in front of them. Bernard is slouched casually, right foot up on his left knee, like he's at a poetry reading. Zee, however, is at full attention, the anger ripe on her face. Their hands are still bound before them, although the two Almiri who led them here are nowhere to be seen. As I approach, I'm shaking so badly, I nearly drop the gauze several times. Good thing baby Olivia is strapped in, or she'd be floor food too.

*My mother*, I keep thinking—on an endless loop in my brain. *That right there is my mother. I'm going to talk to my mom for the very first time.*

There are so many questions I need to ask my mother: How did she get here? Where has she been for the past sixteen years? Why did my father think she was dead?

Most kids get to start with "goo-goo-ga-ga."

"This would be much easier if you would simply cooperate," Oates says to them, motioning me over. He doesn't move a muscle for the first aid kit that I offer him, so I unwrap the gauze and play nursemaid. Zee has a fair amount of bruises on her face and her arms—lots of small cuts. I guess the Almiri did quite a number on her during the surprise attack. I guess *I* did quite a number on her myself when I sat on her.

Whoops.

Still shaking fitfully, I unscrew the cap from the antiseptic cream and dab a little on my mother's face.

*My mom. I'm touching my mom.*

She flinches and jerks away. Instinctively I grab her chin to steady her and try again, attempting to form coherent thoughts so I can shape them into words. But I have no idea what I want to say to this woman. To my *mother*. I am, for once in my life, totally speechless. For her part, she's staring at me. Like, really intensely. Does she know that it's me? Sure doesn't seem like it. If she did, you'd think she'd pick a slightly more emotional response than simply glaring icy daggers at me as I tend to her cuts. Maybe she's just weirded out seeing a chick with the Almiri?

"I'm already aware of who you and your comrades are," Oates tells Zee while I continue doing my best Florence Nightingale. "But perhaps an exchange of names would be in order? I'm Captain Lawrence Edward Grace Oates, although most of the chaps here simply call me Titus."

Baby Olivia sleeps silently at my chest, unaware of the momentous family reunion that is going on right in front of her.

"And?" Oates prods when there is absolutely zero response from my mother. "Madam, you are . . . ?"

Zee shifts her glare from me to Oates, upping the intensity from "level-four scowl" to "full-on face melt." But if there's one dude she won't win a staring contest with in this place, it's the stoic, centuries-old Victorian Brit.

"Zada," Bernard informs Oates after a few moments of awkward dueling glares between them. "Zada Khoury. We all call her Zee."

"Well, then, Zee," Oates continues. "As to the matter of why you are here . . ."

I try to follow the conversation as best I can, to learn more about this woman I clearly don't know at all, but all I can do is stare at her as I dab more cream on her cheek, taking in every centimeter. She is short, I notice, and scrappy.

"We came to rescue *this* asshole," Zee says, gesturing with her head at Bernard. Despite her well-formed muscles, my mother obviously hasn't been eating enough. Her clavicle juts right through her thermal. "Which"—she rounds on Bernard—"is beginning to seem like a colossal misallocation of resources." Her straight dark hair is cropped close to her head, and although she has a few wrinkles around her eyes, she wears her age well. "Weeks of planning, dozens of assets reassigned, and we get here and find you're just *hanging out* with our oppressors like this is some sort of Burning Man." She's aged a lot from the photos, but dur, they were all from, like, twenty years ago.

"She thinks you're gonna lock us all up and, like, throw away the key," Bernard tells Oates, in a tone that practically drips with an eye-rolling *"women."*

Oates shakes his head at that. "Bernard and I have been having discussions of a very different sort since he arrived," he tells my mom.

Zee merely scoffs. "Let me guess. Talks of love and understanding and a détente with the Almiri."

"I told you she's a cynic," Bernard says with a sigh.

My mother is beautiful, really beautiful. More than the pictures gave her credit for. But I don't see a smidge of me . . .

"Just be clear on this, *Almiri*," Zee spits. "Bernard here does not speak for the movement. And we are not so gullible as to think your kind wishes to come to any sort of 'understanding.'"

"You might find our priorities more in line than you realize, madam," Oates offers.

Zee immediately rejects the notion with a laugh. "I have a lifetime of experience concerning Almiri priorities," she tells him disdainfully.

She does?

"That may be true," Oates responds. "But you have no such experience with me."

You know that dream where you show up to history class six weeks late and everyone is gabbing on and on about the Smoot-Hawley Tariff, and you just know you're gonna be screwed on the final because you have no flipping clue what they're talking about? Well, that dream seems like a safe, cozy place compared to how lost I am at the moment. What movement is my mom talking about? And how does she know anything about the Almiri? I squeeze a bit more antiseptic out of the tube and onto my finger, while in her papoose Olivia gives me a gentle sleep-kick.

"Look, babe," Bernard interjects, and for a long second my neural transmitters are so assaulted, I can't hear anything else. *The dude with the musty beard calls my mother 'babe'?* Ew ew barf barf ew. I steady my breathing and do my best to focus, reaching once again for my mother's face.

Maybe, I think, despite the initial evidence, this woman really *isn't* my mother. Because as hard as I search, I can't even find a hint of my face in hers.

"Oates here is an okay dude, all right?" Bernard goes on. "I'll totally vouch for his upstandingness."

"I should have left you to rot the last time you tried to pull a stunt like —"

But Zee doesn't get to finish, because I have dropped the antiseptic on her foot.

*Her chin,* I realize suddenly. *I have her same angular chin.*

"Miss?" Oates is looking at me curiously as I scoop the tube from the floor. "Are you quite all right?"

"Um," I start. Like I said — brain-mouth connection no worky. "May I speak to you in the corner for a moment?"

Oates narrows his eyes ever so slightly as he considers my request, following up with a quick nod. He gestures to the door. I struggle with the cap on the cream like the world's biggest chromer, then finally give up on the whole thing and walk to the corner.

"Everything all right?" Oates's voice is a whisper, his eyes darting to the captives in the chairs several meters away.

"Uh . . ." I'm not entirely sure how to answer that question. "No?" I answer at last.

He nods. "Tell me, then."

I look over Oates's shoulder to my mother, who is staring at us with equal parts curiosity and rage. "So . . . that woman?" I say slowly. "Zee?" Oates nods again. I bounce Olivia gently while she snores. "Yeah. She's sort of . . . my mom? My dead mom? And, like, she hasn't figured out who I am yet? And I don't really know what to say to her."

Oates takes this new information in and seems to process it carefully. Then he does what, I suppose, any good Brit would do in such a situation. "I'm going to make some tea," he replies.

"But—" He's moving for the door. He's not really going to leave me *alone* here, is he?

"Where do you think you're going?" Zee asks, possibly thinking the same thing as me, although probably not for the same reason. "That's it, run to tell your masters about your latest catch!"

"If the conversation does not go to your satisfaction," Oates tells me, handing me his toy popgun, "you have my full permission to shoot her." I stare at the thing, bewildered, before tucking it into the only convenient spot I have available to me—Olivia's papoose, the hilt snuggled against my baby's cheek.

I'm not gonna lie. The girl looks pretty cute with a gun.

"Er, thanks?" I tell Oates.

He only nods in return, then exits.

I stroll back to Zee, doing my best to hold my head up high. This is it. The moment that will change my life forever. *You're my mother*, I open up my mouth to tell her.

But she has no time for me. Instead, she turns to Bernard. "Explain yourself, Bernard," she bellows at him. Honestly, if I were the dude, I'd at least pretend to be a *little* chagrined, because I know for a fact that this lady packs C-4.

But Bernard only shrugs. "I knew you'd never come on your own, so I had to find a way to get you here."

Zee's up on her feet in a flash. With one swift sweep she kicks out the front legs of Bernard's chair, landing him flat on his back. She looms over him, glowering. "Why, Bernard?" she shouts. "Why would you do such a thing?"

"These guys aren't our enemies, Zee," Bernard says,

looking not at all put out that someone looks ready to rip his throat out. "They've been oppressed by the Almiri power structure too. It's like, they're prisoners, right? But it's a prison of their *mind*. We need to set them free. These guys could be our way in. Unless, of course, you'd reconsider my idea of going straight to By—"

Zee moves to kick him in the balls, but Bernard raises his bound wrists in surrender. "Okay, okay! No, then. So this is our best shot."

"I'm through with these ridiculous schemes for some sort of flower-power reunification," she heaves. "We should've left your sorry ass to freeze out here. And *you*"—she jerks her chin in my direction, suddenly turning her venom on me—"I didn't know the Almiri had started keeping pets."

*Zuh?*

"Zee," Bernard says quietly, picking himself up off the ground. "The baby's a girl."

Zee stops, her spaz attack momentarily put on pause. "Oh God." She looks at Olivia, then me, squinting hard. "You don't even *know*, do you?"

"Look," I say, putting my hand on my hip. "I'm starting to get really annoyed at everyone acting like I have the slightest flipping clue what any of you are talking about. And anyway, there's something I need to—"

"Man, I totally thought you *knew*." Bernard settles himself back into his chair. "Okay, what's the best way to put this?" He rubs the back of his right hand with his left palm. "We're, like, the coming together of the yin and the yang."

I roll my eyes. "Not helping," I tell him.

"The offspring of Almiri and humans," he clarifies.

"You're Almiri?" I say skeptically. But I guess you could say I'm . . . intrigued. "Both of you?" That doesn't make sense.

Bernard shakes his head. "No. See, usually when an Almiri impregnates a human, she gives birth to another Almiri. But sometimes there are"—his eyes drift to Olivia—"anomalies."

I follow his gaze to the cooing baby in my arms. "She's not the only one?" I ask, staring at her perfect little face. Her bitty nose, her tiny curving earlobes. The spot on her left cheek where the Almiri starkiss once lay, a perfect constellation of freckles. "This has happened before?"

"Oh yes," Bernard says. "It's extremely rare, but it happens."

"But . . . how?" I ask. "I thought the Almiri could only—"

"Every once in a while," Zee pipes up, and her voice sounds calmer now, steady. Although there is still more than a trace of fury in it. "A long while, when one of those perfect Almiri males impregnates a human host, the fetus mutates. It keeps many of the genetic markers from the father, but it does something the Almiri find loathsome: it takes on genetic attributes of the host mother as well."

"Whoa," I say.

"Right?" Bernard agrees. "Total trip, I know."

"They call us *Ibrida*," Zee spits, and I feel her anger rising again. "'Of the sow and the boar.' A unique genetic species from two distinct ones. *Mules.* The irony, of course," she adds, with almost a laugh, "is that unlike real mules, *we* can breed freely."

"Wait, what?" I ask, snapping my eyes up in her direction.

"Really?" Because I may still be learning about these Almiri fellows, but one thing I do know—when an Almiri mates with a human female and produces an Almiri baby, the mother is left infertile. As in, no more kids, ever—Almiri or otherwise. Which means, if the Almiri aren't super-duper vigilant, they could easily wipe out the human species all together. That's what happened on their original planet, thousands of years ago. And they were so worried it would happen on Earth that they established the Code. And we all know how well that went down. But if these mules or whatever are different . . .

"So, what you're saying is, if someone had one of these *anomalous* babies, instead of a regular Almiri, then . . . they wouldn't be barren afterward?" When Zee nods in the affirmative, I nearly do a little hop 'n' squeal. "That's wonderful!" I exclaim. *I'm not barren.* Just knowing that one less thing has been taken away from me, that I still have, like, *options*, is almost as good as discovering that I have a hidden set of wings.

"Wonderful?" Zee's eyebrows shoot up. "Certainly not the way the Almiri see it."

"But . . ." I'm confused again. "You'd think they'd be *thrilled* to—"

"They claim we threaten their very existence," Zee tells me. "Because we can breed with both Almiri and humans—"

"And other hybrids," Bernard cuts in.

"And other hybrids," Zee agrees. "But no matter whom a hybrid mates with, the result is more hybrids. Which is why the Almiri believe that we *mules* have the capacity to wipe out both 'pure' species. So they lock us up when they get the chance. Or worse."

"Worse?" I press my hand against Olivia's back.

"At first, they thought only to cloister the girls. They didn't realize that some of the boys born had the same genetic mutation. By the time they realized that there were both males and females out there, breeding with the general population, it was too late to effectively control us, so they began taking more extreme measures. They claim to be a morally superior species, so they would never degrade themselves by killing us," Zee snorts. "They prefer a more gradual form of genocide."

When I raise a questioning eyebrow, Bernard lifts his bound hands, so that I can see it—on the back of his right hand where he's always scratching. There is a dark red splotch in the center, like a sunburst. Like a rash you might get from a vaccine.

"Forced sterilization," Zee finishes.

"No," I say. I don't believe it. I just don't. Sure, Byron said Olivia was "dangerous." Sure, he sent her here, and all of us with her, just for knowing about her. But he assured me that was only temporary. "They wouldn't."

But even as the words come out of my mouth, I have to wonder. How much faith do I have in the Almiri? Am I willing to risk my daughter's future on it?

Zee gives me the most contemptuous glare I have ever seen produced by someone other than Britta McVicker. "It's too late for this one, Bernard," she says, still staring at me as she speaks. "We don't have time to open her eyes to the truth. I say we take her hostage, see if we can use her as leverage."

"Dude, I'm *right here*," I say, snapping out of my daze. This is not really turning into the happy family reunion I was hoping for. "Maybe just cool the hostage talk."

Zee—my mother—shrugs. "If you're not with us," she replies, "you're against us. And if you're against us—"

"Then it's totally fine if I shoot your ass?" I say.

I have Oates's popgun trained right at her forehead. I've got a baby in one hand, a gun in the other, and I'm staring down my mother from the end of the barrel. So basically your typical Tuesday.

She just rolls her eyes. "Please stop wasting my time with that toy." So, at least we know she's smarter than Alan. "But nice attempt at making me think you'd ever have the steel to shoot somebody."

"For your information," I spit back, "I *have* shot somebody before. A Jin'Kai that was in my way up on the *Echidna*."

*RANDOM TV INTERVIEWER: Elvie Nara, if there was one thing you'd like your deceased mother to know about you, what would it be?*

*WIDE-EYED, SINCERE ME: What a great question, Stew. Well, I guess if I thought about it really hard, I'd have to say that I'd want her to know that I've shot somebody.*

Zee stares at me blankly. "Jin-what?" she says, for the second time that morning.

"Guys, guys, guys," Bernard says, rising again to stand between us. "We're really getting off on the wrong foot here. This is not how I wanted you to meet my lady love, Elvie."

At that, my mom's face goes suddenly taut.

"Elvie?" she whispers.

My face is just as strained. *"Lady love?"* I squeak.

She's gazing at me, finally really taking me in. And it's

the first time that I've seen her look like anything other than a butt-kicking rescue ops leader all day.

Well, ever, actually.

"Holy shit," she whispers. "Elvan, is that *you*?"

"Uh," I say, suddenly feeling superuncomfortable, like I should straighten out my top or stand with my shoulders back or something. Man, I really do have terrible posture. "I go by Elvie now," I tell her. "But, yeah, it's me."

And I wait for her to hug me. Well, try to hug me with her hands shackled. To jump up and down and screech and holler and cry and gush and ask me how I'm doing, how old I was when I lost my first tooth, how the sophomore sock hop was, how I like my pizza.

She does none of those things.

"I can't believe my daughter turned into an Almiri sympathizer," she says simply.

"Zee?" Bernard asks. He's looking utterly confused. Which is not a new state for him, although given the current situation, it seems totally warranted. "Er, do you still want to take her hostage?"

And all of a sudden it hits me, like some sort of totally obvious boulder to the noggin: if my mother is a hybrid, and my daughter is a hybrid . . .

"I'm a *mule*?" I ask. I'm loud enough that Olivia begins to stir, squirming and writhing, clearly getting hungry, but she's just going to have to wait.

"Don't you ever use that word," my mother scolds. "That's what *they* call us." She sits up a little straighter. "We are *Enosi*. 'The Union.' And you should be proud."

"Enosi?" I work the word over in my mouth.

"I know, right?" Bernard chips in jovially. "'Enosi,' 'Almiri'—all these far-out names that end in *i*, it's so old-school sci-fi."

I shake my head. No way is this happening. There must be some mistake. I'm just a regular teenage girl.

You know, except for the whole alien boyfriend thing, and the half-human child.

"But I'm not like an Almiri at all," I say. "I don't have, like, superpowers or anything."

"No, Elvan, in most ways you are just like any other human girl," she replies. "But you're *not* a human girl. Because for one thing, your biochemistry is incredibly adaptable to environmental conditions. Haven't you ever noticed that you don't get as hot as other people, or as cold, or as sick?"

"I get hot," I tell her. I do not want to be a weird alien freakazoid. I'm just a girl, dammit. "And I get sick plenty."

"But not for long, I'll wager. Think, when was the last time you were sick for more than twenty-four hours?"

I think hard on that. And I can't think of an instance. Even when I was four and Dad thought I was getting the chicken pox, I only got a few welts and then they disappeared the next morning. Dad thought it was just a false alarm, an allergic reaction or something. Could it be that I beat the bug that quickly?

"How long have you been here, Elvan?" Zee asks me.

"Almost two weeks," I say. "They moved us right after—"

"It's very cold down here. You and the baby must be freezing."

"Well . . . ," I say, realizing what she's getting at. "We were at first . . ."

"But not anymore," she says. "Because your body is adapting."

So maybe *that's* why I've been noticing the hair on my forearms and legs getting thicker. I thought it was some sort of awful post-baby hormonal thing.

"We might not be as strong as them, Elvan, or as fast, or as brilliant, or as beautiful, as they all claim to be," Zee continues. "But we've got something they lack. Flexibility. We don't need to change the world around us to fit our needs. Where they stand still, we *move*."

*That which remains still cannot survive.*

I don't want to believe it. I do not. But the baby in my arms is proof in more ways than one. I shouldn't have been able to feed her that first time, not after so many days without breastfeeding. A normal human wouldn't have been able to.

But my body adapted.

"Do you understand now, Elvan?" my mother says. "Do you see why they hate us, why they've persecuted us for years? Do you see why it's ridiculous to assume you can trust any of the—"

"No." I cut her off again. "You don't get to do that. You don't get to waltz in here after sixteen years, and find out you're my mother, and then tell me how to think." I do my best to wrangle the squirmy little creature in my arms. The kid is getting *hungry*. "I have a brain," I tell her. "And I can use it myself."

"Let me know when you decide to do so."

I must've imagined it a million times, what it would be like to have a mother. Someone to tuck me in bed at night when my dad had to work late. Someone to chaperone my school field trips to Amish Country. Someone to yell at me when she caught me sneaking out late to watch flat pics with Ducky.

But I never pictured this.

"They fear you, Elvan. That must be why you're here, in this place. Your very existence is the greatest threat they have to their grip on this planet. You're Enosi, and there's nothing these monsters wouldn't do to destroy you."

Suddenly I'm having a total lightbulb moment. Everything that's happened in the last few months—everything that, at the time, seemed pretty random—is beginning to come into a dim sort of focus. When I was at the Hanover School, didn't Dr. Marsden always say I was "special"? And he lied to his superiors about me too. And when he had the chance to kill me, he didn't. Because he *knew*. Somehow Dr. Marsden knew about me.

And he was up to something.

"The Almiri didn't put me here to destroy me," I say, realizing the truth as the words tumble out of my mouth. "They're protecting me. Or, at the very least, protecting themselves."

"Why would they protect you?" Zee asks. "What, other than you and your child there, would they need protection from?"

"A shift in the balance," I say.

"Sorry, Elvie," Bernard says. "I'm afraid I don't get what you're talking about."

"Well, isn't that a nice turn of events?" I say. But I don't really have time for smug amusement. Because, yes, the more I think about it, the more it becomes clear to me that if Dr. Marsden knew about my being a hybrid—or Enosi, or whatever—he must have been planning on using that to his advantage. And if his other allies, like the construction worker phonies who tried to capture me during my labor, know what he knew . . . well, that could be dangerous for a lot more folks than just me.

"I think it's time we got Oates back in here," I say. "Oh, and by the way, you could've at least mentioned how cute your granddaughter is. That's sort of the polite thing to do." I shift so my mother has a better view of my now-screaming baby. "Olivia Colette," I tell her as she studies me coolly. "I named her after you."

"So that's pretty much the scoop," I sum up, reaching around the feeding infant at my chest to take a swig of Oates's chamomile tea. I gotta say, having a baby is a surefire cure to helping any girl get over exposing-yourself-aphobia. Because, hell, a tiny thing like Fear of Nip Slip is *nothing* compared to the excruciating screams of a hungry infant.

I settle back into my seat as I finish filling in Oates, Zee, Bernard, and my dad (Oates was kind enough to bring him along under the auspices of "carrying the tea") about my theory concerning Dr. Marsden, the Jin'Kai, and their unknown but undoubtedly douchey plans for the hybrids in general and me in particular. Dad already knew most of the facts, so he's only piped in a couple times, to debate a point of interpretation.

Zee seems dismissive of the entire scenario, as if warring alien factions are somehow too far-fetched for a woman who claims to be a superior genetic species born of two different worlds. Bernard, predictably, looks confused.

Oates, meanwhile, has been sitting quietly, taking in my every word.

I look across the table at Dad as little Olivia chows down on her lunch. "You okay, Dad?" He's examining the contents of his teacup hard-core, and I'm a little worried that I may have overloaded his circuitry with questionable facts. Dead wife's not so dead; newly minted best friend is his not-so-dead-wife's lover; daughter's some sort of alien-human hybrid . . . Even Harry Nara couldn't have had the foresight to make crisis folders for all of *that*.

But when he looks up, my father seems the picture of tranquility. "I accept reality and dare not question it," he says to the table.

"Walt Whitman?" Oates asks, warming his hands on his own cup.

Dad jerks his gaze in Oates's direction, surprised, I suppose, that someone got his totally esoteric citation. "Indeed," he says with a smile.

"A wise philosophy in times like these." Oates shifts in his hard wooden chair to face me. "So, Miss Elvie, to make absolutely certain I understand"—he pauses for an infuriatingly long sip of tea. *Sssssssiiiiiiii* . . . (this guy is a perfect fit for Antarctic living, because I swear his default pace is "glacial") . . . *iiiiiiiiiiipppppp*—"you're positive that Byron and the others at headquarters are well aware of the threat of these Jin' . . . ?"

"Kai," I finish for him. "Jin'Kai. And yes, they do know they exist. Before the *Echidna* crashed, Cole downloaded Dr. Marsden's files for Byron to examine. But . . ." I shift Olivia ever so slightly so I can take my own midsentence sip of tea. Delightful. "Marsden was hiding information from his superiors. He told me as much. He must have had personal files, files we weren't able to access before we escaped." I set the teacup back in its saucer with a *click*. "Byron and the others should be looking for the wreck. If it's at all salvageable, it may be possible to find Dr. Marsden's personal files. Then they'd know what we were dealing with."

Oates takes in that information and then, without another word, rises from the table and leaves the room. I turn to the rest of the group to see what they make of *that*, but they aren't much help.

"Why should we warn the Almiri of anything?" Zee wonders. "So these Jin'Kai fellows want to wipe out the entire Almiri race. I say we'll all be better off."

It is a strange feeling, realizing you have more sense than your own mother. I sigh as Olivia pulls away from my chesticular area, letting me know that she's finished eating. "Because," I tell my mom. And it occurs to me, as I'm zipping up my thermal suit, that my mother has probably never done what I just finished doing. Having abandoned us right after I was born, there's a decent chance she never even held me. "The Jin'Kai aren't just a threat to the Almiri anymore. They literally want to *take over the world*. And if they think that they can use the Enosi as a means to an end somehow—if they're already doing experiments on girls like me to find out what

121

makes us tick—then they're a threat to everyone. This isn't Almiri versus Enosi. This isn't Almiri versus humans. This is Jin'Kai versus every single person on the planet Earth. Right, Dad?"

Dad leans forward, face scrunched up in heavy concentration. "Here's the thing I wonder," he says, swishing his cup so hard that a little tea slips out the side. He doesn't even notice. "If you're not dead, then who did we cremate?"

Ugh, Dad. Not helping.

Zee shrugs her shoulders as if the answer to Dad's question is as silly as asking how long one's legs should be to reach the floor. "Some friends broke into the crematorium with a body bag filled with butcher's scraps."

"Pleasant picture." Dad lifts the teacup to his lips but doesn't sip. "And I'm guessing your self-inflicted coma was induced with a Tetrodotoxin Chromate variant?"

"Hydrolyzed gyromitrin," Zee replies.

*Slam!* goes the cup in its saucer. "Hydrolyzed gyromitrin?" Dad cries, his voice dripping in disbelief. "Do you know how *dangerous* that is?"

"Excuse me?" Zee is sitting straight as a rail. I'm pretty sure the hairs on the back of her neck are at attention too.

"You could have done permanent damage to your liver!" Dad continues, practically choking on spittle. "There are a dozen other neurotoxins you could have used instead."

"It's what I had available. What difference does it make now?" Zee asks.

"Only that it was irresponsible in the extreme!" Dad shouts. I haven't seen the veins in his forehead bulge like this since I was eight, when Ducky and I mixed Pop Rocks and GuzzPop in the back of his brand-new car.

"What business is it of yours how I poison myself?" Zee says, her voice getting shrill.

"Guys," I butt in, "maybe now's not the time—"

"Elvie, please," Dad says sharply. "I'm having a discussion with your mother."

"A discussion?" Zee bellows. "More like a lecture. Where do you get off . . ."

Suddenly I feel woozy. I rise up and, just as Oates did, make my way briskly out of the storage room without saying a word.

Neither Cole nor Ducky are anywhere to be seen in the canteen. Only Clark and a few of Jørgen's cronies.

"How's it going in there?" Clark asks me.

"Where's Oates?" I reply.

Clark peers at me for a moment, as if debating whether or not to respond, but eventually motions to the entry hallway. "He's up topside. Said he needed to check something."

"Thanks."

As I exit the climate-controlled stairs and make my way up into the cabin, the cool air hits my skin, settling my nerves a little. But they quickly return to unsettled status when I hear Oates's voice.

"Don't you give me a lecture on 'need to know,'" he declares loudly. It might be the first time I've ever heard the dude raise his voice. "You didn't think this aggressor was a threat we might need to protect ourselves against?"

The response comes from a distorted—yet familiar—

voice. "The threat of the Jin'Kai discovering a couple of prisoners marooned at the South Pole was minimal."

I pause at the top of the stairs, just listening. Thankfully, Livvie is full from her recent feeding and feeling groggy, so she's content simply to listen too. I rub her back slowly, one hand on the door.

"A minimal threat?" Oates shouts. "You've hidden their existence from me for fifty years, you ponce!"

One step farther up the stairs, and the door swooshes closed silently behind me. I look around and find Oates sitting at the table in the corner, hunched over the old ham radio. He clutches the speaker in his hand.

"Lawrence," comes the voice again over the radio. I recognize it now as Byron's. "You are no longer privy to security matters. This should not come as a surprise."

"I'm privy when it suits you," Oates says. "When it has to do with protecting your precious—"

"BUUUUUUUUUUUUUUUUUUUURRRRRRRRRRRR-RRRRRPPPPPPPPPPPPP!"

And that would be Olivia, ruining my eavesdropping moment. I'm starting to figure out why spies never bring babies along with them.

Oates stops midsentence and turns to look at me.

"Sorry," I tell him, feeling my face burn. "I shouldn't have . . . I was just . . ."

"Oates?" blusters Byron's voice from the radio. "Is that her?"

"Never mind the girl," Oates retorts, turning his attention back to the radio. He waves me away, but I stay put, patting Livvie's back. "The matter at hand is these Jin'Kai chaps and their apparent knowledge concerning the hybrids."

"*Good girl,*" I whisper into Olivia's tiny curled ear. "Good job with the burping." But my focus is on the conversation in front of me. So Oates is a prisoner, but he has private powwows with Byron on this antique radio? What do they do, chat about baseball?

"We have the files from the *Echidna,*" Byron tells Oates. "There is no mention of any experiments involving *Ibrida.*"

"I have it on good authority that there may be files still aboard that would speak otherwise."

There is a long pause from the radio. I walk over to the table and stand next to Oates, who doesn't bother to shoo me away this time. Instead, he actually pats my hand in a reassuring manner before he continues speaking.

"Byron, if these cousins of ours are up to something, we should know about it." He is beginning to sound much more calm. Determined, even.

"I'll see about getting a task force together," Byron answers finally. "If I can get the other Council members to agree—"

"No time for politics," Oates cuts in. "Within weeks the weather will warm, and the ice will melt. The thing could be completely underwater by the time your people get here."

"Wait," I whisper. "The *Echidna* is *here?*"

"Oates, don't do anything foolish. You don't have the manpower, or the *authority*—"

"Feel free to extend my sentence, then, if you must," Oates says, rising from the table.

"Oates! Don't you drag that child on some damned goose chase! I'll know if you—"

With that, Oates shuts the radio off and turns to me.

"Everything all right downstairs, lass?"

"The *Echidna* is in Antarctica?" I ask him, incredulous. I suppose it makes sense that a ship that big would be pulled toward one of the poles, but . . . "How do you know?"

"A crash that size could not go unnoticed," Oates says matter-of-factly. "Carnage like that, a place like this . . . Even a blind man can spot fire in the ice a hundred miles out." He shoves the radio back into the corner. "I informed our little Lord Byron of the crash when it happened. That's when we got to discussing your coming here for a sojourn."

"Why were you talking about me with . . ." My eyes bug out. "*Lord Byron? That* Byron"—I point to the radio, as though I think he's inside it—"is *Lord flipping Byron?*"

"Mad, bad, and dangerous to know," he says. "We go way back, he and I."

That explains the ugly-ass oil painting on the wall of Byron's study, the one with the mustachioed dude in the headscarf. My tenth-grade English teacher, Mrs. Kwan, would practically *crap* herself if she knew who I'd been talking to. She might even rethink that B- she gave me.

"Holy shit balls," I say, in the spirit of being poetic. The head of the Almiri goon squad isn't just 1950s heartthrob James Dean. He's also an eighteenth-century Don Juan—and the freaking boringest poet I've ever read. Even the baby can't believe it.

"*Buuuuuuuuuurp!*" she burps again. And this time she leaves a little spit-up on my shoulder.

"Come, let's get down below," Oates says, heading for the

door in the floor. "We've many preparations to make, and I don't work well on an empty stomach."

"Preparations for what?" I ask.

"You're the one who said these files were important," Oates tells me as the door swooshes open. He takes one step down before turning to me. "And you know the ship." My confusion must be evident, because Oates steps back into the room again, as though to better explain. "The man's been keeping information from me, and I won't have it. Our expedition leaves at dawn."

"Our . . . expedition?" I gasp.

"There's no time to waste," Oates calls, descending out of sight. "I will put on the tea, and then we'll begin."

# Chapter Six

# IN WHICH THE ICE BEGINS TO CRACK

"Elvie, I know you're kick-ass and everything," Ducky tells me as I hug baby Olivia even tighter in the papoose slung around my arms. "But maybe you don't take the infant on a five-day dogsled trip to an alien spaceship crash site."

I shake my head, staring at Liv's tiny flecks of eyelashes as she sleeps so peacefully. It's only four in the morning, but thanks to the wonders of the Antarctic summer, it's bright enough that it feels like midday. "I'm not leaving her, Duck. I'm her *mother*, for God's sake. I'm the one who knows how to feed her and change her diaper. I know what all her cries mean."

"How are you going to change her diaper when you're huddled on the back of a sled going thirty miles an hour in below-freezing temps?" Ducky's really not backing down. "Elvie, I'm sorry, but you're being unreasonable. Your daughter needs to stay here. Maybe you should too. Let the others handle it."

"I'm the only one who's been on the ship," I argue.

"Cole's been on the ship," Ducky corrects me.

I raise a wary eyebrow at him. "And you really want *Cole* in charge of saving the world?"

Ducky thinks on it for a good hard second before letting out a sigh. "No," he concedes. "But the baby, Elvie, I'm serious. Even if it's not too much for you, it will be for her. Even if she is a half-alien superbaby."

I turn to my dad, who is loading up one of the dogsleds with what appears to be 500 kilograms of pemmican. Dad takes in the situation in one glance—me holding my baby close, my pleading eyes. And he responds in typical Harry Nara style.

"It's not for me to say what's right for you, Elvie. Besides, you already know."

There is a lump in my throat that I can't gulp down, no matter how hard I try. But I know Ducky is right. If I want to go on this adventure to save the planet, the safest place for my baby is without me.

Stupid planet.

The crash site recovery team is composed of six people— er, *beings*—and was decided on by a near-unanimous vote, by both the Almiri and the Enosi. Oates insisted that the hybrids have a say—over the protestations of Jørgen and a few other grumpy Guses—and at least one representative. As it turns out, they got two: Zee, because she's a major pain in the ass, and Bernard, because he's the only one of the Enosi with a damn clue about Antarctic survival. Cole and I are making the journey because, as my bestie pointed out, we know the ship. And Oates is coming too, of course, to handle the dogs and because, well, he actually knows where the *Echidna* came down. And, y'know, he's Oates. The last slot was a little less obvious, but in the end, reason won out. My father rounds out the team because he knows the layout of the *Echidna* as well as Cole and I do, maybe even better, and we might very well need his technical know-how depending on the extent of the damage to the ship. It'll be much harder to find anything if, say, we can't get the doors to open (assuming there are still doors, of course). And I don't mind saying that the thought of my daddy tagging along on my little icy slumber party puts me *much* more at ease.

At the moment, Oates has put me in charge of inventory. Oates estimates the *Echidna* is about a two-day sled ride from here, but he's packed enough supplies for nearly a week—two days there and two days back, one day at the site, plus one day to err on. Along the way we will sleep in a tent, perched on the ice, with nothing but a thin thermal sleeping bag to shield us from the cold. I can only imagine how thick my forearm hair is going to get after all this.

I scan the list.

One thermal tent. Six thermal sleeping bags. Two heating pods for cooking and, if it gets bad, warming the tent. Four canteens to fill with melted snow, for drinking. Food for the dogs. One replacement runner for each sled. One can of oil for the sled runners. One first aid kit containing bandages, gauze, antiseptic, stitching. Our rations for the journey: six loaves of hardtack bread, two boxes of protein gel packs and vitamin powders, approximately nine billion kilos of pemmican, and, obviously, two tins of tea. Lastly, our "covert ops" gear, which is really just a nice way of saying "nerd stuff": two lap-pads, some cables and climbing gear, and a tool kit for fine wire work, in case we have to hardwire ourselves into the *Echidna*'s computer systems for any reason. The files we're hoping to find will most likely be on a separate, non-networked machine, which will make locating them more of a hassle, but we'll still want access to the main computer systems to make sure we can move around the ship.

Honestly, I can't imagine how Pontius and the other dogs are supposed to haul all this crap stacked on just two sleds. I look longingly at the snowmobiles that the Enosi rode in on. My mother suggested we take them for our trip, seeing as they can go twice as fast as the dogs, but Oates merely scoffed at that. This morning, when we came outside to pack, we found out why: the overnight freeze had iced over the motors, and the mobiles were useless—just hunks of metal rusting in the snow.

Oates has been adamant that the supplies be divided between the two sleds—so that, he explained, if half of us sled down a giant crevasse or something, we won't *all* die for lack of food. Which, when Oates mentioned it, did not make me feel all warm and fuzzy inside, but at least you know the dude is planning ahead.

It takes us a good two hours to pack up, check, and double-check all our supplies, and another hour for Ducky to pry Olivia out of my arms for the last time as the waterworks break and I become a sniffle monster. But finally I let her go. Cole rubs my back in little circles as he blows kisses at our daughter.

"She'll be fine, babe," Cole says. "She's going to be with her uncle Ducky."

"I pumped tons of milk last night," I remind Ducky through the sniffles. "It's—"

"The bottle in the refrigerator marked 'baby milk,'" Ducky says. "I kinda figured. And she has to be burped after every meal. And she doesn't like when her socks bunch up by her toes." He offers me a sympathetic smile. "I'm going to be the rockingest babysitter the girl ever had."

I laugh through my sobbing. "She's never had a baby-sitter."

"Victory by default, then."

A few meters away, Oates is giving some last-minute instructions to Rupert, to whom he seems to have left the met-aphorical keys to the metaphorical castle. (Jørgen, no shocker, seems to be not-so-metaphorically pissed about it.)

"Make sure our guests are treated well," Oates continues. "*All* our guests."

Rupert nods his handsome head. "Of course," he agrees. "One big, unruly family."

Jørgen—who's *supposed* to be securing the supplies on the back of the sled but seems to be too busy being a humbug to tie even a slipknot—grumbles loudly under his breath toward Oates. But when Oates turns to face him, the sourpuss goes back to work.

As Cole makes his way back to Oates, I shoot Ducky a wor-ried look. "If that xenophobic douchetard of a Swede so much as *sneezes* in Livvie's direction—" I hiss, but he cuts me off.

"Clark and Rupert have my back," Ducky assures me qui-etly. "Besides, this little lady's round-the-clock security guard is sporting some serious *guns*." One arm still grasped tight around Olivia, he flexes his pathetic bicep in a clear effort to make me laugh, and dammit, it totally works. If there's anyone I'd trust my baby with, it's Ducky, pathetic biceps or not. I know he'll care for her like she's his own child.

"Thanks," I say genuinely. "And . . . sorry. You know. About yesterday."

He shrugs off the apology. "I was just being a grump."

"Yeah," I agree. "You were. But you weren't wrong, either."

The cabin door opens and Zee heads out, carrying the last of the ice-climbing gear. Three hybrids follow her outside—hanging on every word she says, like she's the mama duck and they're her obedient little ducklings.

Ducky snuggles Olivia close as he watches them. "I still can't believe that's your *mom*."

"That makes two of us." I tickle Olivia's chin as I watch Zee. I wonder if Ducky thinks we look alike at all. We have the same chin, same severe eyebrows. But I definitely got Dad's cheekbones.

I turn back to Ducky to ask if he sees the resemblance, but he's not looking at my mom anymore. A certain skinny redhead is occupying far more of his attention.

I laugh, poking him playfully in the side. "She's cute," I tell him honestly. "You should, I don't know, ask her to tea or something." His face turns into a beet. Like an actual beet you could chop up and serve on baby spinach with a nice vinaigrette.

"Why should I do that?"

"Like, duh. You clearly *love* her."

"No, I don't," he counters artfully. "*You* love her." And then, not one second later: "You really think she'd go for me?"

"Of course she will," I assure him.

No way she'll go for him. She's five years older, at least, and pretty, and she seems, well, *worldly*. And Ducky may be Ducky, but he's still . . . Ducky. But like a good PIP, I challenge him with a wiggle of my pinkie finger till he finally gives in.

"All right," he says, sighing, as our fingers lock in the unbreakable bond of pinkie oaths. "But if you come back and find me a shattered shell of a man, it'll be on your head."

"I accept all the consequences," I tell him.

Oates finally finishes up with Rupert and makes his way to me. "Enough with the long good-byes," he says gruffly. "This is a brief foray into the wilderness, not a yearlong trek. We must head out now if we hope to make the first leg by nightfall."

I nod and gulp. "Okay," I say. But I can't tear myself away from my baby. She's still sleeping so soundly, curled up in Ducky's arms. She doesn't even know I'm leaving. When she wakes up and someone besides me is holding her, will she totally freak out? Will she writhe and wail when Ducky tries to feed her from a bottle instead of a boob? Or by this time tomorrow, will she completely forget I even existed?

"Now, child," Oates says again. I dart my eyes in the direction of the two sleds. My dad, Cole, and Bernard are already climbing on board.

"One sec." Oates nods brusquely, then heads to the sled to harness the dogs.

"Hey, Elvie?" It's Ducky again. I think he's going to give me one last reassurance about my daughter, but he does not. Instead, he says: "Be careful out there, all right?" And for the first time he looks deadly serious.

I smile, glad to finally have the chance to reassure *him*. "I'll stay well away from Yetis, I promise," I say.

"No, I meant . . ." He shuffles his feet. "You remember those freaky Jin'Kai heavies that nearly lopped off all your heads back on the *Echidna*? The, uh, Devastators?"

"The Almiri aren't great with nomenclature," I admit.

Ducky shifts Olivia up on his shoulder for a better grip. "I know you never actually saw them, but I did, on your phone . . ." I can't tell if his face looks so pale because of the reflection off the snow or because of something else. Whatever it is, I don't like it. "I know there probably isn't anything left alive after the crash, but . . . just be careful."

"Duck," I say seriously. "If you want to worry about me, pray I don't get attacked by an Emperor penguin along the way. I hear those guys can be real bastards."

He gives me a tight smile, but I know I haven't eased his worry much. That's when Zee passes us on the way to the sled, zipping her thermal up to her neck. "Come on, Elvan," she calls. "You can gab with Dino when we get back."

"It's *Donald*," I reply, annoyed. But really, what's the point? The lady can't even seem to get *my* name right. So I swallow down my exasperation, and instead squeeze Ducky and baby Olivia up in a baby–best friend sandwich, hugging them hard. "I'll see you in less than a week," I tell them.

The twelve dogs make such light work of the snow that their little puppy paws barely dent the crust of the slick, icy ground as our sleds cruise along. Every once in a while we hit a squishier patch, where the snow has begun to melt in the sun and slush over, but for the most part our first few hours are smooth sailing. Or smooth mushing. Whatever. I'm still learning the lingo.

The good thing about snow travel is that there are no real paths, so you can go pretty much wherever your heart desires. The bad thing is it's hellaciously monotonous. Bernard has taken it upon himself to become the crew's onboard entertainment, "amusing" us all with road-trip games.

"I spy . . . ," he shouts to us, over the *whish* of the sled runners across the snow, "something *white!*"

"For serious?" I mutter to my dad. In my sled it's just me, Cole, and Dad. Cole's in front, in control of our six dogs, which would probably freak me out, except that he's the only one of us who can stand that much wind in his face, so he won the position by default. Dad tugs the zipper of his thermal suit so that it covers a fraction of a millimeter more of the skin at his neck. This suit is good for warmth, but still, with this much wind, it's pretty bitter. And as the only purebred human on this little voyage, Dad must be absolutely *freezing*.

"Bernard's just trying to keep our minds occupied," Dad replies. I don't really get how Dad can defend the guy. Me, if I found out my long-lost spouse had actually been living a totally separate life somewhere else and canoodling a doofus like Bernard, it would be all I could do to not punch them both in the face. But here's Dad, being the bigger man and stuff. Still, I notice he doesn't play along.

*Someone* does, though.

"Ummmmmm . . . ," Cole calls over to the other sled, where Oates is at the helm, with Bernard and Zee curled up behind. "Is it that snow cliff?"

"Bingo!" Bernard shouts back. "You've gotten every one! Who's up for State Names?"

The voyage is quite majestic, scenery-wise, but is not one for the easily bored. Looming straight ahead of us, but not appearing to grow any closer, for all the hours we travel, is an enormous cliff. It must be at least a thousand meters high, and it's pure ice. The sun glints off it, turning the ice a sparkling blue, then silver, then gold. It's amazing how many colors ice can be. And the structure of it is beautiful too. If I squint, I can see faces in the various crevasses and dents—some menacing, some kind. Round about lunchtime, though, it just starts to look like a giant block of Parmesan cheese. Nothing else changes. Ice, snow, ice, snow, jingle-jangle, every here and there a dog poop. I've had more riveting afternoons counting my own teeth.

I wish I had my phone so I could call Ducky and find out about Olivia. Of course, that would necessitate that Ducky had a phone too. But I'd build a cell tower myself if it meant I could hear that precious girl smacking her baby lips just once today. She's probably eating right around now. I hope that's going well. Olivia's never used a bottle before. Is she spitting up? Is she gassy? I hope Ducky remembers the technique I showed him, leaning Livvie forward in one hand and rubbing her back slowly with the other. Dad taught me that trick just a couple days ago, and it's made a world of difference.

I glance over at Zee, sitting straight as an arrow in her sled, staring off at the ice cliff. Did she wonder what I was doing, minute to minute, after she left? And how long was it until she stopped?

"Elvs?"

I snap out of my trance and turn to Cole in front of me. "Yeah?" I say.

He looks at me like I'm a geometry quiz he forgot to study for. "We're stopping for lunch. Didn't you notice we stopped?"

"Oh," I say. "Oh yeah." We have indeed stopped. Oates is unhitching the dogs. "I guess the, uh, ice glare is getting to me."

While I help Oates with the dogs, Bernard and my dad unpack our lunch rations, and Cole powers up the electric heating pod so we can melt some ice for drinking.

"Watch it," Zee scolds him. "We want water, not steam." Chagrined, Cole dials the temperature on the pod down by half.

"I still can't believe you walked all the way to the camp," Cole tells Bernard as we're digging into lunch. We've all perched atop one of the sleds, chowing down. I'm trying to make my food last, since there isn't much of it, but all I want to do is shovel it into my gourd. I cut myself a thin strip of pemmican from the tin, then squeeze a line of brown protein gel on top like frosting.

Yum.

"Sure did, friend," Bernard replies. "Hoofed it all the way from the Iceberg Hotel on McMurdo Sound, with nothing but the shirt on my back. Well, the *parka*, that is."

"And a knapsack full of food you stole from the hotel cafeteria," Zee adds. I can tell she's still pissed that she followed his ass here. "Not to mention the book of maps you stole from me to find the place."

So *that's* the big book he's always losing.

"Oh yeah," Bernard says. "And that. But mostly I lived off the land. Like one of the first humans. Just me and the ice. I carved out ice caves to sleep in. Took me almost two weeks, all told. It was crazy."

Dad just blinks. I wonder if his brain's short-circuiting from the idea of setting out on a voyage with such a half-assed plan. But he says nothing. Personally, I'm feeling pretty over-matched in general out here. Even on the *Echidna*, when all hell was breaking loose, I felt like I could get a handle on things. 'Cause even with all the crazy around me, it was my world and my stuff. You need something rewired? I'm your girl. But down here a hammer counts as high-tech. It's very primal, and your biggest concerns aren't some malfunction-ing gravity generators or misbehaving fitness equipment, it's Mother Nature. That bitch is a whole lot rougher, and she doesn't come with an override switch.

Suddenly we hear a whine from Pontius, who leaves his doggy dish to climb the sled and nuzzle into Oates's armpit.

"What is it, boy? What do you see?"

I squint off into the distance, where Pontius and now the other dogs are sniffing and barking, and my stomach tightens into a knot.

There are dozens of them, far off in the distance, little black specks.

"Jin'Kai!" I scream, jumping to my feet.

"Elvie?" my dad says, setting a hand on my arm. "Are you okay?"

"Over there!" I shout. I point in the distance, so they'll all see them too. I blink. I'm not hallucinating. They are certainly there—the Jin'Kai, making their way toward us on foot . . .

Or rather, *waddling* toward us.

"Uh, Elvs?" Cole says. "Those are penguins."

And hey, sure enough, they are. I will my heartbeat to slow, assured that we will most likely *not* be murdered by penguins.

Although Pontius seems less sure about that. He keeps growling and whimpering as the funny-looking birds waddle ever closer.

Curious about the only change in scenery in the past several hours, Oates, Dad, Bernard, Zee, Cole, and I all hop down from the sled to greet our visitors. They sure are silly-looking. Smaller than the Emperor penguins I've seen at the zoo, and with pointy, nubby beaks, white rings around their tiny eyes, and short little wings. "Adélie penguins," Oates informs us. "Also," he warns, although not quite quickly enough, "they bite."

Cole sticks his injured finger in his mouth.

I have to say, the penguins are a welcome distraction. They dance around us, curious, and then run away all at once, sliding on their penguin bellies—only to turn around and head back seconds later for another look. I hear a giggle and look up to see my dad and Zee, laughing as one of the bolder penguins tries to yank a protein gel pack from my dad's pocket. Zee manages to snatch it away from the little guy before he figures out how to rip it open. "Not for you," she tells him sternly. "You'll just have to find a fish somewhere, like all the rest."

Watching them share this moment, I can almost imagine what it might have been like to grow up with two parents. Almost.

My dad laughs again as he takes back the gel pack. "I would've thought you'd let him have it," he tells Zee with a grin. She cocks her head to the side, clearly not sure what he's getting at, but Dad doesn't seem to notice her confusion. "Are these the same type of penguins you fed when you were here all those years ago?" he asks. "What did you say they were called, Captain?" he calls over. "Adélie?"

"Adélie," Oates confirms.

Zee is frowning now. "Oh, Harry," she says, as though she's afraid to disappoint him. "I've never been to Antarctica."

Dad's mouth drops open. "But . . ." He looks at me, but I'm just as bewildered as he is. Dad told me the story of my mother's globe-trekking ways only recently, and they're stories I know he held on to for a long time. To suddenly have them disputed by the woman who told them in the first place . . .

"How else was I supposed to explain that book of maps? Did you really want me to tell you that it was from my previous life as a half-alien hybrid resistance fighter?"

And looking at my dad, frozen into silence, I wonder if in fact this is *exactly* what it would be like to grow up with two parents.

I'm not sure if Cole is with it enough to understand that he's breaking the awkwardness, but somehow he does anyway. "Where are the polar bears?" he asks loudly. And even though he's being doof-tacular, my heart could not be more bursting with love for him, if only for giving my dad a second to recoup.

"No polar bears here," Oates replies, giving Pontius a soothing scratch behind his ears. The husky's clearly still on edge with all the birds around. The other dogs are up on the sleds, growling down at the penguins like elephants whimpering at mice in an old cartoon. "Wrong Pole."

"Oh, right," Cole replies.

"You know," Bernard says, waddling around with the penguins like he's one of them. I'm pretty sure that at any moment he's going to start squawking. "Fifty years ago we would have been swimming instead of standing right now."

I wrinkle my nose. "Huh?"

"Climate change, man," Bernard replies.

"He's referring to the Summers That Weren't," Dad explains, and I nod quickly to let him know that he does *not* need to fill me in (again) on one of his all-time favorite history lessons.

"What's the Summers That Weren't?" Cole asks.

I groan, faking my own heart attack as Dad starts in on the story (and the general state of our current educational system, and blah blah blah . . .).

Basically, about sixty years ago, the environment was in real rough shape, thanks to the pollution given off by pre-fusion-tech fossil fuels, among other things. The seasons started to fluctuate, really strangely, and climate change in general was getting to be a real pain in the ass. Then, starting in 2031, the winter actually lasted for four years. Four straight years with nothing but cold. It snowed everywhere—from Philadelphia to Sydney—at the same time. Frozen pipes became the bane of the beach bums in Santa Monica. I think the main reason my dad likes this particular bit of history so much is that a few weeks after he was born, the temperature in Philadelphia climbed above 10 degrees Celsius for the first time in four years, and within a month there were actually blossoms on the trees. All over the world the climate began to resume its regular cycles. According to most scientists, this "mini Ice Age" was finally halted because of the Universal Energy Reform Act and the overhaul of tech thanks to breakthroughs in fusion power, but Dad likes to refer to himself as the "Sun Baby."

"Wait," Cole says, slowly taking in all this new information. "So we're, like, walking on ice right now? Like, *just* ice, and then water? Is that safe?"

The guy has a point. Suddenly I'm more panicked than Pontius with the penguins.

"It's at least two meters thick," Zee replies dismissively, climbing back onto the sled, "and hard as shale rock. Not to mention"—she reaches for one of the huskies, who growls at her—"that we don't have much of a choice. So let's get going, shall we?"

I roll my eyes as I gather my things. "I suppose we shall," I mutter before hoisting myself up onto the sled. "You okay, Dad?" I ask, leaning over the seat back to resecure the supplies. Tuckered out from his history lecture, he's standing beside our sled quietly, watching my mom and Bernard across the ice.

"Just thinking," Dad says with a quick, not-so-convincing smile.

"Thinking how ludicrous it would be to leave for a thirteen-day walking tour of the frozen tundra without a plan?" I say with a smile.

Dad smiles back, slowly wrenching his gaze from the other sled. "Maybe I've been putting too much stock in plans," he tells me.

Which, coming from the King of Planning, is perhaps the most disheartening thing I've ever heard.

My father seems to want to be alone with his thoughts, so I climb up to the front seat, snuggled next to Cole for warmth as he mushes our dogs, following the path laid out by Oates. Honestly, he's not too bad at it. My Coley may just have a future in dogsledding.

I guess all this wind and sun is really getting to me, because before I know it, I'm waking up from a nap I didn't realize I'd taken. Cole's left arm is wrapped around me tightly and my head is on his shoulder. We are still mushing.

I may or may not have drooled a little.

"How long was I out?" I ask Cole, straightening up to relieve my achy back. He loosens his grip around my waist to give me some wiggle room but doesn't reposition his arm.

"About an hour, probably. I figured I'd let you sleep, since you've been getting up so much with O-Co lately."

I blink, surprised. "That was really sweet, Cole, thanks." He's smiling off into the distance, a happy, thoughtful smile I've never seen before. It looks nice on him. "What are you thinking about?" I ask as I snuggle into him a little closer.

He shakes his head. "It's silly."

"Tell me."

He looks down at me, and I set my chin on his shoulder so that I'm looking up into those gorgeous blue-green-blue eyes, and that constellation of freckles on his left cheek that I've always been so smitten with. "It's just . . . ," he begins. "When I was a kid, I knew exactly what kind of car I wanted. A red

Apple Caracal. I was, like, five," he says defensively when I start to laugh. I bite my cheeks and nod, urging him to go on. "And, anyway, I had it all figured out—I mean, what color the car would be, and what I'd look like when I drove it, and even where everyone in my family would sit. And while you were sleeping, I . . ." He scrunches up his face, like he knows what he's about to say is ridiculously goofy. Which, of course, only makes me want to hear it more. "I realized," he finishes, gesturing to the sled around him, "that I pretty much have exactly what I dreamed up when I was five."

"You dreamed that your Caracal would be pulled by dogs, and that my dad would be snoring in the backseat?"

Cole laughs. "No," he says. "I dreamed that I'd be at the wheel, with a pretty lady at my side, and a *baby* snoring in the backseat. Driving to my mother's for Christmas dinner." He shakes the bittersweet memory from his head. "I told you it was silly. I was five."

"I think it's sweet."

"You do?"

I nod. "I used to think about stuff like that too," I tell him.

"Oh yeah?"

I settle my head back on his shoulder. "Yep. Only in *mine* it was a Mark VI, and I was heading to my job at NASA. And, obviously, I was the one driving."

Cole grins. "That's my Elvs," he says. "I guess I'm fine with sitting in the passenger seat sometimes."

"Cole?" I whisper, pulling away slightly.

"Mmm?"

And I'm just about to tell him, when I happen to glance

over his shoulder to the other sled . . . where Zee is glaring daggers at us. For some reason that stops me before I get started.

"Nothing," I whisper. I lean my head back down on his shoulder. And I decide not to tell him. It's not important anyway.

Only that . . . when I dreamed of driving my car around as a five-year-old, there was no guy in the passenger seat.

Oates declares that we should stop for the evening right around the time my large intestine feels like it's ready to eat itself, but since I don't have a watch and the sun is wonky round these parts, I have absolutely no idea what time it is. Eight o'clock, maybe? It's certainly time for dinner.

We pitch our tent with relative ease, although I cringe every time Oates hammers one of the grounding spike thingees into the ice. I know the ice is hellz thick, but we're still going to be sleeping *on top of nothing but a layer of flipping frozen water*. I'm pretty sure I'm going to have nightmares about drowning in a glass of iced tea.

Dinner is another scrumptious affair. This time I try spreading a little protein gel on top of my hardtack to give it a bit of flavor. The experiment is a failure. Meanwhile, Oates has a pot filled with water boiling over the heating pod to make his precious tea.

"Are you sure that's safe?" I ask for, like, the umpteenth time. "We're not going to melt through or anything, are we?" Oates looks up at me and, very seriously, gives me a shrug. I can feel a pit forming in my stomach, and then after giving me an appropriate amount of time to panic, he gives me a smile. And I can't help but chuckle in nervous relief.

"I'd just like to say, sir," Dad says, chewing on a piece of pemmican, "that it is a great honor to be out adventuring with the great explorer Captain Lawrence Titus Oates."

Oates's smile fades, and he focuses again on the water for his tea.

"Were you, like, famous?" I ask, curious. Dad is a big buff on explorers and expeditions, like Columbus to the New World, Magellan circumnavigating the globe, Sergio Altair traveling through the volcanoes of Tharsis on Mars, and whatnot. I think he just got a kick out of reading all the manifests and journals detailing the explorers' intricate plans to not die while doing something that, at the time, seemed absolutely crazy.

"Famous?" Dad says, as if I've just said the most insulting thing ever. "Why, Captain Oates is legendary."

"Legends are tales told to make sense of the senseless," Oates says. "And rarely do they hold much in the way of value or truth."

"Word," Bernard agrees.

I roll my eyes. Now my curiosity is piqued about this man—or Almiri, whatever—who keeps showing new layers itty bit by itty bit. But his face has grown dark, and I'm pretty sure he's done talking on the subject. "Well, whoever you are," I tell him, "I'm glad to have you on our side."

"That's *it*." Zee slaps her can of pemmican down on the heating pod, knocking it from its snow perch.

"Careful!" Oates hollers, grabbing the pod at its base. "This is a vital piece of equipment, and if it breaks—"

"I've had enough of this Kumbaya shit," Zee screeches. "Elvan." She turns to me. "This man is not 'on your side.' Nor is this twit." She waves a dismissive hand at Cole.

It's my turn to slap down my food. "Oh, but *you're* on my side?" I snap back.

"More than you know, Elvan." Zee shakes her head at me sadly. "I've been trying to help you since the day you were born."

I snort. "Yeah, it was really helpful how you were always not there at all," I tell her.

My father puts a hand on my arm, as though to shut me up, so I do. But only for him.

The wind rattles eerily.

"I think it's well past time for me to turn in," Oates says suddenly. "I'd advise all of you to do the same shortly. You will need your rest."

The sun, by the way, is blindingly bright at this point. I swear, I'll never get used to this.

"I know I'm beat," Bernard adds, and he's gone too.

Cole remains on his ice chair until my father stands and offers him a hand.

"Cole?" he says.

"Oh, thanks, Mr. Nara, but I'm not ti—"

"Come on, son."

Cole looks from me then to Zee, but I refuse to meet his gaze. I don't exactly want to sit out here and fight with my mother . . . but I don't *not* want to either.

Finally Cole makes up his mind. "I'll be right inside the tent if you need me, 'kay, Elvs?"

*Where else would you be?* I think. *Honolulu?* But I offer him a tight smile.

It is silent between Zee and me for a long time. I listen to the muffled sounds of the men rolling out their sleeping bags in the tent, settling in for the night. Pontius snuggles happily at my legs, and I pet his warm, thick coat, not thinking much of anything.

"I loved your father, you know," my mother says at last. "Leaving him—leaving you both—was one of the hardest things I've ever had to do."

"Guess you never tried Zumba," I say to the ground.

After a few more moments of awkward silence I finally pipe up again. "Why did Dad think your name was Olivia?"

Zee tosses a pebble of ice into the distance absentmindedly, like she's skipping stones on a lake. "Olivia was the name I took on when I . . ." She trails off. Shakes her head, as though she's started the story at a bad angle. She purses her lips and tries again. "I was born Zada Khoury," she says softly. "My mother was human. She had no idea that there was anything unusual about me, or that my father was Almiri. Even the Almiri didn't know about me at first—my father, for his own reasons, chose to hide his indiscretion from his comrades. But when I was just about your age, the Almiri found out what I was and came for me."

I know that my mom is telling me all this because she needs me to understand some things. And okay, yeah, I'm interested. How many times did I dream of having this very conversation with my mother—where she came from, and where she went? Only somehow, in my dreams, it went very,

very differently. I scratch Pontius a little harder behind the ears and do my best to listen.

"I had to run," she says, "and hide. No matter where I went, the Almiri did their best to smoke me out. I was young, and terrified, and . . ." Her eyes drift to the distance, where she's tossed the stone. "One day I woke up, and I decided it was time to start fighting back. I ferreted out more people like me, clusters of Enosi who had also been in hiding, and we learned to help one another. We started to organize. I knew it was exactly what I was meant to be doing. And then, well . . . then I met your father." She picks up another ice pebble but doesn't throw it, just studies it in her hand. "I thought I could go back to being human, I really did. I changed my name and tried to forget what I was. I suppose deep down I knew I couldn't hide in plain sight forever. I always lived just on the edge of fear, worried they'd track me down sooner or later. But it was a lovely, lovely dream, being with your father, one I didn't want to wake up from." She looks up at the sky. "But when I discovered I was pregnant . . . well, I guess I thought there was a chance that if I wasn't around, the Almiri wouldn't ever find you. If you were just a little girl with a human father, they'd never . . . so I left." She looks at me finally, staring so intently that it's unnerving. "And I know you'd do exactly the same thing, Elvan, if you thought it would help *your* daughter."

I close my eyes. Picture my precious baby. Would I do the same? Would I abandon my daughter in hopes of protecting her? Honestly, I'm not sure. What I *do* know is that I'm thoroughly tuckered out.

I'm about to tell my mother good night, that we'll work

on Mother-Daughter Bonding Round Two tomorrow, but she beats me to the punch.

"I want you to end your relationship with that Almiri boy," she tells me.

"*Excuse* me?" I say, practically choking on the last traces of my pemmican.

"I said that I want you—"

"I heard what you said," I interrupt. "I'm just shocked you think it's any of your business." And *that* at least has her stunned enough that I manage to get out another sentence. "That Almiri boy's *name*," I tell her, "is Cole Archer. And maybe you had a good reason for leaving me and Dad. I believe that, really. But you *left*. And you can't just expect that everything that happened while you were gone is yours to change." I give Pontius one last pat, then rise to my feet. "I will see you in the morning," I say.

Zee does not wish me good night.

Two minutes later I find myself with the others, slipped into our thermal bags—which are, for serious, crammed right up against each other. I listen to the breathing of my traveling companions slow as they nod off, one after the next, and I wonder how so much tension and awkwardness can fit into such a tiny tent. I squeeze my eyes closed, but sleep doesn't come.

"Elvs," Cole whispers softly into my ear as we snuggle much too closely. I guess he can't sleep either. "Elvs?"

I shift my ear toward him so he knows I'm listening, but I don't respond.

"It must be nice to have your mom back," he whispers. "After all this time. Right?"

I think about Cole's dream of driving to his mother's home in Milwaukee with his imaginary family for Christmas. I think about how, thanks to the illness that took her life more than two years before I met Cole, that's never going to happen. And suddenly I feel very guilty for the way I've behaved with my own mother. Not for her sake — but for his.

I close my eyes against the still-bright evening outside the tent, and do my utmost to settle into sleep.

I do not sleep well. I would toss and turn, except that there's nowhere to toss and turn to. I can't help wishing that now that my mother is finally in my life, I could find a way to make more of an effort to stop being such a raging asshat to her all the time. But then I do some more not-tossing-and-turning and wonder, Why isn't *she* the one making the effort?

When I finally drift off, I have fitful dreams filled with the eerie thunder from the day of our arrival.

*Crack-BOOM!*

*Crack-BOOM!*

"Wake up!" comes the call, much too early. Someone is shaking me. "Elvs, wake up!" Cole. I must've slept more deeply than I thought.

"Cole?" I sit straight up, bringing the top half of my sleeping bag with me. Outside the tent I can here Oates shouting and the dogs howling. "What's going on?"

"I don't know," Cole says, "but Oates is freaked out. We have to move now."

Cole looks sufficiently freaked himself, inspiring me to jump straight out of my sleeping bag and into my boots and thermal. I'm pulling the last boot on, the thermal dangling off one arm, as I come hopping out of the tent. And that's when I see it. The meter-wide hole in the ice, just at the edge of the dogs' tarp.

"Oates!" I shriek. "What happened? What's going on?"

"Stop standing around, girl, and grab the gear!" he shouts at me. There is another thunderclap.

*CRACK-BOOM!*

"A storm?" I ask, still fuzzy. The dogs are going apeshit, and Oates has a hell of a time getting them into their harnesses.

"That's no storm," Oates says as he wrestles with the dogs. And that's when I do a head count. Two sleds but only eleven dogs.

Oh God, I think, as I look back at the hole in the ice, the black water sloshing around beneath it.

Pontius is gone.

# Chapter Seven

# IN WHICH OUR GROUP REALIZES THEY'RE GOING TO NEED A BIGGER FLOAT

"Move your ass! Move!" Oates shouts at no one in particular. He's strapping the remaining dogs into their harnesses, while Dad and Cole frantically pack all our gear onto the sleds. Bernard and Zee, meanwhile, are whipping the tent poles out of the ice so quickly, they nearly spear me several times.

"Leave that!" Oates says as I move to help dismantling the tent. "The food and the heating gear only!"

"Leave the tent?" I ask, incredulous. What the hell is going on? "But what are we supposed to use for—"

I'm cut off by another incredibly loud *CRACK-BOOM!* Only this time I don't merely hear it. I feel it.

In the ice.

"Leave it all!" Oates shouts. "Get on the sleds!"

Booming ice seems to be all the incentive we need. Each of us instantly drops what we're doing and jumps aboard the sleds, me with Dad and Cole, Zee and Bernard with Oates.

Oates and Cole frantically urge on the dogs, and we take off. There's another *CRACK-BOOM!* which jolts the entire sled. The runners bounce up several centimeters off the ice and slam back down with a *thud*. But the dogs keep running, like creatures possessed. I may not have any idea what exactly it is we're running from, but those dogs sure seem to.

"Is the ice breaking apart?" I shout at my dad over the chaos. "I thought you guys said it couldn't do that!" I look behind me, and sure enough, the ice is breaking away. But there's something . . . *else* there too.

"What the hell is that?" I scream. Back at the campsite something beneath the ice pushes through to the surface. It's dark and smooth, glistening with beads of water rolling down its sleek shape. The ice around it disintegrates, and our tent and all the supplies we were forced to leave behind plunge into the black water.

The dogs yelp and skitter on, running ever faster.

"Is that a *submarine*?" I holler. Holy shit. Of all the ways I imagined the Jin'Kai might track me down, this wasn't one of them.

But then the shadowy form turns sideways in the water. And although I'm not super up to speed on my maritime craft, even I know that submarines don't have *eyes*. For a second one large black eye meets mine, and then in a flash the creature dives deep into the murky depths of the ocean again.

What. Duh. *Fuh*.

Dad hollers something at me, but I lose it in the wind. We're whipping along far faster than we've gone before, the dogs tugging the sleds forward until it seems their harnesses might snap.

Cole urges the dogs even faster, trying to keep pace with Oates beside us. The *CRACK-BOOM!*s are beginning again, closer together now, sometimes overlapping. The ice all around us trembles and cracks. I look down and see a dark shadow racing along after us under the ice.

Hunting us.

One jolt hits directly beneath us, and again the entire sled lifts into the air and slams back down with a smash.

Whatever the hell is underneath us, it means business.

I twist around in my seat to grab at a box of protein gel just before it tumbles to the ice. What few supplies we'd managed to secure are dropping quickly away, sinking down into the newly forming cracks around us.

Suddenly Oates veers away from us, breaking hard to the right. He's shouting something to us, but again, I can't hear it over the cacophony of creaking ice, barking dogs, and wind. He's pointing to his left, directly ahead of us. I turn to look. In front of us the ice is groaning and breaking free as something pushes through from below.

"Cole!" I scream. He's got his head down to keep the wind out of his eyes, and he doesn't seem to hear me, so I slap him on the back. Just in time he looks up and sees where I'm pointing.

We veer to the left with exactly enough of a head start to avoid the *giant black torpedo shooting through the ice*, in the exact spot we would be now had we not abruptly shifted course. A spray of water and ice shards rains down on us. The enormous black creature twists and turns, giving us a view of what look to be two small wings and a white underbelly.

No, not wings.

Fins.

A *colossal killer whale* is trying to murder us. Seriously, my life would be less weird if we were actually being chased by aliens.

The whale crashes down on the surface of the ice, shattering the crust and parting the water in a tremendous splash. Our sled rocks with the wave, but thankfully we manage to avoid getting blasted to smithereens. This time.

There is one moment, before the beast submerges himself again, when I swear to goodness he looks directly at me with his enormous round black eye. And it's like I can read his thoughts, exactly what he's thinking in that moment. He doesn't see humans, or Almiri, or hybrids.

He sees meat.

The creature dives into the sea again. His huge tail rises up and slaps the side of our sled with a mighty *thwack*. The sled pitches over on its side, and we have no choice but to dive off as it flips and crashes down. My momentum sends me skidding on my stomach over the smooth surface for several meters. I spin around to see the dogs dragging the overturned sled away from us. Their harnesses scrape between the ice and the sled for several seconds and then snap free, sending the dogs skittering in six different directions across the ice. Dad and Cole run up beside me and lift me off the ground.

"Come on, Elvie!" Dad shouts. "To Oates."

Oates is at least fifty meters away but has circled around and is heading back our way to retrieve us. But between us lies the large rift of icy seawater where the whale broke through. As we run toward Oates at an angle to circumvent the hole, the whale pops up again, his massive head bobbing almost playfully on the surface. He stares straight at us, and if I didn't know any better, I'd say the shitbag was *smiling*.

Smiling with rows of enormous, sharp-ass teeth.

The piteous whining howls behind me cause me to swivel my head. All around us the ice is breaking free, and large black snouts shoot out of the water. At least half a dozen of them, strategically positioned to trap the loose dogs inside a perimeter. They grab the canines, clamping down on the poor things with a crunching of bones that stifles their pathetic last yelps before pulling them down to a watery grave.

We're surrounded.

The ice underneath us begins to shift, swaying with the waves like a toy boat in the bathtub. Not because one of the whales is beneath us, but because the entire surface as far as I can see is now breaking apart into smaller and smaller floes, bobbing on the surface like ice cubes in a giant drinking glass.

"This way!" I shout, tugging my dad and Cole behind me and running along the length of the rift as I assess the least-damaged path. Oates seems to see it too and changes his course to run parallel to ours. He passes control over to Zee and moves back on the sled, attempting to unfasten something.

We're only about thirty meters or so apart from each other, but there's no way to bridge the gap as more and more of the ice breaks free. The ground beneath us has, in a matter of minutes, almost completely disintegrated. I hop from one bobbing chunk of ice to another as Dad does the same. Cole has leapt several lengths ahead of us before realizing that he's essentially abandoning us and turns back.

"Elvie!" he screams at me. "Don't look back!"

Which, of course, is my cue to look behind me. And sure enough, *that* was a bad idea.

Two whales are behind us, their tall dorsal fins slicing through the water as their massive heads plow through the broken ice. They're not in a hurry, these two, as they swim brazenly along—they *know* they've found the buffet bar. The sheer size of the whales is enough to make me dizzy. From snout to tail, each is easily twelve meters long. In other words, I am currently being chased by two good-size trucks with teeth.

Cue the *Jaws* music.

Beside me, Dad slips as he jumps from one floe to another, landing awkwardly on his knee. I hop over to him and try to help him up.

"Elvie, just go!" he shouts. "Go!"

I ignore him, obviously, and continue tugging ('cause, *dude*, what daughter would actually leave her own father to be eaten by killer whales??). But suddenly I'm swooped up from behind and completely lose my grip on my dad. For a moment I'm positive that I'm about to be whale food, but quickly I figure out that Cole has me in his arms—and, to my horror, is hopping away from my father.

"Cole, what are you doing?" I cry. "My dad!"

Dad is waving us away, all heroic-like. Behind him the two whales grow ever closer, snapping at the surface like my dad's the tastiest shrimp scampi they've ever seen. I flail blindly at Cole, punching his shoulder and slapping his face. "Let me *go*!" I holler. But to no avail. Cole continues on, farther and farther away, leading me to goddamn safety. The whales are right on my dad now; their jaws wrench open—

Leaping across the ice like a Wuxia master, Oates lands directly on top of the foremost whale, brandishing the dog snare-pole in his left hand. Wielding it like a harpoon, he plunges the long rod directly into the whale's blowhole. Immediately the beast lets out a raging, gurgling cry, and blood spouts everywhere.

A now death-red Oates jumps from the creature as it sags beneath the water, the snare-pole still lodged in its head. "Look out!" I screech, although I know he's too far to hear me. But I can't help myself—a second whale is rearing up just in front of him, jaws open wide. I cower against Cole's arms, watching in terror. The orca is big enough that it could easily swallow Oates and my dad in one gulp, but Oates doesn't even seem fazed. In a flash he's pulled something from his side—and between the white-blue glow and the smoke pluming from Oates's glove, I piece together that it must be one of the heating pods, cranked up to max. Oates's hand must be completely barbecued under his glove. I can't even imagine the pain. The whale sure can, though, because as Oates hurls the pod into its gaping maw, the creature immediately rears back in agony, instinctively shutting its mouth, which just makes the situation that much worse. The whale thrashes erratically away from Oates and my father, sending huge waves crashing in every direction. Oates lifts my father off the ground and races away from us toward the remaining sled. Cole sprints quickly across the floes with me still in his arms toward the solid ice farther up ahead. Looking back over my shoulder, I see four dorsal fins appear behind Oates and my dad. They crest above the surface as they swim in pursuit of their prey.

When we finally reach a sturdy patch of ice, Cole drops me

on my feet, and I immediately start running around the edge to the sled, which Zee has brought to a stop as they wait for Oates and Dad. In all the panic I never got my thermal zipped up properly, and I'm soaked through all the way to my unmentionables. Between the cold and the sheer terror, my teeth are chattering so loud, I can't hear anything that Cole is yelling at me. So we simply keep running—Zee and Bernard and the sled a jittery blur in front of me. As we race, I twist to watch Oates and Dad speeding just ahead of the whales—who are lifting themselves out of the water and crashing back down, shattering floes and sending them flying in their wake. Here I've spent the past several weeks panicked about aliens, I realize, and it's the freaking animal kingdom that's going to do us all in.

Cole and I scramble on board the sled, then frantically wave on Oates and Dad. The instant they grab on to the side, Zee takes off again. When the ice gets solid, the whales turn and begin swimming alongside the sled, dangerously close to the spot where Dad and Oates are clinging for dear life.

That's when I notice Bernard. At the edge of the sled he is leaning way over, clenching another heating pod in his hands like a quarterback getting ready to toss a long pass.

Our *last* heating pod.

"No!" I scream as he twists the dial on the pod. But it's too late. Bernard tosses the heating pod at one of the pursuing whales.

And it bounces harmlessly off its snout.

Even so, perhaps sensing that these glowing rocks pose some sort of threat, the whales abruptly abandon their pursuit and dive below the surface. Bernard is still cheering several minutes later when, well clear of the orca threat, Zee slows to a stop so Dad and Oates can climb all the way on board.

"Woo-*ee!*" Bernard cries. Now that we've stopped momentarily, the wind is no longer whishing past my ears, and for the first time I can make out actual words. My heart, I fear, will never return to a normal rate again. "Almiri-Enosi Alliance one," Bernard says with a grin, "killer whales zero!" Then he suddenly drops his hands and his grin all at once, as if he realized something terrible. "Oh, wait. Man, they're endangered, aren't they? And we just, like, killed a whole bunch of them."

"I'm more concerned with the endangered species known as Elvie," I say through chattering teeth. I help my dad sling his last leg over the edge of the sled, and hug him tightly. "If you ever, *ever*, try to sacrifice yourself so that I won't get eaten by whales again, I swear I will punch you right in the mouth," I tell him, squeezing tighter.

"Understood," Dad replies with his usual good humor. But as I hold him, I can feel that he's trembling just as much as I am.

"We've neither cause nor time for celebration," Oates says. He's swung himself into a seat easily and is inspecting the wake of our run-in with the whales. "We've lost most of our supplies and must press forward."

"Allow a moment to appreciate the victory, man," Bernard says. "After all, it's not every day that a humble professor of advanced dance ethnography is victorious when going *mano a mano* with a killer—"

But that's as much as he gets out before all hell suddenly breaks loose again. The first whale that shoots through the ice crashes down on the rear of the sled, missing Bernard by millimeters.

The second whale has better aim. Before any of us can react, the monstrous animal snaps its jaws down on Bernard's torso with a sickening crunch. Zee screams out, but there's nothing she can do as the whale tosses Bernard's bloody body straight up ten meters into the air and then grabs him again, biting straight through his midsection, killing him instantly.

One hopes.

The ice now completely gives way beneath the sled, and we splash down into the water. In front of us the dogs scramble on top of the ice as the sled weighs them down. Frantically we dart off the sinking sled onto the ice. Another whale surfaces and reaches out for my mother, but Dad pulls her back just in time and the hunter misses his prey. The whales—four, is it, five?—all turn their attention on the sled, biting and tearing at it, slowly pulling it down and dragging the dogs closer and closer to the water.

"No!" Oates cries out. It's the closest thing to anguish I've ever heard from him. He runs toward the dogs as they claw futilely against the ice, trying to break free from the harnesses, which are pulling them down into the water, where the whales wait eagerly. I try to make a move for Oates, but Zee grabs my arm.

"No, Elvan," she says. "We need to run."

"To the cliff!" Dad screams. He and Zee start running toward the high cliff face that lies several hundred meters away.

I just stand, paralyzed, watching Oates. He's leapt onto the sinking sled and is trying in vain to loosen the dogs' harnesses. One of the whales takes a bite at him, but he ducks the rows of teeth deftly and delivers a shocking blow to the creature's snout with his fist.

It takes a certain kind of man to punch a killer whale.

"Elvie, now!" Cole says. "While they're distracted."

Cole yanks me out of my reverie, tugging me along beside him as we sprint away—but I can't help gazing back at the man who saved my father's life, and is now trying to save the lives of his beloved dogs. The whales are all over him, snapping with their jaws and slapping with their tails. The surrounding water grows redder and redder, although from Oates's blood or the dogs', I can't be sure.

The last thing I make out before I look away is Oates and the final remnants of the sled slipping beneath the surface.

We spend the night in a crevice in the side of the ice cliff, waiting to see if the whales have had their fill yet.

It's tight enough that we remaining four have to practically sit on top of one another, which is actually just fine with all of us, because without the tent or any heating pods the cold is brutal. The cave does spare us from the wind, though, which is some small comfort. Cole, Zee, and I try to form a protective shell around Dad, who is clearly the least able to withstand the icy temperature. Still, it's not like I don't feel the cold *at all*. It's numbingly cold. I can barely bend my fingers, my joints are stiff, and the tips of my ears are practically burning. A normal girl would be half-dead from hypothermia by now. But as I keep discovering more and more, I'm not a normal girl.

We watch, silently, as the sun sets across the ice. Through the thin wisps of clouds, the sky blazes orange, then red, then a deep burgundy, and finally a brilliant royal purple, until it sinks . . . down . . . into nothingness, and we are plunged into darkness.

Black. It is pure icy black, all around us.

"What are we going to do now?" I ask in a whisper. I'm afraid of the whales catching scent of us again, afraid of dying from the bone-chilling cold and never seeing my beautiful daughter again. Hell, at this point I'm getting pretty seriously concerned about the possibility of Yetis.

"We have no choice but to move forward," Zee says quietly. I think it's the first time she's spoken since the attack. I listen to her breathing, trying to judge how she must be feeling.

"How are we going to make it with no supplies?" Cole asks. "We're a full day out, even if we still had the sleds. And we can't even melt ice for water."

"Yeah, it was a shame that Bern . . . that we lost the heating pods," Dad answers. I listen for a change in Mom's breathing but hear nothing. "In any case," Dad continues, "Olivia—Zee—is right. We really have no choice but to go on. The way we came is, obviously, not passable anymore. We'd have to circumvent too much ground to make it back to camp. Finding the *Echidna* and figuring something out there is our best bet."

"But even if we find it," I ask him, "what do we do then? How will we get back?"

"Well," he says, "we improvise." And he lets out a little snort, like he just can't believe the situation he's currently found himself in.

Beside me, my mother lets out a snort too. But it isn't snide or dismissive. It's a real laugh.

"Zee?" Dad continues, his voice thick with concern. "I'm sorry about your friend."

She doesn't respond. But in the dark she reaches out her hand, searching for my father's glove. She finds mine instead.

I give her a sympathetic squeeze.

"Our main concern," Zee says after a moment of silence, "assuming we make it through the night, will be to find some food."

"Like what?" Cole asks. "Penguin? You think we could bludgeon them with our boots?"

"That might not be necessary," Dad replies, and I feel him shifting slightly inside the cocoon we've made around him. "I have four packs of protein gel and two packets of vitamin powder on my person."

"You do?" I ask, both elated and suddenly wary. "How?" And then, more pointedly, "Where?"

"On my person," he reiterates obstinately.

"*Where, Dad?*" I repeat, fearing the worst.

He lets out a sigh of resignation. "In my socks," he answers, and my chest relaxes in relief. "If we ration them out, they should last several days."

"You've been carrying around food in your socks this whole time?" Cole asks. "Like, even while you sleep?"

"Always be prepared for any situation," my father says, and I can't help but smile. Maybe, just maybe, we will make it through this whole disastrous adventure alive.

I close my eyes and do my best to sleep, picturing my beautiful baby Olivia back at the prison, awaiting my safe return.

Chapter Eight

# IN WHICH THE FAMILY NARA VISITS A GHOST SHIP

The last thing I ever thought I'd long for in my entire life is to set eyes on the L.O.C. *Echidna* again, but after two long days of trudging on foot along the foot of the ice cliff, spending the intervening night huddled in another crevice that we carved out with small ice shards, the dark spot on the horizon is the most beautiful thing I've ever seen. I'm practically homesick.

"Is that it?" I cry into the wind. Cole, whose eyes are considerably better than the rest of ours, squints into the nearly impenetrable white haze that blankets the ice field stretching out before us. The dark spot is a good half mile away, and its location will require us to leave the safety of the cliff and venture out into the open. That means the wind, which right now is only balls cold, will suddenly turn megaballs cold. It also means there will be nowhere to run to if our friends Jimmy Orca and the Orcettes decide to come back for a second helping of people food. So before we start chasing phantom ghost ships, I want to be sure.

"It looks like . . . something," Cole says helpfully.

"Is it the ship or not?" Zee asks. "Harry can't take much more of this cold."

"I'm fine," Dad says, although he's quivering so violently, I'm afraid the vibrations in the snow might start an avalanche.

"You're not fine, Harry, look at you," Zee admonishes. "You're chilled to the bone."

"I can manage," Dad starts, pausing for a round of teeth-chattering spasms. "We need to be sure before we head out."

"Obviously," Zee replies. "We should send the Almiri out to investigate. He can signal us if he gets a positive view from closer up."

"The Almiri's name is Cole," I inform my mother for the umpteenth time.

Zee rolls her eyes. "Well, *Cole*, would you mind taking a closer look for us?"

"Uh, sure," Cole tells her. "Yeah, no prob. If it's the ship, I'll just, like, wave my arms, like this." And then he waves his arms over his head back and forth to demonstrate. Honestly, I want to say something snarky, like *Oh, but if you go all jazz hands on us, we should stay put, is that it?* But it's been sort of a long three days. So I just nod before he trudges off across the ice toward what, we hope, is our destination.

When he's out of earshot, I wheel around on Zee. "Look, I know you don't like the Almiri. I get that. You've been pretty clear about it. But lay off Cole already! He's been nothing but lovely to you. He also happens to be the father of your granddaughter, like you care."

Zee has a very strained expression on her face. Her mouth is a thin straight line. "I apologize," she says coolly.

And then we stand, shivering in the snow, and wait for Cole to do something. Jeez, you'd think the superhuman might be a tad quicker about things. I glance at Zee several times, trying to think of something to ease the tension, but nothing comes to mind. Dad, meanwhile, keeps busy by swinging his arms and kicking his feet in what I hope is an attempt to avoid turning into a life-size FrozePop, and not the onset of some sort of brain-freeze delirium.

Finally, when Cole is almost nothing but a speck, he whirls around and begins jumping up and down, waving his arms like a doofus.

"Well, there you are," Mom says. She starts walking across the ice. "It appears your boyfriend has found what we were looking for."

"He's not my boyfriend," I say, startling myself. I mean, I guess Cole and I never officially had the whole "I'm your girl-friend, you're my boyfriend" chat, but I always figured that was because chats like that are sort of moot when the hypothetical girlfriend and boyfriend already have a very real baby together.

At least I *think* that's why we've never had that chat.

Dad is raising a frozen eyebrow in my direction, like even he's surprised by this sudden revelation. I try to shrug it off. "He's just . . . Cole," I explain lamely.

"Well," Zee says, the kind of "well" that means that what you said makes you sound like a total chromer. "Let's not keep your *Cole* waiting."

• • •

All the relief I felt when we first spotted the *Echidna* has abandoned me now that we're standing at the base of the crash site. In place of that relief there's a pressure weighing down on my chest, making it difficult to breathe. Unless the air has magically grown exponentially denser in the past five minutes, I'm pretty sure that this is the beginning of a panic attack. Gaping up at the remains of the ship where I nearly died half a dozen times just a few weeks earlier, I'm suddenly wondering why I was so desperate to come here in the first place, just to get some stupid computer files.

Granted, those stupid computer files could provide info that would help protect me and my baby, not to mention shift the balance in a war that will determine the fate of the entire planet. But, still.

The wreck juts out of the ice at a fairly low angle. The back end—maybe about a third of the ship or so—is visible above the ice, meaning that whatever's left of the front end is submerged underwater. The thick layer of ice we're currently perched on—which I can only assume formed up around the wreck after the ship crashed through, solidifying it all into one massive shipsicle—creaks and moans under the stress of the massive cruiser. More likely than not, the ship is slowly sliding down into the depths. It could probably break through completely and plunge into the darkness at any moment.

"We're gonna be in for a world of suck if water has flooded the lower levels," Cole says, scouring the ship's exterior to find a point of entry.

"Well, Dr. Marsden's office was fairly far back," I reply. "So with any luck it won't be flooded."

"We got all the files from his office," Cole reminds me. "I thought you wanted to check out the maintenance locker where he was hiding."

Right. I shake my head, trying to remove the freeze from my brain. *Stay sharp, Elvie*, I tell myself. *You're going to need all your wits about you today.* "Yeah," I say. "Right, the maintenance locker." The maintenance locker on the bottom of the ship, where Dr. Marsden was manipulating me and the rest of the Hanover girls like puppets, sending more than a few of us into the arms of untimely death. Where I nearly lost Cole. Where I shot my former physician and confidante three times in the chest, close enough to feel the heat off his wounds before he toppled over the edge of the railing. Chances are, that's where we'll find any secret files Marsden was hiding from his superiors. There or on his corpse.

"Dearheart, are you all right?" Dad asks beside me. "You look pale."

"I'm fine," I lie, trying not to tremble. "Let's just find a way in and get this over with."

Easier said than done. While there is a butt-ton of structural damage all over the ship's exterior, there's no real serviceable way to get inside on the ground. After taking about fifteen minutes to carefully pick our way around the perimeter, we finally determine that the only opening that looks feasible for us to tackle is a good forty meters aboveground, near what appears to be the rear end of the lido deck. It is, I surmise after a good two minutes of blinking at the sun glare off the ship, the hole created when the Almiri rescue ship exploded, thanks to Dr. Marsden's sabotage.

Well, at least the dude did *something* helpful.

"Great," I say with a harrumph. "So not only do we have to climb all the way up there, but then we have to backtrack all the way down to the hull section."

Dad looks up at the icy surface of the hull and whistles. "I sure wish we hadn't lost the climbing gear," he says.

"It's only a few dozen meters," Cole says nonchalantly. "Piece of cake."

"Cole," I say, darting my eyes not-so-subtly toward my slightly paunchy middle-age father. Cole makes a face like he just got an easy question wrong in Trivial Pursuit.

"Oh," he says. "Right. Well, the outside is pretty banged up. We should be able to find decent handholds."

"I don't know, Cole," I say. "I think it might be too dangerous." I'm superskeptical, and not just because I'm pretty positive Dad's going to bite it only a meter off the ground. I don't fancy the idea of *me* getting halfway up the icy metal wall and then slipping and bouncing all the way down like a pachinko ball either.

"There's no point wasting time chewing it over," Zee says, finding a few low-lying grips. "This is the only way in. So we might as well get started." And just like that, she's climbing slowly but steadily up the side of the wreck.

My mother is remarkably spry, but even so, after a few meters she loses purchase on one of the grips and slides right off. Cole catches her before she can land on her butt, and she wriggles out of his arms like he has mutant cooties.

"Are you o—" Cole starts, but Zee cuts him off right away.

"I'm fine," she says—pretty nastily, considering Cole just

saved her tailbone from a real whomping. "Just need to try again."

"There's no way we can all make it up that way," I tell her calmly. Like I'm explaining to a two-year-old that the square blocks can't fit in round holes.

"There's no other way, Elvan," she replies. "What would you suggest?"

"I suggest we let the superdude here climb up and see if he can find something to lower down to us. There's probably all kinds of crap up there. Chances are, there's something we could use."

Zee looks mad, and I can't tell if it's because she thinks I don't believe she can make the climb, or because my idea is just way better than her brilliant trial-and-error-butt-flopping-on-the-ice method. Nevertheless, she nods in reluctant agreement.

"Right-o, be back in a jiff," Cole says, and before I can blink, he's already halfway up. In another moment he's disappeared into the crater. From overhead I hear him whistle. "This place is a *mess*," he calls down. "I mean, if you thought it was trashed before . . ."

"Cole!" I yell up. "Be more productive!"

"Right," comes the reply. "Productive. Good."

Me, Dad, and Zee stand around in awkward silence for a few moments, waiting for Cole to find something useful. I feel like we're playing an eyeball-only variant of hot potato: I dart my eyes back and forth between my parents, always looking away the second they return my glance, and they're doing the same thing. Our eyes bounce around like that for a while, until finally Zee breaks the silence.

"I could have made the climb," she says indignantly.

"I have every faith," is Dad's warm reply. My mother looks at him and searches his face, as if wondering if my sarcastic nature has become contagious. When she studies that earnest gob of his, though, she seems to realize (or maybe remember) that Harry Nara doesn't have a sarcastic bone in his body. The smile that creeps over her face then is the first real emotion other than contempt or anger that I've seen from her since her semihuman moment in the ice crevice after Bernard died.

I rub my dad's arm gently through his thermal sleeve, mostly just to keep him warm. He leans down and whispers in my ear, the pitch of his voice at clear Dad Frequency.

"So you and Cole are having problems?" he asks quietly, so Zee won't hear. "Is it something you want to talk about?"

"No. Not problems," I say as I take my hand back. "Maybe a discussion for another day, Dad. When we're not, like, about to scale an icy metal wall."

"Right," my father says. "Right, good call."

"Hey!" Cole cries from up top. "Guess what I found?" Before we can start playing Twenty Questions, two long cables come snaking down the side of the ship, the length hitting the bottom with several meters to spare. Cole emerges from the hole and slides down the side, gripping one cable in each hand as he goes. He lands on the ice with a soft thunk and spins around to face us, smiling.

"Nice job," I tell him. "Where'd you find them?"

"In that utility closet where we found your classmates from the On Your Own class," Cole replies.

"How do you know it's the same closet?" I wonder.

"Well, there were twenty-odd sacks of flour wearing diapers all over the floor." He frowns. "I'm sad to say most of the flour babies did not survive the crash."

"Well, worst-case scenario," I say as I gather up one of the cables, "we don't find any useful information, but we whip up a few dozen cupcakes for the trip back."

"I don't think the kitchen's still functional, Elvs," Cole adds, serious. I think I hear Zee snort, but it might be my paranoid imagination.

"Just . . . help me tie this up, you goof."

The climb up takes about ten minutes. Even with each of us tethered to the cable, the surface is so slick that we have to watch our footing very carefully as we pull ourselves up the line. I've got one line wrapped across my shoulders and around my waist like a harness, and Dad has the other. Zee shimmies up the line ahead of me, and Cole climbs just behind Dad. Cole wanted to side with me, but I made sure he went with my father in case the old man slipped and needed catching. Which turned out to be an excellent plan, since Dad loses his grip no fewer than three times on the way up.

Exhausted and with beads of sweat frosting over on my forehead, I finally make it to the opening, and soon enough I find myself back in the belly of the beast.

The lido deck is just as trashed as Cole described, although I don't know what I expected from a cruise liner that barreled headfirst into the ground from outer space. Honestly, I'm amazed that the thing's still in one piece. Because of the angle that the ship landed in, the floor is tilted fairly steeply, like a funhouse of suck. It's not impassable, but it does require a little forethought before each step to avoid face-planting. The wall that separated this outer area from the pool inside is completely smashed away, and it looks like all the pool water was flung against the far wall, along with lounge chairs and assorted pool toys, where it all promptly froze into a sort of mural. Over time, snow and frost has accumulated along the exposed wall, and I'm thankful that most of the cloudy ice obscures some of the more morbid objects I imagine came in with the pool water.

"Well, lead on, MacDuff," Dad says to me brightly. "You're our guide now. Which way?"

"Funny how I always end up the guide on this boat," I grumble. I point to the door on the opposite wall, which has remained mostly shielded from the elements. "We can go through there and see if the stairwell is passable. If it is, we can take it all the way down to the bottom level. If not, we're going to have to zig-zag arou—" Dad grabs my arm as I'm about to lead the group to the exit.

"Hold on a second, dearheart," he says, his voice suddenly deathly serious. He walks over to a wall console that used to sit next to the side entrance into the pool area. The screen on the console is completely gone, leaving the guts of the wiring underneath exposed.

"What is it?" I ask as I walk over to him.

"Elvie," he intones gravely. "Tell me what you see."

I stare at the panel for a few moments. I want to say it's just a bunch of junk, but I know my dad, and he wouldn't halt our search before it even began without good cause, so I take another look. LED backlights, all pulverized, magnesium filaments . . .

"The power coupling," I say.

"What's a power coupling?" Cole asks.

"They're conduits for the electricity these computer consoles use," I explain. "Like wiring but without the wires. One module is connected directly to the power source, and it transmits the energy along a beam to one or more satellite modules throughout a piece of equipment."

"So what's wrong with the power coupling?" Zee asks, stepping forward to take a look for herself.

"It's missing," I say.

"Not missing," Dad says. "Removed. Very precisely, I might add."

"Which means . . . ?" Cole asks. The freezing sweat on my brow starts to thaw a little bit as fresh perspiration wells up underneath it. I swallow hard to get the lump in my throat down before I answer.

"We're not alone."

"What do you mean, we're not alone?" Cole asks. "Just because a couple of pieces of junk aren't there doesn't mean much. They could have fallen out or been crushed by something, or—"

"No," Dad corrects him. "The seals that lock the modules into place are intact. These have been removed manually. And that's not all." He shifts over to the poolside wall, which has been broken through. The steel panels that used to reinforce the plaster foam outer wall have mostly buckled and bent, or come loose altogether, leaving mounds of now-frozen dust at the base. Dad bends down and brushes away one of these piles, revealing a perfect twenty-centimeter-diameter hole in the floor.

"This is where the titanium supports should be anchored," Dad goes on. "Even if this wall was blown out on impact, it shouldn't have collapsed completely. And the support frames would still be here." He stands up and dusts off his pants. "Those supports have been removed too. And that's no easy task."

"Meaning," Zee says, "that whoever's here has access to some pretty heavy machinery."

"Or they're very strong," I say, almost in a whisper. We all stand in deathly silence for a minute as Dad and I look at each other, quietly assessing the new threat. Finally, Cole adds his two cents.

"So what are we talking about here? I thought you guys said this was the wrong pole for polar bears."

"Oh, Cole, for Christ's sake," I start in on him. "The Jin'Kai are here!"

But Cole just shakes his head. "That doesn't make sense," he replies. "Desi sent out the misdirecting distress signal, remember? There's no way the Jin'Kai could have located the crash site."

"Not those Jin'Kai, you beautiful moron. The ones who were already here." He blinks at me, still not understanding. "The Devastators are still alive."

"We need to leave this level—*now*," Zee says, suddenly very tense.

"Right," I agree. "But we better be careful—"

"Not that way," she says, stopping me from moving to the door. I freeze, listen carefully. Far away—but much closer than I'd like—I hear the sound of metal on metal.

Boots. Heavy boots on stairs.

And they're getting closer.

"Come on!" I scream-whisper, and I bolt toward the side door to the ruined pool area. The others fall into place beside me, slipping and sliding as we do our best to run down across the icy floor.

"Where is this headed?" Zee huffs as she runs.

"The pool?" Dad asks, huffing even harder. "That will just lead us to the locker roo— My God, Elvie, you are a clever little rascal."

"Don't get too excited just yet," I say as we careen past the side of the now-empty pool, thankfully devoid of any of the frozen corpses I was afraid of finding. "This might not be any safer."

We make it to the locker room. The rows of lockers, which are about two and a half meters tall and twelve lockers deep, have collapsed like dominoes. I maneuver around them, fingers pinching the walls for a grip against the incline, and head to the opening in the wall to the back left. Above, the sign remains hanging: DIRTY LAUNDRY.

"Where does this lead?" Zee asks, looking down the dark chute.

"Down to the main laundry room," Dad chimes in. "If I'm not mistaken." He knows he's not. "I'll go first. It could be a very bumpy ride." And he swings his leg over the edge and hoists himself inside. It's a tight fit for him, but he's got enough clearance that he should be able to slide down easily, assuming the chute hasn't buckled and broken anywhere along the way—which is entirely possible. But seeing as the other option is facing a group of ruthless extraterrestrial meanies that Cole once described as a cross between the Alien and the Predator, I'm willing to take my chances. Dad looks at me and nods, his expression a mix of fright and exhilaration.

"See you down there," he says, glancing down one last time. "Hopefully." And with that, he lets go. The clunking sound of my father sliding down the metal chute echoes up.

Without waiting to hear any kind of confirmation that he's landed, Zee hops over the edge as well. "No time to make sure it's safe," she says, then releases her grip and follows her former husband, making considerably less noise as she slides. I start to climb in after her when Cole stops me.

"Elvie, this is nuts," he whispers. "How are you so certain the Devastators are still alive? They were trapped in that shuttle when the ship crashed."

"Yeah, at the back end of the ship," I counter. "If those things are as badass as you claimed, do you really want to lay odds that they couldn't survive?" Cole makes a face like he's actually trying to calculate the odds. If he calculates even twice as quickly as he diagrammed sentences back in Mrs. Kwan's English class, we could be here all day.

"Into the laundry chute, pretty boy," I say, climbing into the opening.

I let go of my grip on the edge and start gliding down the chute. Well, not so much gliding as banging back and forth against the sides like a human (er, hybrid) pinball. The incline on the chute is so steep that it's mostly a freefall, like the "Death by Water" slide at the waterpark down the shore that Ducky and I were gaga for when we were little. Only, instead of water waiting for me at the bottom, there might just be a jagged pile of burning metal shards, or something equally as pleasant.

After only a few seconds I hear the telltale sound of Cole jumping in the chute behind me, and I make a mental note that if I'm not impaled by something on the way down, I better tuck and roll when I land so that I don't get smushed under 95 kilograms of dumbass. Seriously, first he drags his feet, and then he gives me a head start of less than three seconds before he comes barreling down after me? Timing is not Cole's strong suit.

I can see the light at the end of the tunnel, so to speak, and it doesn't appear to be jagged or on fire or anything like that. I exit with a *fwoosh!* and touch down first with my feet, the jolt riding up through my knees and into my hips before I curl up, pitch forward, and roll like a toddler in kiddie gymnastics out of the way as Cole lands with a heavy *thump* right behind me. My momentum nearly sends me crashing into the wall, but Zee is there to catch me.

"*Whoop!*" Cole screams out. "That was awesome!"

I'm a little dizzy from the ride down and especially my landing (which I'd reckon would earn me a 6.5 from the international judges). I shake my head, trying to clear away some of the fuzzies.

"Cole, only you would think that was fun," I mutter. I glance at Zee, expecting her to join in on the Cole-bashing, or at least look like she wants to. But she's giving me that same tense grimace she had up on the lido deck.

"What?" I ask. Cole has tensed up too, moving into a

defensive crouch. Zee's eyes move past me over my shoulder. I turn around, following her gaze. There is my father, leaning against a table, rubbing his knee.

And staring down the barrel of a gun.

I suck in my breath when I see who's holding the gun on my father. I've seen a lot of crazy shit lately, but this might be the first thing that seems absolutely paranormal. A little ragged and a lot scruffier than the last time I saw him, it is none other than the man I very clearly remember shooting. Three times. And that was *before* Cole dropped him face-first off a ten-meter catwalk.

"Jesus Christ," I tell Dr. Marsden. "How many times do we have to kill you?"

# Chapter Nine

# WHEREIN OLD ENEMIES BECOME NEW NOT-SO-MUCH ENEMIES

I have to say, Dr. Marsden looks genuinely surprised to see me. Almost as surprised as I am to see him—although, to be fair, I think I get the edge, seeing as I was pretty sure he was a pancake of guts at the bottom of a space wreck.

"My goodness," he says, taking a step away from Dad. "Elvie Nara. I can honestly say I never expected to find *you* here." He keeps his gun waving somewhere between Dad and Cole, making it look like the weapon's just lazily drifting around, although if he felt like it, he could easily shoot either one of them between the eyes without another thought.

"The feeling is, obviously, mutual," I reply. "You know, most dudes would take three point-blank shots to the chest and a long fall onto their face as their cue to shuffle off the mortal coil."

"What can I say? I'm resilient." His eyes are wide, and I can tell he's in a very deliberate physical position, anticipating any potentially threatening move on our part.

"We really did surprise you, didn't we?" I ask.

"I wondered if the Almiri might send a detachment at some point," he answers, moving an almost imperceptible half step back toward the door. "But after the first week came and went, I figured I was on my own down here."

"We're not here on behalf of the Almiri." Like that's any of his beeswax.

Dr. Marsden narrows his eyes at me, curious. "You're not?" He takes a second look at our ragtag band of adventurers. Two teenagers, a skinny middle-age woman, and a slightly frumpy, well, Dad-like person who twisted his knee barreling down the laundry chute. Marsden turns to Dad, tilting his head to the side inquisitively. "So that would make you . . . ?"

"My father," I answer. "Harry Nara. Mind not pointing a gun at him, please?"

Suddenly, and quite unexpectedly, Dr. Marsden breaks into that brilliant smile of his. "Well, I'll be," he says, all warm and fuzzy and stuff. "Mr. Nara." And to everyone's surprise, Marsden immediately lowers his gun, tucking it away in his belt behind his back. "It's a pleasure to meet you. I had the good fortune to have your daughter as a student and patient here at Hanover before we became, well, rather Earthbound. Dr. Marsden, but, please, call me Ken." And if *that* seemed screwy, what Marsden does next is absolutely Phillips-head bonkers. He actually *extends his hand* to my father. Eagerly, even. Like this was a PTA meeting or something.

Confused, Dad reaches out cautiously to accept the shake. "I admit I'm at a bit of a loss," Dad says as Marsden pumps his hand energetically. "You *are* the gentleman my daughter shot a while back, are you not?"

"Well, you know, misunderstandings," Marsden answers with a shrug, as if I'd dented his fender in the school parking lot. "Water under the bridge. Or ice, as it were." Marsden widens his grin to show his pearly white teeth, laughing at his own cheesetastic quip. It's that warmth that made me kinda crush on the good doctor—you know, before I learned he was a homicidal maniac. So I can sort of forgive Dad when he returns the smile.

Cole has a little more experience with Marsden—but unfortunately, he's still Cole. Seeing that Marsden has pocketed his weapon, he springs forward.

*"You murdering Jin'Kai bastard!"* Cole bellows as he lunges at the doctor.

"Cole, no!" I scream, but it's too late. In the blink of an eye Dr. Marsden has registered Cole's attack, and the warmth and geniality vanish from his face. In one fluid show of exceptional strength he tightens his grip on Dad's hand and spins him about in front of him, so that Dad becomes a human shield between him and Cole. With one arm wrapped around Dad's waist, still holding tight on his hand, Marsden brings his other hand up and clamps down on Dad's throat. Cole stops dead in his tracks, still several meters away from them.

"Easy, boy," Dr. Marsden growls menacingly. His face has gone completely dark, and his eyes, so kind and inviting just moments ago, have turned deadly. "We're all going to be friends today, wouldn't you agree?"

The air is heavy with the tension, and somehow the

room seems to grow fifteen degrees colder. Marsden's grip on Dad's throat is not so tight that my father can't breathe, but the doc's not about to let go anytime soon, either. And even if we could get near the guy, Marsden's still the only one of us with a weapon. Every muscle in my body is rigid, watching my father's panicked eyes.

"Cole," I whisper, trembling. "Please."

Frozen in his attack stance, Cole doesn't take his eyes off Marsden. But when he hears my voice, he wavers slightly.

"Listen to your girlfriend, Almiri," Marsden says, his tone taunting.

"He's not my boyfriend," I whisper back.

"Wait, what?" Cole asks, suddenly confused.

"Elvie," my mother says behind me. "Not now."

Finally, after another tense few seconds, Cole relaxes and stands up straight, raising his hands in submission, retreating three steps back.

Marsden smirks wickedly, but he releases his grip on Dad's throat. "Sorry about that, Harry," Marsden says, slapping Dad's shoulder good-naturedly as Dad exhales a relieved breath. "Race war and all that. You understand."

"I suppose," Dad says, massaging his throat. But when the doc lets go of his hand, he takes several steps away from Marsden.

"So, now what?" I ask. "You call your goon buddies down here and we all have a party?"

Marsden arches an eyebrow. Man, he does have handsome eyebrows. *Shake it off, Elvie.* "Buddies?" he asks.

"Quit the act," I snap. "We heard the Devastators up on

the lido deck before we decided to ride the laundry chute. We know that at least some of them survived the crash with you."

"The . . . 'Devastators'?" Marsden asks, barely stifling a laugh.

"That's what the Almiri call them," I say. I'd laugh myself if our lives weren't on the line. "So they're not great with names. Whatever, the ugly big dudes that you called to the ship after the Almiri attacked."

"Ah, yes, the 'Devastators,'" Marsden replies. "Yes, they're here. Some of them. But as I said before, *I'm* here on my own. And I'm not the one who called them, Elvie. I really assumed you would have deduced that much by now."

Huh?

"This isn't the place for conversation," Marsden contin-ues. "Their movements have been fairly restricted, but they're starting to branch farther out as they require more parts. Come on, follow me." And with that, the dude actually has the nerve to turn his back on us and head for the door, as if we were all good friends and not, you know, mortal enemies who've recently tried to kill each other. "Watch your step, it's rough going through here."

Cole and I exchange a look, which pretty much conveys our simultaneous thought.

W.

T.

F.

"Elvie?" Zee whispers. She's remained mostly quiet this whole time, and I realize that she knows the least about the Jin'Kai and Dr. Marsden out of any of us. If *we're* confused, she must be completely dumbfounded. "Shall we go?" she asks.

"Now would be better than later, ma'am," says Dr. Marsden.

"My name is Zada," Zee says. "I'm Elvie's—"

"Let's just back this convoy up a bit," I interrupt, turning from Mom to Dr. Marsden. "Just so we're all on the same page here, let's be clear on a few things. You are an evil alien bastard whose compatriots were planning on swapping out my baby with one of your own little lab creations. For whatever reason, you decided not to. Great. But I'm not, like, handing you the Humanitarian of the Year award or anything, because please let us not forget that you *blew up a ship*, killing at least a dozen Almiri who had come to rescue us. Not to mention that you beat the living shit out of Cole and threw him off a catwalk. And you tried to kill me. Like, a lot."

Dr. Marsden just lets out a sigh, like I'm still not getting it, whatever "it" may be.

"Elvie," he says, shaking his head in an *aw shucks* kinda way. "I hate to disagree, but I very much never tried to kill you. And I'd love to explain everything to you, I really would, but for right now you're just going to have to trust me."

"No, Elvie," Cole says next to me. "Don't." Dr. Marsden shoots Cole a *look* but very quickly refocuses on me, holding out his hand expectantly. With a sharp jerk of his chin he motions for me to follow him.

"There is nothing you could possibly do to make me trust you," I tell him coldly.

Marsden rolls his eyes, as if I'm being a great big pain in his alien butt. Then, as though making up his mind about something, he strides back into the room, heading directly toward me. As Marsden gets closer, Cole takes a half step sideways to put himself partially between us. Dr. Marsden reaches behind his back, and I suck in a deep breath, half expecting him to blast me right then and there . . .

. . . And then he *hands me his gun*.

"This way," he says. "Please." And he turns and walks straight out of the room.

The four of us look at one another, baffled. I cradle the weird alien weapon in my hand, bobbing it up and down to get a feel for its weight. It's heavier than an Alimiri weapon but still pretty light, made out of a brownish metal with a smell that's thick and tangy.

"Well," I say finally. And before I can think better of it, I head out the door after Dr. Marsden.

The others follow. Because, well, what the hell else are we going to do?

To say that it's not easy going outside the laundry room is an understatement. It seems that these lower passageways took the brunt of the shock when the ship crashed. The walls have crumpled inward, and the ceilings have caved as well. Debris has been spewed all over the ground. We're walking "downhill" now, along the tilted floor, and it's not as icy here as it was up on the lido deck, but that's a small comfort when we're forced to crouch down to avoid eating wiring.

"So, you said you heard the others up on the lido deck?" Marsden says, leading the way. "I take it you came in through the opening up there?"

"Through the crater left by the explosion," Cole replies, the chill in his voice matching our surroundings.

Marsden ignores his tone. "They must be looking to scavenge some finer components. Most likely they've exhausted the feasible parts on the lower levels."

"Scavenging parts for what?" Zee asks, snaking over a large collapsed coolant compressor that's fallen through the ceiling.

"As far as I've been able to piece together," Marsden tells us, "they've been trying to build a skiff to get them out of here." He pauses to maneuver around the next part of the fun house—the hallway ahead looks like somebody picked it up and squeezed it, then left it for dead. Marsden drops to his hands and knees to get through. "Watch your hands, there are some aluminum shards."

"A skiff?" Dad prompts as he crawls behind Marsden. Dad's huffing and puffing quite a bit, and I think his knee is probably bothering him more than he wants to let on. Chances are, he re-sprained it on the way down the chute, although he's trying to keep up gamely.

Marsden's voice echoes through the pinched hall. "After the crash," he tells us, "it soon became clear that there was no power on the ship. The generators are completely pulverized. There's no way to send any sort of signal, so they began to gather components to build a makeshift craft to get them out of here."

"Why not just walk?" I ask. "They're big baddies, right?" From what Ducky has told me and the way Cole describes them, these guys are about as nasty as they come.

"The Kynigos are not accustomed to the cold," Marsden says. "They have very durable exoskeletons for high temperatures but no internal mechanisms to generate sufficient body heat to survive the climate here. Too long exposed to the elements and they'd be dead."

"The *keeny ghost?*" I ask.

"You can keep calling them Devastators if you wish," comes Marsden's dry reply. "And again, I'm not entirely certain about the skiff. I've only been able to glimpse bits and pieces of it. But based on their comings and goings since we crashed, I think it's a fair assumption."

"And you've been, what?" I ask. "Hanging out, catching up on your reading?"

"Let's just say I've been keeping a low profile."

Man, if the Rasputin of baby docs wants nothing to do with these guys, you *know* they're bad news. "Do they have any idea you're still alive?" I ask.

But Cole has other concerns. "What good is a toboggan made out of broken spare parts going to do them, if there's no way to power it?"

"There's no power *on this ship,*" Dad chimes in. "But with the right component parts from a vessel like this it wouldn't be much trouble to jerry-rig a light fusion engine."

"I can see where your daughter gets her ingenuity, Harry," Marsden tells him.

"Thank you, Doctor," Dad says, and I can tell he's tickled pink.

"Please," Marsden corrects him as we finally exit the squeeze box. There's a general sigh of relief as, one by one, we all rise to our feet again. "Call me Ken. And the lovely lady"— he offers one of his warm smiles to Zee—"I take it this is your mother, Elvie?" I nod. He may be a murderous SOB, but he's a *perceptive* SOB. "Another crossbreed," he says, inspecting my mother up and down in a way I'm not altogether comfortable with. "Amazing. But"—he turns back to me—"I thought you said your mother had died."

"A lot can change in a week," I tell him. "So you knew I was a hybrid all along."

"Yes, and now so do you, it seems. The evolution of the species the Almiri were so desperate to extinguish. You have become of keen interest to us, Elvie."

"Just what is it about the hybrids that makes them so interesting to the Jin'Kai?" Dad asks, the last of the group to rise to his full height. I give him a hand as he winces at the pain in his knee.

"I didn't say the Jin'Kai," Marsden says. "I said 'us.'"

Once my dad is firmly on his feet, I look around and realize that we've come to the medical suites—or what's left of them, anyway. The floor and walls are damp and frosty.

"Has this area flooded?" I ask nervously, wondering if Dr. Marsden isn't just leading us to a watery grave.

"This area was underwater after the initial impact," Marsden says. "The cruiser broke through the ice, and we were completely submerged for, oh, fifteen minutes, maybe twenty. The prow caught the worst of it, flooding the bridge all the way through the hangar and into the engine/repulsor stores. This area was one of the last places the water reached before the ship crested and came back up."

"And the ice just froze up around it," Dad says matter-of-factly. "Extraordinary."

"Nothing does the trick of reviving you after getting shot like waking up submerged in freezing water," Marsden says wryly. "We're holding steady for now, but I have no faith that the ship will stay above sea level much longer. That's why your arrival is so fortuitous. Now, Harry," he goes on, taking Dad by the arm and leading him into his old examination room, "let's see if there isn't something we can do about that knee of yours. There must be some bandages still in their wrapping."

Zee follows Marsden and Dad into the exam room, leaving me and Cole behind, both of us still experiencing massive character-shift vertigo.

"What's he up to?" Cole whispers to me. "Wasn't too long ago he wanted both of us dead."

"All I know," I answer, "is that he could have vaporized us all in a heartbeat back there and he didn't. Whatever he's up to, we'll have to get it out of him, fast."

I turn to join my parents, but Cole touches my arm to stop me. "Elvie, we can't trust him," he says.

"Yeah, dur," I reply. "But we need to find out what he's doing, and we can't exactly do that in the hallway."

"Okay," Cole says, thinking it over. "But, like, we should be clever about it. Sneaky."

I open my mouth to tell Cole that cleverness has not exactly proven to be one of his strengths, but I shut my yap instead. I've been snarky enough for three lifetimes, and poor, sweet Cole doesn't deserve any of it. "Good plan," I agree. "Now, c'mon, let's not leave the grown-ups alone too long."

"'Kay, only . . ." Cole's hand still lingers on my arm. "What did you mean before, when you said I wasn't your boyfriend?"

I kiss him on the cheek. "I was trying to throw Marsden off

balance," I say with what I can only hope is an encouraging smile. "Y'know, sneaky?"

He moves his hand from my arm and touches his cheek where I've just kissed him. "Yeah," he says, smiling back. "Yeah, sure."

I enter the exam room, Cole right behind me. Dad is up on the exam table, which is, of course, tilted at such a teeter-totter angle that he's forced to grip the edges to keep from sliding down. Meanwhile, Marsden is wrapping a thick tan bandage around my father's pant leg, chatting and *laughing* with my parents like he's the family MD.

"Normally this would go against the skin," Mardsen says. "But I figured it was a bit chilly in here to have you strip down to your skivvies."

"Quite," Dad agrees with a laugh.

Uh, hello? When my Dad found out that Randy Bird had thrown a basketball at my head in sixth grade PE, he practically led a campaign to have him expelled from the school, and now he's sitting around *chortling* with my attempted murderer? "I want to know what the hell your game is, Doc," I say, hands tight around the ray gun.

I hope that was sneaky enough for you, Cole.

"Elvie!" my parents say in unison. As if I'm a disobedient child.

"Dad, Zee, you don't know what this guy is capable of," I tell them. "And I'm not buying the 'Good Doctor' act one bit. So tell me what you're up to, Doc, or I'll fry your ass with this goofy ray gun of yours, and this time I won't stop till I know you're good and dead."

Marsden smiles and continues wrapping Dad's knee. "Don't be too hard on her, folks, she's not wrong," he says. "It's no use arguing that we are anything beyond allies of convenience." He looks up at me. "Yet allies we are."

"Not yet," I answer. "Not till you tell us everything that's going on. Why you're hiding from the Keeny . . . Kyni-goats . . ." Damn, it's difficult to be threatening when you can't even pronounce half the words you're saying. "*Devastators*," I say at last. "And why you're so interested in hybrids. Everything."

"Well," Marsden replies lightly. As though angry girls with ray guns shout at him every day. Maybe they do—I don't know, I haven't been reading the dude's diary. "I imagine we're both interested in the crossbreed situation, Elvie. That is why you're here, isn't it? Looking for any files you might have missed detailing my tests?"

Like I said before: perceptive.

Dr. Marsden finishes fastening the bandage on Dad's knee and rises up, sauntering over to the nearby counter and lackadaisically browsing through the cabinets, looking for who-knows-what.

"Your questions are interrelated, Elvie, so I'll give you one big, messy answer. The situation, in a nutshell, is this: The Almiri see you as a threat. My brothers the Jin'Kai see you as a nuisance. I see you as a savior." Mom, standing beside Dad, lifts her head on her neck a little, listening. "And I'm not alone," Marsden continues. He finds some gauze packs and a slender pouch of antiseptic gel and takes them out. He walks back over to Dad and gingerly lifts up his hand—and it's only then that I realize that Dad's palms are practically shredded. I guess he had even more difficulty navigating the hallway than I thought. "The Kynigos, or 'Devastators,' are what you'd call the old guard of the Jin'Kai," Marsden goes on, beginning to clean and dress Dad's wound. "They're not a very flexible bunch, and they like to get their way. It was their . . . *enthusiastic* approach to breeding that forced the Jin'Kai's hand when it came to reappropriating the other Pouri colonies. Unfortunately, we as a species don't seem to have learned much from our mistakes. There was a notion that, with time, more worlds with viable hosts would be discovered beyond the original six colonies. I'm sad to say that this notion never quite came to fruition. And here we are, on the cusp of taking the final colony, which will buy us, what, a hundred years? Two? Our growth is exponential. We need another solution."

"I've got a great solution," Cole suggests. "We wreck your sorry asses and send you all packing back into outer space."

"Let me be very clear about this," Marsden replies, his voice deathly serious. "You have no chance, *no chance*, to survive the war that is to come. My predecessors have not just conquered but *consumed* five other worlds before this one. I am part of the vanguard generation, sent to Earth to quietly create a foothold for our fleets that are en route."

"Fleets?" I ask, already feeling the dread rising in me. "How many?"

"More than you can count," Marsden says bleakly. "And more than this modestly populated little rock can sustain. Fifty years ago a small band of us arrived on the planet, and today we already outmatch the Almiri strength." He turns to Cole. "The Earthbound Jin'Kai represent less than two percent of the total strength of our forces. Your kind lost this fight before it even began."

Okay, so dread officially risen. If what Marsden is saying is true, then a few files in a computer aren't going to help us any. After all, how are a bunch of ones and zeros going to help against an intergalactic force of highly advanced warriors who outgun and outnumber us by a factor of who-the-shit-knows?

But Marsden isn't done there. "Our inevitable military victory won't help us survive long after your demise, however," he continues.

"Is that supposed to, like, cheer me up?" I ask. "That you guys will be dead too, eventually?" I roll my eyes. "Hey, we can stop now, guys. Mission accomplished! Woo-hoo!"

Marsden ignores my little bout of sarcasm. "As I see it, there needs to be a change in the Jin'Kai culture if we are to bring to an end our history of self-defeating genocide. I am one in a minority of the vanguard who believe that there is a way to prevent the tragedies of past mistakes. And all of my work has been toward achieving this end."

"Your 'work,'" Cole growls, "included the slaughter of countless numbers of our offspring." I have to say, I'm pleasantly surprised that Cole's the only one of my cofighters not taken in by Marsden's good nature. I guess, 'cause, you know, the doc tried to break open his face and stuff. "How many sites like this ship were there before we found out about what you were up to?"

"Enough," Marsden answers coolly. "My work was progressive but ultimately useless . . . until I found you, Elvie." He turns and looks me right in the eye. "I knew from the first bio-scan that there was something different about your baby. After I ran more tests on you, I realized what I had in you: the answer. A host with the ability to carry an infant without becoming infertile. After still further tests I found even more good news: You weren't a fluke. The genetic indicators in your DNA pointed to hereditary traits." He points to Mom. "The mutation was dominant, and that meant it held the solution to our ever-encroaching crisis."

"You were looking for a way to replicate the 'mutation,' as you call it," Zee says, nodding like this all makes perfect sense. Like the doctor's discussing how much garlic to add to the marinara. "To find what made us different from our Almiri fathers."

"And I was *this close* to finding it," Marsden tells her. "Until, of course, this buffoon and his cohorts came and ruined everything."

Cole glowers under the accusation. "You mean when we saved everyone on this ship," he says.

"Did you, now?" Marsden muses. "I wonder, what was the school enrollment *before* your little visit?"

"You mean before you started *drowning*—"

"Cole!" I put up a hand to shush him, which startles him into silence. I can feel Cole getting hotter, and he's got every right. But the last thing we need right now is Archer vs. Marsden, Round Two.

"None of this explains why you're hiding from your buddies upstairs," I put in.

Marsden turns his attention back to healing Dad's hands. "When the Almiri attacked, the faculty went to our containment contingency plan, and reinforcements were contacted.

But I knew that when they came, all my work would be in danger of being exposed, and destroyed. The Jin'Kai can be just as set in their ways as the Almiri. What I was doing—looking for a way to alter our species—would have been considered tantamount to treason."

"It was Fred who contacted the Jin'Kai." I realize the truth as the words come out of my mouth. "The cook. He contacted them, and you killed him for it."

"And you've been hiding like a rat in the walls ever since," Cole says.

"How have you survived?" Zee asks. And, honestly, I'm not thrilled with the way she's eyeing at him. I mean, I'm not gonna lie—the dude's good-looking. But that's not what seems to be interesting my mother. She seems actually . . . taken in by his rhetoric.

"I was fortunate enough to secure a stash of food from the vending machines," Marsden answers.

"Is that what the others have been living off?" I ask. "Pregnant-lady ice cream flavors?" I snort at the idea of all those badass predators on a major sugar high.

"Not quite," Marsden says. "You trapped a full squadron of Earthborn Jin'Kai and Kynigos in that shuttle before you escaped, am I right?"

"At least a dozen or more," I confirm.

"Well, in these past few weeks I've spotted only four Kynigos and no Earthbounders," he says. "So you do the math."

Yee-uck.

"Elvie, you must see what I'm getting at here," Marsden continues. "Almiri, Jin'Kai, it doesn't matter. The two species have built-in expiration dates. The precious Code isn't going to hold forever, and what then? Eventually we will both go extinct and take the human race with us. You, and those like you, are the only hope for any of us."

To my horror, Dad has joined my mother in the nodding-in-agreement thing. Can't they see that the dude is a scheming rat? A scheming, conniving, homicidal, duplicitous, majorly hunky rat.

Still . . . he kinda has a point.

"So what are you proposing?" I say. Beside me, Cole bristles. But I decide, for the moment, to listen to the doc.

"What I'm proposing is that we help each other in order to *help each other*," Marsden says, tossing the last of the cleaning gauze in a heap in the frozen corner. He hands my dad a cream to apply to the scrapes. "You want to see my research? I'll give it to you. On one very reasonable condition. I need off this ship. So do you. So we help each other get free. And when we're free, I'll show you everything."

"You'll show us first," I say, stroking the gun with one hand for emphasis.

"Very well," Marsden says. "We can gather my records before heading to your transport."

"Transport?" Dad asks, giving me a look.

"Well, you didn't walk here, did you?" Marsden asks with a smile. But when no one answers, his smile slowly fades. "Did you?"

"We came via dogsled," I explain. "But it sort of got . . . eaten."

Marsden frowns but doesn't seem flustered. He merely

shakes his head as if weighing his options. "Then I suppose we must resort to a variant on my original plan."

"Plan?" Leave it to my father to cheer up at any mention of a plan.

Marsden turns to my dad, like he knows the guy's his best shot at supporting what I am almost positive is about to be a truly preposterous scheme. "With any luck that skiff the Kynigos are building down there is close to operational. If we can find a way to neutralize them—"

"*Excuse* me?" Cole says. "Elvie, this is so totally a trap."

"Let's hear what he has to say," Zee puts in.

I nod in agreement. "If it *is* a trap," I tell Cole, "then we're already in it." Cole harrumphs, totally exasperated with me, but he doesn't say anything else. I turn back to Marsden. "You give us your files. We help you get control of that skiff thing of theirs. And then we head back to the camp at Cape Crozier."

"An Almiri camp?" Marsden asks disapprovingly. "So this lot"—he jerks a thumb at Cole—"can arrest me?"

"We came to find your research to show the Almiri, to show them that the hybrids aren't a threat to them," I say. "If your work is as convincing as you claim, then who better to show it to? Who knows, you might even be able to convince them to work *with* you."

Marsden thinks on this for a while. "I don't trust them," he says finally.

"Perfect," I reply. "'Cause I don't trust you."

He gives me that big smile again, his eyes twinkling in what always appears to be admiration. He throws up his hands in resignation.

"Very well," he says. "I suppose it's only fair that if I ask for your faith that I show some in return. Then it's agreed. There's just one more thing that I'm going to need from you."

"And what's that?" I ask, narrowing my eyes.

"First," he says. "You're going to need to promise that you won't freak out."

# Chapter Ten

# IN WHICH AN ICE-COLD DIP LANDS OUR HEROINE IN HOT WATER

"Elvie, this is crazy," Cole says in one of his trademark "duh" statements of obviousness.

"Keep your voice down," I say. "They might be in there right now."

Cole, Dad, and I are making our way down the ladder slowly, heading toward the familiar maintenance entrance to the hangar bay. It's harder than it should be—due to the tilt of the ship, the ladder is pitched about forty degrees, and it feels more like climbing down the side of a steep, icy hill than anything. At least last time we needed to come down this way, we had a cable to tether us. Now we're forced to shift from one rung to the next with the knowledge that if we let go, we're going to slide down a long way, with only our chins slamming into the remaining rungs to slow our fall. It's terribly cold down here, worse than the rest of the ship, and even through my gloves my fingers burn with the chill. From what Marsden said, a good deal of the hangar is now underwater, with multiple potential hull breaches. Normally the part of a sinking ship you'd want to *avoid*. Except that, as part of Marsden's plan, this is exactly where we need to be.

"I don't understand why you two need to be doing this," Cole says. "If the Devastators are building their ship down in the hangar, that's almost definitely where they're going to be."

"That's what the distraction is for," I tell him.

"Yeah, like that's going to work."

"You doubt my programming skills?" Dad chimes in through heavy breaths as he eases one leg down to the next rung. Cole is beneath me on the ladder while Dad is above me, and I suck in my breath every time Dad makes a move, afraid that he's going to slip and make a squashed Elvie sandwich. As if on cue, the rung breaks free as Dad puts his weight on it and he loses his grip.

"Ow!" I holler as the frozen rung hits me in the face. Luckily, Dad finds another handhold and steadies himself.

The broken rung *bongs* and *clatters* as it makes its noisy way down to the bottom of the chute. The three of us freeze, holding our breath and waiting, but after a few minutes it becomes fairly clear that no one has been alerted to our presence.

"Sorry," Dad whispers down to me, chagrined.

"No worries," I reply, rubbing my forehead as we start down again. I return to my conversation with Cole. "Look," I say, "we have no idea if that thing they're building is up and running yet. And the best two people on board to figure that out are the inimitable Harry Nara and yours truly." To be honest, this part of Marsden's crazy plan is the one I mind the least. After several days of feeling completely out of my element while having to contest with, y'know, *the* elements, I'm glad that the task set before me is to deal with wires and circuits instead of wind chills and wildlife.

"It just seems that big tough Dr. Marsden should be the one facing off with these guys, instead of traipsing off to find some baby that's probably long gone."

Dr. Marsden insists that the Jin'Kai baby—the one that my classmate formerly known as Other Cheerleader gave birth to only minutes before the Devastators decapitated her—is still very much alive, and that the Devastators are keeping it somewhere on the ship. Marsden claims that he only wants to protect the child by "rescuing him" from a bunch of meanies who don't care about him. Personally, I think Marsden doesn't want the other Jin'Kai unearthing any "off the books" tinkering that may have gone on while he was engineering those rapidly developing fetuses. If I'm right, it might mean that the good doctor has already started experimenting with mutating the Jin'Kai DNA to create hybrid attributes.

"Would you rather Marsden was the one with the escape craft while we were off on some wild baby chase?" I ask. "At least this way he can't run off without us." Not that the idea of running off without *him* hasn't crossed my mind—he's already given me his top-secret files, which apparently fill two heavy-duty hard disks. I've got them tucked safely in the inner pocket of my thermal. If it weren't for the fact that I gave him my word, I would have very few reservations about blowing this popsicle stand without him.

"Yeah, we'll just get our faces eaten by monsters," Cole adds cheerily.

"Not if Oliv—sorry, Zee—has anything to say about it," Dad puts in. "Assuming those explosives that Ken gave her are functional."

Yeah, consider me not so thrilled that Marsden and my mom set off together to play their roles in this little *Mission Impossible: Freaky Alien Edition*. Not that I think Zee is gullible by any means, but when Marsden was going off on his whole rant about how hybrids hold the key to saving the planet, he knew *exactly* what audience he was playing to. And I worry that maybe Mom simply heard "hybrids good; Almiri baaaaaaad" and turned off her thinking beanie after that.

"I still say it stinks," Cole says, letting go of the last rung and sliding down the final meter to the ground. "Marsden obviously had a lot of this plan already worked out before we showed up, so why didn't he ever try it on his own?"

"I imagine it's a happy coincidence that he found himself with four partners," Dad suggests. "Being able to put every action into play concurrently eliminates a lot of the risk of being discovered and having your later actions countered by a cognizant opponent."

"Dad, please don't call us his 'partners,'" I groan as I slide down the last stretch of the wall. Cole catches me as I land. "This is still Dr. Marsden we're talking about."

"After what he's told us, Elvie, there isn't even a sliver of a crack in your picture of him as a villain?" Dad follows us down to the ground, and both Cole and I brace him as he lands. He grunts, then tries to play it off like he's totally fine as he rights himself. "Your view of him is so intractable?"

"Dad, he tried to kill me," I reply. "How tractable do you expect me to be?"

"I'm not saying you should love the man. Or trust him completely. But it seems to me, the more we learn about the reality of this invisible war and all its factions, all these densely layered moving parts, that things might be more complicated than just good guys and bad guys."

"Good guys don't leave a trail of bodies in their wake," I tell him, with perhaps slightly more conviction than I feel. But now is not the time for philosophical debates. Instead, I gesture down the walkway to the maintenance hatch that leads to the hangar. "Let's see what we've got down there."

We cram into the maintenance staging area, and I am overcome with a nauseating sense of déjà vu. *It's okay,* I tell myself. There's plenty of oxygen in here this time. Plenty of breathable air.

And freezing water.

And, possibly, killer bad guys.

I seriously *hate* this hangar.

"I can't see anything," I say, trying to peek surreptitiously through the small window on the door. "It's all foggy."

"Here," Cole replies, and he reaches up and starts wiping the window with his thermal sleeve. The reaction from my father and me is nearly simultaneous as we both grab Cole's arm and yank it down away from the window.

"What is wrong with you?" I hiss. "What if they see you?"

"Oh," Cole says after a moment of letting the thought register. "Right."

I roll my eyes. "Well, now that it's done, you might as well check if you can see anything."

Cole grimaces at me, then slowly slides his head into the window to take a look.

"I see . . . *something* . . . ," he says, squinting. "Could be them. Three of them, looks like."

I poke my face in next to his to see for myself, but the window is already mostly fogged over again, and all I can see is a few dark blobs that could just as easily be giganto penguins.

"Are you sure?" I ask.

"Pretty sure. Yeah, there's definitely three of them."

"Well, let's hope those Almiri eyes of yours are sharper than your noodle," I say.

Cole leans back, arms over his chest. "What now, then, oh captain, my captain?"

I cock my head to the side. "Did you just finally learn about snark?" I ask, a small smile creeping across my face. Cole simply shrugs, but I can tell he's hiding a smile too. "Well," I say in response to his earlier question, "now we wait."

We wait what seems like a long while, although that could just be because of how small the staging area is. But at last we hear our "go" sound—clanking noises from far away, somewhere past the hangar in the promenade.

"Is that them?" Cole whispers.

As if in response, loud metallic voices suddenly reverberate all around us. *"You cannot cele-brate until you AM-bu-late!"*

"That sounds like a pretty enthusiastic yes to me," I say, smiling at my dad. He's grinning ear to ear, incredibly pleased with himself that he was able to rewire the fit-bots in the health and wellness center and get them up and running in a matter of hours. When Marsden brought up the need for a distraction, my mind immediately went to the insane training droids that nearly killed us last time around. I figured that a band of overly zealous Japanese-designed aerobics machines would be a far more clever distraction than running around shouting "Ooga booga!" and hoping the Devastators would chase us.

"Is it working, though?" I ask Cole. "Are they moving?"

Cole takes another peek. "They're moving to the promenade," he says, and then a moment later nods and turns to me. "They're gone."

"Gone?" I ask. "Or just out of sight?"

"Only one way to find out."

Cole eases the long handle on the hatch, which opens without the normal *hiss-pop*, since there's no pressure differentiation between the staging area and the hangar when the ship isn't in space. But Cole has only cracked the hatch a few centimeters when water starts seeping in.

"Shit," I whisper. "It's flooded."

As Cole continues to open the hatch slowly, the water streams in more quickly, pooling around our feet. When the hatch is wide enough, Cole pokes out his head to get a better view. I half expect some crazy weapon to lop his noggin right off, but he pulls back inside, head safely in place.

"This end is flooded about half the way up," Cole says. "We're going to have to swim ten meters or so."

"That water is freezing," I argue. "We can't swim in that."

"Sure we can," Cole says. I make eyes toward my Dad. Naturally, Dad picks up on the subtle gesture more than Cole does.

"I'll be fine," Dad assures us. He pulls the hood up on his thermal and tightens the zipper under his chin. "Waterproof," he reminds me, slapping the chest of his thermal. "Keep your hood on, and try not to get your head wet."

Cole is the first out, dropping into the icy water, completely submerging. He comes up, hood down, hair wet, and shakes himself like a dog.

"Brrrr! Bracing," he says. "It's pretty deep—careful coming in."

I find the submerged half ladder with my foot and use it to ease slowly into the water so that I don't splash Dad like laser-brained Cole just has. Even in my thermal, the water hits my system like a shock. I'm thankful that my hybrid DNA has helped me adapt to the cold, but right now I could go for a little of Cole's seeming imperviousness. I push out a few strokes and tread water. The hangar is only half-flooded, but thanks to the tilt of the ship, all that water is pooled on our side. On the far side of the hangar I can see the make-shift skiff, floating at the edge of where the water meets the slanted floor like the surf of the beach. It looks like a long skeletal speedboat with a duel-pronged prow, a large rough steel shield covering the front like a backward clamshell. For being cobbled together from spare junk pulled from the wreck, it's pretty impressive. Whether it will work or not, however, remains to be seen.

Cole makes sweeping broad strokes toward the skiff while I wait for Dad, who is very gingerly lowering himself into the water. I can tell from his face that the cold is biting at him as much as it did me, probably much more so. But I know we can't go slowly here. Dad won't be able to stand the chill for long before risking hypothermia and frostbite.

"Come on, Dad," I say encouragingly. "It's just like when you taught me to swim at the public pool in Belmont Hills. You just have to jump in."

"As I recall," Dad says, gritting his teeth as he eases his way down, "during your first swimming lesson you clung to the edge of the pool until I bribed you with the promise of doughnuts."

"If you get in now, I'll buy you a chocolate-frosted Boston cream. Promise."

"I'm moving, I'm moving," he tells me when I try to urge him forward. "The spirit is willing, but the body has testicles."

Dad finally manages to get all the way into the water without getting wet above the neck, and we swim over to the edge, where Cole waits with the skiff. He's not even looking at the skiff, though. Instead, he's examining the walls of the hangar.

"Look at these dents," he says. In truth they're more like deep gashes or violent puncture wounds. They pierce at least thirty centimeters deep in some places, and travel one over the other from about waist-high until they reach the hangar exit. The long docking nozzle that used to be situated over the exit has been torn away (in fact, I can see some elements of it repurposed on the skiff).

"They're handholds," I whisper. And then I gulp. "Jesus, do you think they made them with their *fingernails*?"

"More like claws, I'd wager," Dad puts in.

"Well, they're convenient for me, at least," Cole says. Silver lining and all that. "Good luck with the skiff."

Just as Cole begins to place his hands and feet in the

lowest-lying grips, I touch his shoulder. He pauses and turns around.

"Don't worry," he tells me. "I've got your back. Can't warn you if they're coming back if I don't go up there."

"I know, it's just . . ." I touch his beautiful face with my hand, and then I lean up toward him and let the surprising warmth of his body lure me closer.

And then I kiss him. He kisses me back.

I want to stay in that kiss forever, where nothing's confusing at all. No murderous baby docs with shifting alliances. No angry mothers or sad-sack fathers. Not even any boyfriend-girlfriend conversations waiting in the wings to be had. In that kiss there's just Cole and me. The two of us, together.

But a girl can't live inside a kiss.

Pulling away, I unzip my thermal and reach inside, removing the ray gun that Marsden handed over to me. I offer it to Cole, but he refuses it.

"Keep it," he says. "If one gets by me, you'll need it. Besides, if I run into them, I'm supposed to just lead them to one of those charges your mother's setting all over back there, right? Boom goes the dynamite."

"Be careful," I say, putting the gun back. "Don't do anything that, well, you would normally do."

Cole smiles and shakes his head. "Have that motor running when I get back, 'kay?"

My chest clenches, and I have to breathe deeply to work out the tightness as I watch him scurry up the wall and disappear through the exit into the promenade.

Toward the monsters.

"Elvie, come look at this," Dad says behind me. I turn around, and he's already nose-deep in the skiff, poking around the covered interior. I climb into the craft and sit next to him. He's squatting on the ground, fiddling with some loose nylon tubing that's running from the area that appears to be the cockpit back under the "floor," which is built from catwalk grating. The tubing ultimately leads into a jumble of gears that resembles the inner workings of an old clock or something, which I can only assume is the motor.

"They must be using these as the sensor relays," Dad muses of the tubes. "Perhaps in lieu of traditional pedals. They look like kitchen hosing, like from a sink's handheld sprayer. Outstanding."

Dad's voice is filled with excitement, but it also sounds a little shaky. I bend my head down to look at his face as he continues examining the ship. He's incredibly pale, with a faint bluish color in his cheeks. He's gritting his teeth together, barely managing to keep them from chattering.

"Dad, you're freezing," I say. "We need to warm you up."

"Now, now, Elvie," he replies. "There's no time for that. We must stick to the task at hand. Can you look behind me to see if there's a power flow to the engines? Since they don't seem to have installed any buttons, I'll just tug on some of these wires and see if we get a response."

I shuffle out of the interior and around to the back end of the skiff to check out the engine. Here the Devastators have attached a series of eight beam loaders. Typically, people use beam loaders to single-handedly move large, heavy pieces of equipment around, but in this array it looks like the Devastators have upcycled them into makeshift repulsors—which, in theory, should help push the skiff over the ice, and also keep it afloat if it were over water. These suckers really are ingenious.

"Okay . . . now," Dad says. I watch, but nothing happens. "No?" Dad asks. "How about now?" Another few moments of silence.

"Nothing back here," I tell him.

"They must not have gotten around to installing some of the power couplings yet. Do you see them anywhere on the ground nearby?"

I scan the floor of the skiff, but there's not much to see. We're tilted enough that things could have rolled into the water, but I doubt the Devastators would've left valuable pieces lying around like that. And I seem to recall, from my previous time spent memorizing the layout of the ship at my father's request, that there are several tool compartments lining the wall down here. Our buddies might have stashed some couplings in one of those.

I locate the half-meter-wide panels just off the floor and start pulling open the closest one. Since these would normally operate automatically with sensor activation, there are no handles to grab, so I'm forced to dig my fingers around the edges and pull. Fortunately, the magnetic bonds are shot, but I still manage to cut up my hands pretty badly for my trouble.

Plus, no power couplings.

"How did they think they were going to get the skiff out of here?" I ask as I yank open the second, and then the third compartment. Nothing and nothing. "Even if they could open the outer door, it's underwater. The whole compartment would flood immediately."

"I believe they've been worrying an opening over yonder," Dad says, gesturing absentmindedly toward the front wall in the flooded area without ever taking his eyes off what he's doing. Sure enough, along the wall just at the surface of the water there are huge score marks running several meters high and across, like someone has been slowly and deliberately cutting away at the hull with an energy cutter. Like, say, a ray gun.

"That must have taken *days*," I say, practically whistling through my teeth. "But what happens if they—"

The sound of splashing water interrupts me, like something emerging from beneath the surface. I whip around to look at the water, expecting a Devastator ambush.

Instead, what I find is something altogether different. A small, raven-haired boy of about six years old. Stark naked, and standing knee-deep in the freezing water.

Zuh?

"*Dad*," I whisper. My father pokes his head up from the skiff and follows my gaze.

"Oh my," he says. "Is that the child Marsden was talking about? I thought he said it was a baby."

It's barely been a month since Other Cheerleader gave birth to her little bundle of Jin'Kai joy, but the creature that Marsden implanted in her when he swapped out her Almiri child was engineered to develop quickly (according to Desi, our own personal Jin'Kai defector). I guess I assumed the baby's growth would normalize after it was born. But either Marsden made some sort of mistake . . . or he hasn't been telling anyone the extent of what he's been up to from the get-go.

One month old, and the kid looks ready for first grade.

"Hello there," I say, smiling. I take a step toward the kid, and he instinctively backs away, his face frozen in a look of wary curiosity.

"*Bok choy,*" the kid hisses at us. At least, it *sounds* like "bok choy."

"I don't think he understands English," Dad offers helpfully. Because, you know, I hadn't figured that out. I hold out my hand and take another step forward. The kid tenses up, crouching even farther into the water. I'm amazed that he can stand the cold. I'm not sure that even Cole could handle the temperature buck-naked like that.

"It's okay," I coo in the soothing voice I used on the neighbor's awful cat when I was trying to coax it out of whatever space in our house it had managed to steal into. "No one's going to hurt you. Just come over here, all right?"

"*Bok . . . choy?*" the kid says, cocking his head to the side like a puppy.

"That's right, bok choy. Sure."

I take another step, and then another. I'm only a meter or so away from him now, my feet just at the edge of the water. The kid holds his hand out toward me, more in a mimicking gesture than anything else. I reach the final gap to take his hand and . . .

"*Bok choy!*" he screams, and with a sudden burst he jumps *over my head* and runs past me to the wall. I topple over, startled.

"Bok Choy, no!" I call after him. But it's too late. Before

Dad can even untangle himself from the skiff, little Bok Choy has scampered up the wall and disappeared the same way Cole went.

"Shit!" I shout, climbing back to my feet. We don't have any communicators or anything, so there's no way to tell Cole there's a teeny-tiny Jin'Kai coming up behind him. And if the kid catches the Devastators' attention . . .

"Go," Dad says, reading my mind. "Get him. I can handle this."

"You sure?" I ask.

"Piece of cake."

I'm not nearly as spry climbing the wall as Cole or Baby Bok, but I manage to get to the top easily enough and pull my way over to the open exit. I find myself in the promenade gaming area, which is completely dark, given the fact that there's no power or windows. All of the game consoles appear to be broken, but they're still standing, giving the little bugger plenty of places to hide. It's incredibly icy, and I have to be careful not to slip backward as I walk uphill. Whenever possible, I latch on to one of the consoles and pull myself forward, bracing my back against one or another before pushing ahead. I scan the dark room for any sign of movement. I'd call out again, but I'm afraid there might be someone else lurking about whose attention I most certainly do not want to attract.

"Here, Bok Choy," I whisper under my breath. "Here, little alien freak baby. Er, *big* alien freak baby."

After I've made it about halfway through the long promenade, I see a shadow flicker out of the corner of my eye. I turn just in time to notice the shadow disappear into a stairwell leading up. I move to the stairs as fast as I can without falling on my ass. When I get inside the stairwell, I hear the pitter-patter of tiny feet on the stairs above me. I bolt up the stairs after him as fast as I can—which is no easy task, seeing as the stairs are, you know, *slanted*. This kid's flipping fast for a one-month-old, but I can just see a flash of alien tush as he bolts out of the stairwell onto a level two flights above me.

I run out of the stairwell and realize that he's led me to one of the sleeping decks, where my old stateroom used to be. The kid could be in *any* of these rooms, and there's dozens and dozens of them—there's no way I have time to search them all. Those fit-bots will only distract the Devastators for so long, and the makeshift explosives Marsden has been cobbling together and Zee's been setting up—on the off chance we could lead one of the meanies into them—aren't guaranteed to kill them either.

I'm searching for a naked needle in a haystack, and my time is ticking away fast.

My mind races as I make my way down the shadowy hallway, peeking around each door, and then, finally, it bumps into something. A real desperate shot in the dark, perhaps, but the thought is as good as anything I'm going to come up with.

"*I love you . . .* ," I start, my voice quiet but strong. "*A bushel and a peck. A bushel and a peck, and a hug around the neck.*"

It works on Olivia, I figure, so why not on this kid? Unless, of course, he's gotten used to Devastator lullabies, which probably sound like cats being pushed through a wood chipper.

"*A hug around the neck, and a barrel and a heap . . .*"

There's movement down the hallway about four rooms down. I continue singing quietly, channeling all the inner calm I can muster into the words. *Calm, calm, calm.* I get down on my knees and move no closer.

"*A barrel and a heap, and I'm talking in my sleep about you . . .*"

First I notice the little fingers wrapping themselves around the frame of the door, and then, seconds later, a pair of little eyes peeks out at me.

"Hey, buddy," I say gently. "Why don't you come over here?" He's hovering in the door now, probably confused why this weirdo stranger is singing to him. But I guess even he figures it's better than running.

"*I love you, a bushel and a peck. You bet your pretty neck I do . . .*"

The alien scamp inches out into the hallway and takes a few furtive steps toward me. When I reach out my hand, though, he freezes, letting out a stream of "*Bokchoybokchoy-bokchoy!*"

"It's all right," I say, reeling my hand back in slowly. I gradually shift my legs underneath me so that I'm sitting cross-legged, and I pat the frozen floor in front of me. Bok Choy relaxes some and inches closer. Then slightly closer. He is staring at my face, fascinated. I don't know if there are any reflective surfaces where he's been kept, but he seems to be able to distinguish the difference between me and his current caretakers—I look like him, and I'm guessing those other dudes don't.

Point: Elvie.

I pat the floor again, and his gaze goes to my hand. I

move it in a circle, and he follows it with his eyes, round and round. And then, before he knows it, he's standing right in front of me.

"Boop," I say as I touch his nose with my finger. And wouldn't you know it—this creepy, accelerated-growth-having alien child *laughs*. Bright, joyful children's laughter, ringing down the halls.

Loudly.

"Okay, *shhh*," I say, putting my finger to my lips. "Quiet. *Shhhh*."

"*Boop!*" he shouts, touching my nose with his finger. "Bok Choy!" He runs his hand down my cheek, over and over, fascinated with my skin.

"Yes, Bok Choy, boop. Now let's be superquiet so we don't disturb any—"

"*Bok choy!*" he screams again, still laughing. Only this time he's not talking to me. He's looking over my shoulder. Suddenly my nose is filled with an unmistakably pungent odor, a smell I've only experienced once before. The acrid stench invades my nostrils with violent ferocity, causing my eyes to fill with water almost immediately. Slowly I turn and follow Bok Choy's gaze . . .

*Oh well*, I think to myself as I look up at the redonkulously large creature that has managed to race here all the way from my deepest darkest nightmare just to end up hovering over us in the hallway.

*Life was nice while it lasted.*

# Chapter Eleven

# WHEREIN THE BADDIES GIVE STAN WINSTON A RUN FOR HIS MONEY

Ducky wasn't kidding about how flipping freaky the Devastators are. The thing standing before me in the hallway has a face like a cross between a Japanese oni mask and a prehistoric bonefish. It stands well over three meters high—and higher than that if you count its top two arms, which arch over the thing's massive triangle-shaped head. I say *top* two because the thing has another set of longer, stronger-looking arms in the middle of its torso with very different-looking hands. The top arms have hands ending in four thin articulated fingers, while the second set each have three thick fingers—two long and one stubby. The creature stands on powerful haunches that look like a reptilian version of a minotaur out of Greek mythology, with jagged, sharp cloven hooves, each with three long, sharp-looking toes.

It smells like a zombie's overripe adult diaper.

"*Bok choy!*" Bok Choy greets the beast gleefully, pointing at me for the Devastator's benefit.

The monster arches its back and raises itself slightly higher on its legs, making it seem even taller, stretching its four arms wide.

And then the son of a bitch roars at me.

I don't throw the word "blood-curdling" around a whole lot, because while I'm never one to avoid a good hyperbole, I really don't like the visual the expression conjures up. But that's exactly what my blood does when I hear that awful explosion of sound escape from the Devastator's mouth—it curdles. The animal's deep-purple skin (or is it a shell? I can't really tell, and it seems like an inopportune time to ask. But I will say that the sucker seems to have some sort of exoskeleton like a giant bug or something. It isn't altogether pleasant) seems to shimmer and pulse with a faint luminescence as it flexes, and its four beady eyes—two on each side of its gargantuan head—focus directly on me.

And all of this is, obviously, creepy and awful. But the worst thing about the Devastator is its mouth, for the following reasons:

A) It's huge.

B) It's *huge.*

C) It has, like, approximately one billion teeth.

D) The teeth have *joints.*

Yeah, seriously. Joints. When the monster opens and closes his hinged jaws, the teeth actually bend in and out on what look like *finger joints* connected by thin black muscle tissue. The creature bellows a second time, and the teeth extend outward almost as if they were pointing at me.

Good thing I haven't had much food in the past few days, or I'm positive I'd be sitting in my own feces right now.

To my surprise, Bok Choy also seems startled by the Devastator's roar. Maybe these guys are typically really lenient when it comes to childrearing. Or maybe after seeing someone who looks more like he does, the kid is realizing that giant roaring monsters with six limbs and flexing teeth are not as warm and fuzzy as he'd been led to believe. Bok Choy clutches me in a big hug, peeking at the Devastator over my shoulder.

The beast, obviously not too cool with his child's latest choice of friends, takes a heavy step toward us, its toes clanking on the floor almost like metal. I rise up and hold the kid close to me, keeping him against my chest . . .

So that the monster can't see I'm reaching for my gun.

After easing my hand inside my thermal, my fingers close around the curved grip of Dr. Marsden's ray gun.

"You really feel the need to act tough and scare a little kid?" I scream at the Devastator, who takes another several steps forward. "You think that makes you a badass, picking on either of us? I probably weigh as much as one of your balls. Assuming you have balls."

The creature hisses and snaps at me in a weird syncopated pattern, and I realize that it's probably *speaking* to me. Or cursing me out. Whatever it's saying, it makes Bok Choy even more restless than he was.

"*Bokchoyflexinnachtrauglebok!*" comes the angry goobledygook from the boy's mouth. The Devastator responds with more rhythmic hissing and snapping. Bok Choy clutches me tighter.

"It's okay, baby," I coo. I yank the gun out of my top and point it directly at the Devastator, who immediately freezes.

"Yeah, that's right, not so tough now, are ya?" I say, trying not to shake so hard that I drop the gun (as I've been known to do in the past). "Let's see how tough you look when I blast your ugly face off," I say.

I really should be thinking up some killer one-liners to send my nemeses out on, 'cause these situations continue to present themselves with far more regularity than I ever could have anticipated just a few months ago, and I continue to find myself at a loss. Still, even if I *had* a line worthy of a flat-pic action hero, this fellow wouldn't understand it anyway.

I pull the trigger.

And nothing happens.

My body goes numb. I press the trigger again. Nothing. The gun is dead. In fact, it's probably been dead a very, very long time.

Marsden, you mother*fucker*.

"Okay, so . . . ," I say as the Devastator bares its creepy teeth once more, in what I can only imagine passes for an evil grin in Devastator Town.

"Bok Choy?" I ask my naked little buddy, setting the kid's feet down firmly on the ground. "You want to learn a new word?"

"*Bok choy?*"

"Run!"

I take off down the hallway, grasping Bok Choy by the arm. Thankfully, he seems to have no problem following me. Our only hope is if the north stairwell is still passable. Even if it is, it's all the way at the far end of the deck. And I don't know if we can outrun this monster.

The Devastator starts galloping after us, and I seriously

wish I did *not* turn around to look, because as he runs, his two strong middle arms come down to the ground and serve as a *second set of legs*, allowing him to move at tremendous speed. We've got a decent head start, but the stairwell is so far away. We are, to put it bluntly, screwed.

And then the whole ship rocks, sending us careening into the wall.

What was that? The ice breaking? One of Marsden's explosions?

No time to think. The shock has caused the Devastator to slip and fall, giving us a momentary break as he scrambles to right himself. With a burst of speed I didn't know I had, I make it to the north stairwell and exit the hallway. Bok Choy sprints along easily beside me, seeming to enjoy this game of chase quite a bit.

As soon as we enter the stairwell, however, I discover that the stairs on this level and all those below have completely collapsed. I skate right off the edge and am a hair's breadth away from falling to my doom, but I just manage to reach out and catch the edge of the last stair above my head and hang on by my fingertips, dangling over a two-hundred-meter drop.

Bok Choy deftly leaps over me and lands high up on the stairs right above me. He bends down and grabs my wrists.

"Careful!" I shout, knowing that he can't understand me. Fortunately, he *does* seem to understand that GIANT FLIPPING HOLES = BAD. Even more fortunately, these Jin'Kai fellows apparently gain their strength at a very young age. With minimal effort the little bugger pulls me up onto the stair, saving my life.

At least for the moment.

The Devastator crashes through the doorway, and Bok Choy and I book it up the stairs in the only direction we can go. The ship is starting to shift and turn. It *is* sinking. Why now, I don't know, but the way it's pitching means that the stairs are starting to level out straight, so that climbing them is like running across a ridged floor. It also means the next flight is practically pointed straight up. Impassable.

"Looks like this is our floor!" I shout as we make a run for the door.

We're on one of the old entertaining decks, which was left abandoned when the ship was turned into the Hanover School. It's mostly halls of shops and gimmicky restaurants, creating the feel of a chintzy shopping mall. The floor slants steeply downward, too steep to go in any other direction. We skim down the hallway with the Devastator still in pursuit.

Past all the empty store stalls at the end of the hallway lies the battered remains of an ornate set of swinging doors, one of which hangs loosely from its hinges while the other has broken away completely. It's the old ballroom. I've only been in there once, when the Hanover faculty thought the girls might enjoy a salsa dancing program in lieu of our normal aerobics regimen. That lasted about half an hour before it became clear that when both dance partners are sporting big old pregnant bellies, it's hard to successfully pull off a full dip.

I forgot how enormous the parquet ballroom floor was. It's easily half the size of a soccer field. Currently it's scattered with debris—overturned chairs and tables, fallen chandeliers, and assorted bits of caved-in ceiling. There are huge rows of aluminum windows on this level, so that dancers back in the day got a good look at the stars while they tangoed and waltzed. The sun is streaming in, and as my eyes adjust to the sudden brightness, I can see the ice rotate as the ship continues to move. We are very clearly sinking under the surface. Very soon this ship is going to bite it, and it looks like it's going to take every bit of ingenuity I have to get out alive.

Gee, I could've sworn I've been here before.

Again, Bok Choy and I have no choice but to follow the slope of the room. Judging by the view out the windows, however, a maneuver like that is going to put us below sea level, and I don't know how we're going to make it back out. But I guess we'll just have to cross that ice bridge when we come to it.

A deafening roar behind us clues us in that the Devastator has discovered our whereabouts. I spin around quick and watch as the behemoth barrels into the room, bringing the remaining door off its hinge. The Devastator stands up on just his hind legs and reaches behind his back with his middle two limbs. When he pulls them around again, he is wielding two enormous blades—straight along the back, rounded at the bottom, and running to a sharp point. Each blade is about the size of Bok Choy.

Nice craftsmanship, though.

The Devastator moves toward us, brandishing his weapons, just as the ship is suddenly jolted again. And then again. Two big blasts, one after another. The first blast shatters the windows along the side of the room. The second sends the ship lurching once more, and in a move so serendipitous it seems preposterous, a chandelier that was still hanging from the ceiling breaks free and crashes down right on top of our would-be assailant, covering him completely in rubble.

"Bok Choy," I say, "I'm starting to think that someone up there likes me."

*"Bok choy,"* Bok Choy replies. He's kind of a one-note conversationalist.

I turn back around, and my stomach drops. Water is pouring into the ballroom at the far end, and more is sure to follow as the ship continues its vertical realignment.

"We have to get out of here," I tell my cabbage-obsessed friend. We start back toward the door we came in . . .

And the chandelier lying in front of us flies up into the air. Underneath, the Devastator rears up, fanning his arms out and leaning toward us, gnashing and flexing his grotesque teeth.

The ship bucks sharply and we *sliiiiiiiiiiiiiide* down the steep incline to the side of the room that is rapidly filling with water. The Devastator loses purchase on the ground again (guess those big honking claw feet weren't built for smooth, slick surfaces) and rolls along with us. Just as suddenly, the ship lurches back down horizontally, shuddering with intense force as the aft section slams into the ice. When I manage to lift myself to my feet once more, I find myself standing ankle-deep in the water—which is rising rapidly.

While Bok Choy squats easily in the water behind me, I wince at the icy pain in my feet, looking around for anything I can use to defend myself. But even if there was something nearby, it probably wouldn't do much good against . . .

Against a monster who has stopped just a few meters from us, and looks . . . *nervous.*

The water, I realize. The cold.

*They have very durable exoskeletons*, Marsden said, *but no internal mechanisms to generate sufficient body heat to survive the climate here.*

I turn to look at the water. At the point where the windows meet sea level, the force of the incoming stream is severe. Past that, it shouldn't be too bad. Weak enough for us to swim out, at least. To where, I'm not sure.

But anywhere is better than here.

I turn to Bok Choy and make an exaggerated, cartoony gesture of holding my breath. He cocks his head but very quickly mimics the gesture. The Devastator catches on too, roaring again and pitching forward with blades extended. Before the blades can find their intended target (i.e., my head), I dive under the surface, clutching Bok Choy by the wrist. Right off the bat the blast of water coming in feels like the strongest undertow ever, pushing us sideways away from the windows. I swim forward at an angle, letting the push guide me deeper into the well, until we're past the worst of it. The razor-blade pain of being underwater has subsided, but it's too fast a shift to mean I've adapted. More likely I'm going into shock. I make a conscious effort not to pass out (*always* works), and head for the broken window port that leads outside. Beside me, Bok Choy does an impressive breaststroke, even with my grip on his arm. And as we swim, it becomes evident that he's guiding us even more than I am. Seems this kid is a bit of a water baby.

I don't look behind us as we push forward. There's no point. If the Devastator is there, we're dead. If he's not, I'm most likely dead anyway. So why risk having the last thing I ever see be that douchebag's ugly puss?

We swim through the window and immediately push upward. There is a strong pull on us from behind as the *Echidna* continues to sink, slowing our ascent. We're only a few meters from the surface, but it seems like we're swimming in place. My lungs feel ready to burst, and I'm starting to see spots in my vision. After several moments the ship is completely submerged and well below us. There is a swell underneath us as the ocean swoops in to fill the space, and we get pushed upward and break through to the surface. I inhale deeply—sharp, painful air filling my chest. Blinking the icy water from my eyes, I spot a large, seemingly steady ice floe and swim for it. Bok Choy races ahead and climbs on top, pulling me up after him.

"*Bok choy,*" he says sympathetically, and rubs my face with both his hands.

"You said it, buddy," I tell him. My whole body is quivering. Those weirdos in the Polar Bear Club are friggin *nuts*.

I push myself up onto my hands and knees and look around. There's nothing to see on the horizon, just ice and water. No sign of Dad, Mom, Cole, or Marsden. I do my best to concoct a scenario in which they might still be all right, but the odds are looking slim.

My reverie is broken by the rudest (and, seriously, *still* not dead?) Devastator to ever live, when he shoots out of the water and lands on the edge of our ice floe.

"Oh, for the love of God!" I scream. "How come no one around here just has the good grace to die?"

The creature roars, but it's a far weaker cry than his previous attempts. I also note that he's moving quite slowly as he approaches us. Creaky, like a *geriatric* alien monster. The cold really must be screwing with his system. Sadly, though, it's not screwing it up quickly enough to save us. I back away to the edge of the floe, the Devastator slowly dragging himself toward us, still brandishing one of his two swords. I glance around desperately. I honestly don't know how much more of being submerged in that water I can take. My head is soaked and numb. The ice around us is completely broken up in the wake of the *Echidna*'s sinking, and there are no ice floes close enough to move to. Actually, looking at them, it appears that what few ice floes were relatively nearby seem to be moving away from us.

No, those floes aren't moving.

*We* are.

The ice floe on which we currently find ourselves perched is actually slicing through the water with surprising speed, away from any other solid ice, as if it were being steered. The Devastator seems to have noted this too, and turns from us to look over the side. I look around as well, and after a few moments I realize where we're getting our propulsion from. A series of water spouts shoot into the air at the edge of the floe.

And you know the old saying: where there's water spouts, there's a group of killer whales who have been tracking you for days, trying to eat you.

There they are—four snouts just below the water to our left, pushing the ice floe out into no-man's-land. I grab Bok Choy's hand and run to the other side of the floe. The Devastator decides to take a more proactive approach—he lunges at the whales, slashing the water with his blade. And I guess that tactic was a pretty good one, because in a matter of seconds the water turns red and the whales disappear.

Which is awesome news and all, but I'm not exactly ready to throw a celebratory party, since there's still a *frigging monster with flexible teeth* standing right in front of me.

The Devastator turns his attention back to us, the matter at hand. However, he must not be as good a whaler as he thought, because suddenly I spot, behind him in the water, four dorsal fins, heading right for us. I try to think back to every Nature Channel special Ducky's ever made me watch, searching the recesses of my brain for some tidbit of useful information. Unfortunately, there's not much time, because the whales are going to be on us in a matter of seconds. The only thing that springs to mind is a vague sense that we should not stay on the edge. But I don't want to get too close to Toothy McTootherson, either. I decide to split the difference and take three steps toward the Devastator. He opens his jaws wide and winds up with his blade to make a—excuse the pun—*devastating* downward cut.

That's when the whales, swimming at full force, suddenly dive, right before hitting the ice. The result is a mini–tidal wave that sweeps across the top of the floe and sends all three of us sprawling. The Devastator loses the grip on his sword as his stroke meets the ice and slides backward to the very edge of the floe. His blade remains wedged in the ice.

They're trying to flush us off, I realize. They're trying to force us into the water.

I see the whales now, repositioned and speeding in our

direction again at full tilt. I grab Bok Choy's arm and start running *toward* the Devastator and the whales. The Devastator, now panicked, has the opposite idea, and passes us as he tries to run to the far side. He takes a vicious swipe at us, but I drop to my knees and lean back so that my head is practically on the ice, sliding past the alien warrior and toward the native Earth-born killing machines. As I slide by, I grab hold of the blade stuck in the ice, jolting me to a stop. Bok Choy's momentum takes him past me, and there's a wrenching tug on my arm as I stop him from sliding completely into the water.

The whales reach the floe and again dive under. The wave is even bigger this time and washes over us with a chilling crash. I hold tight to the blade and Bok Choy, sliding around on the surface but holding fast.

The Devastator is not so lucky, and seeing as he was already at the far edge, he gets washed right over into the water. His shriek is eardrum-piercing as he flails and splashes, the icy cold water freezing his joints. He claws at the edge of the ice in a futile effort to pull himself back up, but the whales are already there, waiting, and a maelstrom of churning blood and foam erupts as the four whales make a meal of the screaming alien. In a matter of seconds the would-be conqueror from another world falls victim to the ocean's deadliest predators.

There's a slight lull as the water calms around the floe, but I'm not fooled. The floe has gotten considerably smaller since the whales started attacking it, I realize. They're not going to quit now just 'cause they've had a snack. I huddle up tightly with Bok Choy, still holding on to the blade as an anchor.

Sure enough, within moments one of the whales fires out

of the water like a missile and lands almost the entire length of his body onto the ice, a fraction of a meter separating us. Bok Choy screams in fear as the massive mammal snaps its jaws at us. At this range I can see all the way down the animal's gullet. Its tongue is burnt black, as if someone set it on fire with a match.

Or like maybe it just recently ate an electric heating pod.

The whale and I lock eyes. I know they are highly intelligent creatures, but I wonder if they are evolved enough to understand trash talk.

"Muaah," I say, sticking my tongue out at the creature, wiggling it tauntingly.

The whale seems to get it and slaps the water angrily with its tail. The surface of the floe strains and cracks under the weight, and the blade comes loose in my hand. Without thinking, I lunge forward and gouge the Shamu wannabe right in the eye. It reels back, the blade still lodged in the side of its head, and slinks under the water. The other whales start circling the floe, closer and closer, nudging it, and I see tiny fragments of the ice break off and fall away. Pretty soon they'll have us in the water, and it will be over. Aside from my cutting wit, I am officially out of weapons. The sound of something moving beneath the surface grows steadily louder, and I make out a dark shadowy form shooting up in our direction. Black Tongue is coming for us.

But when it crests, I have another in a series of the "shocks of my life." What comes flying out of the water and passing over my head isn't a killer whale—it's the skiff. It lands with a crash on the surface and comes about, zipping toward us. The plating in the front makes it impossible for me to see who's inside. The whales scatter as the craft comes zooming in. As it pulls up beside us, we get a view of the passengers. Zee is driving, while Marsden and Cole sit in the rear. They're all sopping wet, seeing as the skiff has no enclosed cockpit.

I do not see my father.

"Come on, let's go!" Cole screams, holding out his hand to pull me in.

"Where's Dad?" I shout.

"I'm right here, dearheart." His voice comes weakly from the floor of the craft.

Thank God.

I pass Bok Choy across to Cole into the skiff. Bok Choy freaks out when Cole grabs him, and starts punching him in the face and neck.

"Ow! What the hell, kid, I'm saving you, dumbass!" Cole shouts. He looks at me, all bewildered. "*This* is the baby?"

Marsden pulls Bok Choy away from Cole and says something in Jin'Kai lingo that momentarily quiets the boy. Cole reaches back for me, and I take his hand. Just then the skiff is rocked to the side, and Black Tongue surfaces, locking his jaws on the bottom of the boat. He rips at one of the beam loaders attached at the rear. Cole finishes pulling me into the skiff.

"Marsden!" Cole shouts. Marsden stoops to pick up a small sack that looks like it's filled with gelatin and hands it to Cole. Cole shoves me behind him.

"Go!" he shouts at Zee. She pushes down on one of the nylon tubes running along the floor, which, as Dad accurately deduced, serves as the "gas pedal." As we rocket away, the beam loader breaks off into Black Tongue's mouth, still active. Cole leans out the side and brandishes the gelatin pack.

"Smile, you stupid bitch!" he screams, and tosses the pack right at the whale. Instinctively, the orca opens wide and snaps down on the projectile. The moment the pack is punctured, the gel spurts out. When it crosses the beam from the loader, it ignites in a giant blue fireball. There's a loud pop, and suddenly whale bits begin raining down on us from above.

"*Woo!*" Cole shouts, pumping his fist as he turns back around to me. "You see that! That's the line from that shark flat pic you like so much, right? 'Smile, you stupid bitch?'"

"Close enough," I stammer.

"You're freezing," Cole says, moving back to me and wrapping me up in a big hug.

"You're not much warmer," I complain, but I let him hold me. "The ship sank," I go on, stating the obvious.

"I know," Cole says.

"What happened?"

Zee leans back as she drives. "*Someone* set off too many explosives."

She's looking at Cole, who manages even in this temperature to blush.

"Dearheart . . . ," my Dad says weakly.

"Dad?" I pull away from Cole and look down to where Dad is lying flat on the floor. My heart stops in my chest.

My father is dying.

# Chapter Twelve

# WHEREIN THE BENEFITS OF FUSION-POWERED TRANSPORTATION BECOME ABUNDANTLY CLEAR

I always thought that I was particularly good at holding my shit together in stressful situations. After all, I have, in order, survived a murderous school faculty, a failing space cruiser, a batch of nasty aliens disguised as construction workers, the pretty aliens that had *protected* me from the construction workers, a gang of killer whales, a seriously complexion-challenged baddie from Planet Disgusto, and yet another round with the whales. And I'm still standing. But right now, watching my father struggle for breath as we speed along on the Devastator skiff, Zee at the helm—I am not doing a very good job at keeping calm and carrying on.

"Slow down!" I screech at my mother in the driver's seat, tears pouring down my cheeks. "Slow *down*! The wind's too much for him." We're racing across the ice so quickly that the wind is whistling around the sides of the skiff, blowing over us like a hair dryer set to "freeze dry." It is clearly having an effect on Dad's already damaged skin. "It's too cold. It's too—" I choke on my words, shaking Dad's arm as his eyes flutter closed again. His lips are ice blue, and his eyes are glassy.

"Wake *up*!" I holler.

"Elvie." Cole grabs my arms, squeezing me into a hug that he won't let me out of, no matter how hard I struggle. He's also, I should mention, literally *sitting* on Bok Choy, since the kid has done absolutely nothing but try to hurl himself from the skiff since we set off, and Cole can't seem to think of any other way to restrain him. "We've got to get him back to base as quickly as possible," Cole says calmly. "We can't slow down. It's okay, Elvs. It's okay."

"It's *not* okay!" I scream, struggling against Cole.

Since Cole is busy wrestling with me in his arms and Bok Choy under his butt, he can't make a move when Dr. Marsden moves forward and, to my horror, starts unfastening Dad's thermal suit.

"What are you *doing*? He *needs* that!" I bellow, trying to grab at him, despite Cole's hold on me. "That's the only thing that's keeping him warm!"

Marsden doesn't even attempt to explain himself. When he's tugged the zipper down as far as it will go, he uses his Jin'Kai strength to rip the seam, tearing the suit all the way down the middle and pulling each half off my dad's goose-pimpled body. He pulls off Dad's gloves, boots, socks, everything, leaving him naked except for his underwear. And even though such a sight might be traumatizing on a typical day, I'm much more distressed by the bluish hue of his skin.

His veins are bright purple—I can actually *see* them in his arms, his legs, as though his blood has simply frozen up inside him into a hardened mass.

"*Dad!*"

Dr. Marsden takes something out of his pocket—a plastic pouch that seems to be filled with some sort of liquid. He certainly has a lot of those. He squeezes the pouch in its middle until I hear a small pop, then shakes it vigorously.

"What is that?" I ask. "What are you doing?"

After shaking it another few seconds, Marsden puts the edge of the pouch in his mouth and tears the end away. With practiced speed he squeezes the entire contents out on Dad's chest. It's a clear, thick gel, which Marsden begins smearing all across my father's body. He spreads it to Dad's arms—even working it up underneath the armpits—down to the hands, pausing to get every crevice between my dad's fingers. Dad's digits have all swollen to nearly three times their normal size, the pressure from the inside straining the dark purple skin so badly that I'm amazed the fingers haven't burst right off his hands. Marsden works on my dad's toes, his legs, his hips. I look away as the doc handles my dad's more sensitive areas, tucking my face into the crook of Cole's neck to weep. I don't know what is going on, but I have a feeling I'm about to watch my own father die. And I'm not ready to see that.

"Elvs," Cole coos softly into my ear. "It's okay, Elvs. Look." And he nudges my head up.

"Dearheart."

It's my dad, blinking up at me. And he's smiling with his ice-blue lips.

My heart leaps in my chest. "Dad!" I cry. "You're okay, oh God, you're okay!"

I practically pounce on top of my father to give him a big bear hug, but Marsden stops me.

"Don't touch him," he says all doctor-like. "Give the gel time to work. He's still very weak."

Indeed, Dad's skin is still a ghastly shade, but the veins, already, are less noticeable. He bends his fingers, as though testing their strength. That gel, whatever it was, did *something* good.

"You're a very brave man, Harry," Dr. Marsden says. Then he turns to me. "He's fine for now. Let him rest. He's had a rough day."

I just blink at him. Talk about hard to read. Does this guy want us dead, or doesn't he?

I decide, for the moment, not to think about it too much. For the moment, my dad is okay. And really, that's all that matters.

"I'm not sure this is a better plan," I tell Cole as I examine the "child safety harness" he's whipped up for Bok Choy. Using strips from Dad's shredded thermal suit, Cole has decided to tie the kid to the backseat of the skiff, his hands bound tightly behind him. It's more effective than sitting on him, granted, but . . . "Child Protective Services would have your head on a spike right now," I say.

Cole just shrugs. His bruises from the beating Bok Choy's doled out to him are already healing, but I have a feeling he's well exhausted from trying to rein in the world's most savage (and most enormous) month-old infant. "Seems fine to me," he replies.

"Cole," I say with a sigh. But I don't really have anything to follow it up with. Bok Choy is making a lot of ruckus and thrashing about, just generally being an überhuman pain in the ass—but can you blame him when he has the strength of a He-man but the intellectual and emotional maturity of a U.S. Congressperson? Still, if anyone tied my darling Olivia to a car seat, I would go all caveman on his ass. I glance at Dad, sleeping as well as he can in the seat beside me. Zee and Marsden are at the front of the skiff, doing their best *Flight of the Navigator* to get us back to base, chatting all buddy-buddy. I can't hear them over the engine and the wind, but when Marsden turns and sees me looking at them, he gives me a smile. It's not his usual "charming snake" smile but rather one that seems warm, and honest—perhaps a reference to our harrowing escape, and the confusion we probably both feel about finding ourselves as allies. At least, that's how I read it.

I nod back.

And then, suddenly, I have an unsettling thought. "Hey, Cole?" I say—loud enough to be heard over the rushing wind but not nearly loud enough for the doc to hear me. Cole looks up. "You don't think that . . . Britta . . . ?" I point to Bok Choy. Britta had her fetus swapped too, just like Other Cheerleader. And what if *her* kid was sprinkled with Miracle-Gro too?

But Cole has other things on his mind.

"Ow!" he yelps. Bok Choy has gotten a hand free from his restraint and is bonking Cole repeatedly amidst a stream of "*Bok choy!*"s.

I scooch up right next to Bok Choy and take his hand,

stroking it soothingly. The kid stops flailing and looks at me, his chest heaving. I think back to when I was little, when I'd fall off the swing set or trip on the stairs and start bawling. My father would pick me up, put me on his knee, and start singing a song I thought I'd long forgotten. But as I start in on the melody, the words flow out like they've been inside me all along.

> *"I love you, yes I do, I love you.*
> *It's a sin . . . to tell . . . a lie . . ."*

Immediately the kid begins to calm down.

"It's working," Cole whispers, incredulous. "He likes it."

I smile and continue singing into Bok Choy's ear. I'm glad that I'm able to project my "inner peace" to the kid, but it's all an act. I'm not feeling calm in the slightest. And it's not just the day's deeds of derring-do, or the evil-alien-army-that-could-mean-the-death-of-us-all fiasco. Oh, those are big concerns. But right at this second I'm more anxious about the doting dreamboat smiling down at me. And if I'm being totally honest with myself, I've been kind of anxious about that for a while.

Cole, magnanimous doofus that he is, would do anything I asked him to, without blinking. And that should send me over the moon with happiness. It would send a *normal* girl over the moon with happiness. But that's the thing, isn't it—I'm not a normal girl. In the last year I've gone from typical suburban teenager whose most passionate love affair was with her lap-pad, to (oops!) mommy-to-be, to Rambo-lina-style survivalist, to half-alien hybrid fugitive. Not to mention that the bump in my belly has actually turned into a real-life *person*—a person who's going to depend on me for just about everything that I've always depended on others for.

*"Millions of hearts have been broken,
just because these words weren't spoken . . ."*

I'm changing, in more ways than one, and I'm going to continue to change, adapt, grow with the world around me. But Cole? Since I've known him, he's always been, well, *Cole*. Lovable. Beautiful. Generous to a fault. Which is how he'll always stay.

*That which remains still . . .*

*"I love you, yes I do, I love you.
If you break my heart, I'll die . . ."*

As I continue singing, gently tickling Bok Choy's arm to soothe him, I look up at Cole. I need to tell him. The best thing is to talk to him.

"Want some harmony?" he asks, leaning across the kid's body. "Two voices are better than one, yeah?"

I nod, sniffing just a little between lines, but Cole doesn't notice. It can wait till we get back to camp, I decide. There'll be plenty of time to talk there.

*"So please say that it's true when you say, I love yoooou . . ."*

"Elvs?"

I raise an eyebrow.

"I don't know this one," Cole says. "Can we sing 'Baby, Let's Go to the Prom with All Our Friends' instead?"

The skiff zooms along at approximately five billion times the speed of a dogsled, and we reach the Cape Crozier base before the sun even begins to sink below the horizon.

"Those dudes may suck," Cole says, hopping off the back of the skiff into the snow before we've pulled to a complete stop, "but they're flipping pro mechanics."

"Well, they had a little help from Harry Nara," I say, rubbing Dad's shoulder gently.

Zee puts on the brakes, and Cole helps me with the knots tying Bok Choy to the seat. There's still a lot of fight left in the kid, you can see that easily, but he's grown a lot calmer over the last couple hours. I think he's starting to like me.

"How's he doing?" Zee asks, coming around from the front of the skiff. And I know without looking up at her that she's not asking about the weird Jin'Kai superbaby, but rather about her once-husband.

"He's still sleeping," I answer. "Some of his color's come back, but I'm still worried that—"

"Is it always so quiet around here?" Marsden asks, cutting me off midthought. He's looking around all suspicious-like, as though worried we led him straight into some sort of trap. Which, if I were an evil villain like him, I guess I'd be constantly worried about too. Even the dogs, those we didn't take with us at the start of our journey, are sitting quietly at attention, their ears pinned back against their heads, observing us, but not barking or rushing up to us like I would have expected.

"Dude," I say to Marsden. "Chill out, all right? I told you, these Almiri are cool." And I'm realizing that I sound more like Bernard than I ever thought possible. For a second I think I see a shadow out of the corner of my eye, but when I turn, it's gone. "They'll want to talk to you, listen to what you have to say. No one's going to come barreling out at you with ray guns and slam your face into the snow."

Which is precisely when a horde of Almiri come barreling out of the cabin with ray guns, and slam all our faces into the snow.

"Okay," I say, snorting to push the ice flecks out of my nose. "Now you guys are just trying to make me look bad."

"Shut your trap, mule," spits the muscle man with his elbow digging into my back.

I crane my neck around to look my captor in the face. He's beaming down at me with smug glee. "Jørgen?" I shout. "You gave Captain Oates your word! He specifically instructed you—"

"Oates isn't in charge here," Jørgen counters. "As a matter of fact"—he glances around at our motley crew, half buried in the snow, and smiles—"it seems he's no longer in charge anywhere."

I've heard more touching eulogies.

"That's enough, Jørgen," comes a voice from the doorway. "Just bring them inside." I turn to find Alan, of all people, standing in the doorway, his arms folded across his chest.

"What are you doing here?" I ask.

"Hello, Miss Nara," he says, bland as ever. And then, as

easily as if he were ordering soup: "Search them."

The Almiri quickly begin rummaging around in our clothes, and Jørgen in particular seems a little fresher than is necessary.

"You and your friends failed to follow orders," Alan goes on. "And in the process you've jeopardized our security."

"Got them!" Jørgen says, pulling Marsden's hard disks from the inner pocket of my thermal.

"*We* jeopardized security?" I screech as Jørgen pulls me up and drags me to Alan, before handing him the disks. "If it weren't for us, those files would be twenty thousand leagues under the sea by now!"

We are pushed brusquely through the door into the cabin. Dad can barely stand, let alone goose step, so the Almiri are forced to pick him up and carry him.

The cabin is eerily quiet. And when we get downstairs, we realize why.

Alan has brought dozens of commandos with him, each of them wearing some sort of polar variant on the military-style outfits Cole and Captain Bob wore back on the *Echidna*. They stand at attention, sprinkled down the hallway, guarding each of the doors.

"Where's my baby?" I ask. "Where's Ducky?" I don't see him, or any of the Enosi, either, for that matter. "What did you do with them?"

"Almiri sympathizers in there," Alan barks to his cohorts, ignoring me completely. The soldier in front of the bunkroom door Alan points to stands aside as Cole is thrown inside. Before the door slams shut behind him, I see Clark's face, along with Rupert's and a few of the other friendlier Almiri. Alan continues with the rest of us down the hall.

"I want this scum"—Alan darts eyes at Dr. Marsden, who's vying for World's Best Scowler as he struggles against his captor—"and whatever the hell *that* thing is"—here Alan looks at Bok Choy, who has already bitten his warden half a dozen times—"in the pantry." He shoves me forcefully in my back. "Mules and humans in here." And seconds later I am tossed inside a bunkroom myself. Mom is pushed in right behind me, and the dude carrying Dad drops him carelessly on one of the other bunks. "We will deal with you later," Alan threatens before slamming the door shut.

The room is bursting with hybrids, absolutely every one of my mother's buddies who stormed the prison camp, hanging from the bunks, slouched against the wall, lying on the floor. Talking and arguing and generally sighing at one another. They stare at the three of us who've just joined the party. But I only have eyes for one person out of all of them.

"Olivia!" I cry, rushing over to where she's being cradled, by my one and only Ducky, in a bunk at the far end. "Thank *God* you're okay!" I scoop her out of Ducky's arms as he rises to meet me, and then I squeeze the Duck into such a tight hug, I nearly knock him backward on the bunk. "Ducky, it is so good to *see* you!"

"You're alive," he sniffles, squeezing me back. "Oh, Elvie, I was so worried. When those guys showed up . . . and you'd all been gone for so long with no word and . . . I know you said it might be longer, but . . ." He hugs me again. "I thought you were an icicle for sure."

"You have no idea," I say, snuggling with my precious baby. And, okay, I *know* she probably doesn't know who I am, really—her eyeballs barely work, for goodness' sake—but I swear, when little Olivia hears my voice, she looks right up into my face. And she smiles. "I'm never letting you go again, my precious girl," I whisper.

Ducky has crossed the room to my father, who's now surrounded by a fair amount of curious hybrids. "Is he going to be okay?" Duck asks me.

I look over at my father. He's passed out again, which is not surprising. His breathing is shallow and raspy. "I don't know, Duck," I say softly. Zee sits down on the bed next to Dad and covers him with a blanket. She begins to play nursemaid, asking the other hybrids for assistance. They seem more than happy to oblige.

Duck's eyes fill with concern as he inches back my way. "Elvie, are *you* okay?" he asks me seriously.

I'm not even sure how to begin to answer that. "Captain Oates is dead," I say instead. "Trying to save us. And the dogs. Bernard's gone too." I gulp down the tears that are starting up again and pull Olivia closer to my chest. There is nothing more comforting. "I saw them, Ducky." And when I look up at him, I can tell that I don't need to explain who I mean.

"You . . . ?" He trails off. And then, I guess, things have gotten just a little too serious for him. "How come you get to have all the fun, Elvie?"

At that, I can't help but laugh. I stroke my baby girl's head some more. I just can't get enough of her, really. "Where's her papoose?" I ask Ducky.

"Oh, it was right . . ." He looks around, then spots it on the bunk. "Hey, Marnie, can you hand me that . . . ?"

That's when the redheaded hybrid girl—the leggy, thin one with the long face—bounces up off the bunk where she was just sitting with Ducky and rushes to bring me the papoose. "Here y'are, Elvie," she greets me pleasantly with a medium-thick Scottish brogue. "We're so glad you've made it back all right. Donny's been feert out of his mind."

I take the papoose and raise an eyebrow at Ducky. "*Donny?*" I ask.

And suddenly this broad laces her fair, freckled fingers through my bestie's.

Ducky's face is beet red yet again. But he's also wearing a grin that won't quit. "Uh, Elvie, this is Marnie." He leans in close. "She's Scottish!" he stage-whispers at me.

"*Dur,*" I reply. And I strap Olivia in at my chest, where she belongs. "It's nice to officially meet you, Marnie."

"Likewise," she says with a kind smile.

And honestly, despite all the shit that's going on, I'm happy for Ducky.

Really.

As Marnie's fingers squeeze tighter around Ducky's, I can't help noticing the red sunburst lesion on the back of her right hand.

We are in that bunkroom for a long, long time. Hours, probably. We are not brought food. The guards on the other side of the door let no one out to pee. And, no matter how hard we beg, they make no concessions for my father, who—if left to his own devices much longer—will very surely die. I am a wreck. I sit, slumped, against the wall beside the door. I can't look at my rapidly expiring father. I can't look at "Donny," or Marnie, who for some reason—despite the fact that she has been nothing but lovely—is seriously pissing me off with her face. So I sit. I feed Olivia with what little milk my boobs have to give. Burp her. Rock her gently to sleep. Don't do much of anything, because I hardly have the energy to think.

And then I remember the book of maps.

"Hey," I say softly, approaching my mother where she sits in the corner. I don't know if I'll ever feel comfortable calling her "Mom," but after all we've been through, "Zee" is starting to feel just the smallest bit strange.

She looks up at me, and the adorable, snoozing infant strapped to my chest, and gives us a wan smile. "Hey, your-self," she says. She pats the floor beside her, offering me a seat, and I take it.

"How's the patient?" I ask, eyes darting up to my father.

"About the same. He's fine for now, but he's going to need treatment soon." She notices the thick book in my lap, with the worn edges, and her face brightens just the slightest. "Where did you find that?"

I hand it to her. "Under Bernard's mattress. I thought it might still be there from before we left, and . . . anyway, I thought you'd want it."

"I've been looking everywhere," she breathes. My mother carefully pries open the book and flips her way through its pages, taking in the rivers, roads, valleys, all of it. And it's strange, watching her study a map in a way I used to do myself—with the book she left my dad, back at home—but knowing that she's thinking something completely different while she does it.

"Are you still mad at him?" I ask her, as I rub Olivia's head. My baby girl drools onto the collar of my thermal, and I do not mind in the slightest. "For coming here, I mean?"

The pages crinkle as she turns to another intricately plotted map. "No," she says after a long while. "Bernard and I had our differences, that's for sure. But he did what he thought was right—he always did, that's what I loved about him, I guess. And I can't fault him for that."

"But you think he was wrong, coming here?"

My mother flips another page, and suddenly there we are—Antarctica. Cape Crozier. How weird to be a spot on one of my mother's maps, after all these years.

"I think if he hadn't been such a hardheaded, stubborn ox, we'd still be stuck in the same place we've found ourselves for a while," she replies. "And I wouldn't have found you."

We are quiet for a while more, watching little Olivia's perfect face as she snoozes. When I look back at my mom, she has returned her attention to the book of maps. As she runs her fingers over the hills and valleys of Antarctica, I notice something. Tiny, luminescent blue lights sprinkled across the page. They follow the lines of her fingers, then disappear. "It's *beautiful*," I breathe. The lights are like bitty fairies, traipsing down the page. The map I had at home didn't do anything like that.

She shuts the book closed, looks up at me, and smiles. "You know, Elvan," she tells me sincerely, "I think you may be right."

I tilt my head to the side. "About what?" I ask.

"This problem is bigger than one group's hatred or fear of another," she says. "Sometimes we do need to know when and where to look for help. Finding you, seeing how strong you are, even if not in the way I would have expected, it's made me realize none of us should have to make it on our own."

I think about that. "It can't be easy," I say with a slow nod, "being an avenging freedom fighter hippie ninja all the time."

At that, my mother laughs. "The health care plan is *shit*," she agrees.

Dude, I think we just shared a moment or something.

"Up, mules! Snap to!"

I don't realize that I've fallen asleep—Olivia snoozing soundly across my chest, head tucked under my chin—until I'm prodded awake by the end of a ray gun. "What are you, deaf? On your feet!"

"Jesus!" I hiss. "Would you mind being, like, point-oh-two times less douchy? You're going to wake up my—"

Olivia begins to wail.

"Well, great," I growl. "What do you want now? You've already got all of Marsden's files. Unless you came to help me change Livvie's diaper—"

"We're leaving," the offending Almiri soldier interrupts. "*Now.*"

Ducky is up on his feet in an instant, stepping between me and the soldier. "Where are you taking us?" he demands. Marnie, I notice, is up nearly as quickly, clutching Ducky's hand. But there are more pressing things for me to process at the moment.

"We're not taking *you* anywhere," Alan answers, entering from the hallway. "I have strict instructions from Byron to take only this one"—he jerks his head at me—"her parents, and the baby." He looks in my mother's direction. "Appears the 'Lord' misses his darling daughter."

"Wait, huh?" I say, trying to piece that together. "You mean . . ." My eyes land on my mother, and it is very obvious that there is *an enormous piece of our family history* that she's failed to disclose.

"Now, dearheart . . . ," she begins.

"Elvie?" Ducky says over his shoulder. "Everything okay?"

But I'm too busy rounding on my mother to answer him. "Lord Byron is your *dad*?" I squeak out. "How is it that neither he nor you thought it would be important to let me know—"

And my mother, my flesh and blood, has the gall to roll her eyes. "Let's not get into it right now," she replies. "It's very complicated."

Ducky slowly spins around, and his eyes have gone enormous. "Dude, Elvie," he says in all seriousness. "Are you telling me James Dean is your grandfather?" He does a double-take, from me to my mom. And, obviously, takes the enormity of this moment with the gravitas it is due. "You are totally kicking my *ass* at Six Degrees right now."

"We're leaving," Alan barks again. At the bunk where my father has been gasping for life for the past several hours, one of the other Almiri jerkwads is hoisting him not-so-gently to his feet. "Move it. *Now*."

"But . . ." I glance at Ducky. They're not making me leave him. Not really. "What's going to happen to everyone else?"

"None of your concern," Alan says curtly.

And just as I'm rising up, I feel a soft tug at my chest. At first I think it's Olivia, whose wailing is threatening to make me go deaf again (the girl, I'm starting to discover, does *not* like Alan). But no. It's my mother, attempting to surreptitiously tuck the book of maps into Olivia's papoose. I look at her, a question on my face.

"It's all right, Elvan," she whispers to me as she pats the book down in its hiding place for good measure. "Everything will be fine."

That's the last thing she gets out before she is whisked off her feet and shoved out the door. Baby Olivia and I are not far behind.

I don't even get a chance to say good-bye to Cole.

# Chapter Thirteen

# IN WHICH THE BEST-LAID PLANS FLY RIGHT OUT THE WINDOW

We pull up to the train depot, and Jørgen brusquely yanks Mom off the sled by the elbow.

"Hey, watch it, asshole!" I yell at him. He turns and glares at me with contempt, then reaches to grab me just as harshly, even though I'm cradling Olivia in my arms. I instinctively pull the baby out of his reach. "You really want me telling Byron why his daughter and granddaughter returned covered in bruises?" I ask.

Jørgen glowers at me, his arm still outstretched, frozen in place. I can tell he'd probably like to do a lot more than bruise me, but I'm too filled with frustrated rage at everything that's happened to give a shit. I shoot out a leg and kick his hand away.

"Hybrid or not," I snap at him, "I'm the Big Kahuna's god-damn granddaughter, so you better just slow your incredibly lame roll, tough guy." I guess you could say I've gotten over my shock and awe at the whole being-descended-from-James-

Freaking-Dean thing fairly easily. Possibly because it is among the less weird facts I've discovered about myself in the last week or so.

"From what I hear, he won't be the Big Kahuna for long," Jørgen snarls. "Now get moving."

The guards shuttle me, Dad, Zee, and Marsden onto the train and plop us down into the first car, facing one another. Marsden's face is blank, unreadable, and my mother just stares out the window at our last view of Antarctica. Olivia's stopped wailing, soothed slightly by the sled ride from the prison base, I suppose, but she's still squirmy, and I'm just waiting for her next meltdown. I rub my thumb through her fine, fuzzy hair, thinking about how I could really use a cheering-up from ever-optimistic Cole right about now. But Cole is back at the prison, and who knows what will happen to him. Who knows what *is* happening to him?

Next to me, Dad is not in good shape. His lips are still tinged blue, and his skin is pale and clammy, the remnants of the warm gel mixing with his perspiration and glistening sickly. Even inside his new thermal he's shivering.

"Don't you have any blankets or meds or *anything*?" I yell at Alan, who's standing in the doorway of our train car. He doesn't respond, though, just works his following-orders stony-silence thing. Probably steamed up that he keeps finding himself playing my chaperone to and from the South Pole.

I turn my attention back to Dad, while Olivia tosses restlessly inside her papoose. "Are you okay, Dad?" I ask softly, knowing it's possibly the dumbest question I've ever asked anyone in my entire life.

"I'm fine," my father replies, offering me a weak smile. But he's still trembling.

I take his hand in mine, meaning to be comforting, but he winces at my touch.

"Dad?"

"It's nothing," he says. "Just tender."

"Let me see."

"It's nothing, dearheart."

There's a gentle shudder as the train starts up, beginning its acceleration toward optimal docking speed for our transfer to the elevator. For a long while the quiet thrumming of the mag rail, and my dad's stammered breathing as he slips into a restless sleep, are the only noises that fill the car. Then little Livvie starts up with the pre-wails, kicking against my stomach.

"Liv, shush," I whisper, eyes darting to my dad as his eyelids flutter open-closed. The last thing he needs right now is an infant screeching in his ear. I try to channel all the inner calm I do not feel. "Be quiet, okay? Quiet, honey."

"Elvan, here, I'll take Olivia," Zee offers. She reaches out her arms. "It's about time I bonded with my grandbaby."

Grateful, I lift Livvie out of the papoose and hand her over to my mother, who takes her gently and speaks to her in hushed tones.

"*Shhh*, baby, *shhh*," my mother coos. "It's okay, dearheart. Yes, that's it. *Shhhhh* . . ."

"I always thought that was Dad's thing," I say. My mother looks at me curiously. "'Dearheart,'" I clarify.

My mother shifts Olivia up on her shoulder as the baby's muscles relax into an almost sleep. "That was my pet name for your father," she says quietly, smiling at Dad's figure beside me. "It's what my mother used to call me. Later I learned she got it from *my* dad."

And here I thought the only thing I inherited from my mother was a penchant for sass.

I turn my attention back to Dad, who—even half-asleep—is still cradling his hand with a pained look on his face. Slowly, carefully, I peel off his glove.

I suck in my breath hard. Underneath the glove Dad's fingers have shrunk back down to normal size, but the skin is loose around the muscle, and the fingers are a deep black-purple. I look up at Dr. Marsden, sitting handcuffed next to my mother.

"It's nothing," he says, as if Dad had merely slammed his knuckles in a door. "Just bruising. He won't lose the fingers."

"You're sure?" I ask. "He's not superhuman like the rest of—"

"I'm sure," Marsden replies. "I wouldn't say so otherwise."

"Changing the subject," Dad says, suddenly awake, his voice creaking with effort. I turn my gaze back to him, surprised he's conscious. He pulls his ungloved hand from my grip and cradles it gingerly in his lap. He clears his throat with the effort of gearing up to speak again. "Do we think we're heading back to the States?"

"Wherever we're going," Marsden replies, "it's not a mystery what will happen once we're there. I'll be interrogated, tortured for information. Then maybe killed, if the Almiri are feeling particularly brazen. And you three"—he gestures with his head at me, my mother, and Olivia—"well, we know what's in store for you."

I raise an eyebrow.

"Neutralization of the threat," he clarifies.

"If they wanted to harm them, they'd have done so by now," Dad says.

"It depends on what you consider 'harm,'" Marsden responds. He looks up at Alan, not two meters away and still pretending not to pay any attention to us. "Isn't that right, Almiri?"

"You mean they're going to sterilize us," I say, suddenly noticing that I have been unconsciously rubbing the back of my right hand, just the way Bernard used to.

"What *should* have been done," Jørgen says derisively, "were it not for the sentimentality of a misguided fool."

Byron, I realize, is that fool. My grandfather. It seems that in sending me to Antarctica to freeze my buns off, Byron really *was* trying to protect me—and his great-granddaughter.

"Byron will help us," I say quietly, mostly to myself.

The look on Marsden's face is that of a kindly uncle whose niece is blathering on about Santa Claus. "I think we're past that, Elvie," he tells me. "I admire your persistence in the face of adversity, but your failing is that you always put your faith in the wrong people."

The hum of the train reaches that familiar pitch, and Alan and the other Almiri gather us up to move to the docking car at the center of the train. As we enter, we discover that someone else has joined us too.

"*Bok Choy!*" Sure enough, standing between two Almiri guards, and wearing a small gray jumpsuit, is my new little buddy. Bok Choy is jumping up and down, grinning at me. I swear he looks like he grew another two inches since I saw him last. He's thrilled to see me, obviously, although whatever he's attempting to communicate in his strange, guttural language merely sounds to me like "Alka-Seltzer!"

I will take it.

"Hey, buddy," I say, offering him a small wave. He wrestles free from the guards and runs to me, wrapping me up in a big hug that's a little too tight, thanks to his burgeoning Jin'Kai strength.

"Alka-Seltzer frommle-garb!"

"Oof! Easy, buddy. You're made of tougher stuff than me," I say. But I hug him back just the same. After all, it's not his fault he's a genetically engineered attempt at a Jin'Kai supersoldier. I squeeze his muscly arm. "Alka-Seltzer's glad to see you, too."

At the wall Jørgen snorts.

I round on him. "So what's your reward for turning on the captain?" I ask. "A get-out-of-jail-free card?"

He looks down at me, face dripping with condescension. "When it comes to dealing with freaks like you, I would have gone against that priss's 'orders' for nothing. Getting out of that dump was just a bonus."

"How am *I* the freak?" I ask very earnestly. "You're the one with no balls." And before he can even give me a puzzled look, I have turned Bok Choy out of the way and brought my knee up to smash Jørgen in the groin with all my might.

These Almiri might be superstrong, superfast, supersmart, and super et cetera, but if you whack them in the twig and berries, even they will double over in pain and let out a string of hilarious expletives.

It's the consistencies of life that are truly reassuring.

"Now we don't have to worry about *you* reproducing any-time soon either," I tell him as Bok Choy laughs and claps his hands in approval. *"Bok Choy Alka-Seltzer Plop Fizz!"* he shrieks gleefully, or something close to it.

As one of the other Almiri pushes me back to the wall, Jørgen whips his head up, face flushed bright red like he wants to throw me right out of the train then and there. But he exchanges a glance with Alan, who shakes him off, as if to say "not here."

Jørgen slowly straightens up and takes a few breaths. "We'll see how much fight you have left when they're done with you," he says.

"That's enough, Jørgen," Alan tells him. "Everyone quit talking."

"My hero," I swoon.

The elevator swoops down into view, and pretty soon it and the train are zipping along side by side. The elevator closes in toward us, and then with a magnetic *thunk* the two are docked. The sound of heavy metal clamps locking into place lets us know it's safe to transfer, and the doors slide open with a *swoosh*. We step across into the elevator, me doing my best to shoulder the brunt of Dad's weight, and the guards sit us down on a long vinyl bench—all except Bok Choy, who's busy doing somersaults on the ground in front of us.

I lean across Dad to talk to my mother, who's still cradling Olivia. "I can take her back now," I say.

"That's okay," Zee replies. She smiles down at my precious girl, who has actually done a pretty good job of settling herself. "I think I could get used to this."

I smile, glad to see my mom finally letting her guard down a little bit. No matter what happens to us all, at the very least I have a mother. And that means Olivia gets to grow up knowing her grandmother. I think that, given the hardships she's probably going to face, that's going to be a good thing.

Dr. Marsden is calmly watching my mother bob Olivia up and down. He even smiles and sticks his finger out at the drooling little baby, who grabs it and gurgles happily.

"Strong grip," Marsden says.

"Like her mom," Zee says, smiling at me.

It's a weird scene.

"Sir?" one of the soldiers says, suddenly standing up rigidly straight.

"What is it, private?" Alan asks.

The soldier points out the window port, and I follow the Almiris' gaze outside.

The view from a space elevator window, I am coming to learn, is a pretty impressive sight. You watch the world below get smaller and smaller and smaller, and then find yourself passing through the clouds, then over them. There are airplanes to watch, and billboard projectors hovering thousands of feet above the ground. When you get higher up, you begin to see the occasional satellite still flicking about in the very lowest levels of the atmosphere.

What you rarely see, however, is a hovercraft zooming straight for you.

"Away from the door!" Alan screams, a split second too late. The small dark craft slams into the side of the elevator, sending us all sprawling to the ground. I have to roll to keep

Dad from crushing me as we tumble, and he lets out a grunt as he lands awkwardly on his bad knee. I look to Zee, who is anchored against the long bench across from the door, holding Olivia in a protective shell on top of her chest. Olivia is screaming, and Bok Choy is going to town too, shouting a stream of shrill Kynigos gobbledygook. All of a sudden there is a high-pitched whirring sound coming from the edges of the door.

It's chaos.

The Almiri are all shouting over one another, fighting to be heard as everybody does his best to right himself. Nobody seems to have any idea what's going on—everyone has the same panicked, confused look on his face.

Everyone, that is, but Dr. Marsden. Calm, cool, and collected. Somebody, it seems, knows *exactly* what's going on.

In one fast, brutal motion Marsden rises up and, with his hands still bound, grabs the nearest Almiri guard from behind, and snaps his neck, dropping the now-lifeless body without a second thought. Alan turns to see his compatriot on the ground and reaches for the gun at his side. But before he can draw, the elevator's warning siren goes off—indicating that we've lost pressurization—and in that instant the door behind Alan slides open, revealing six burly, ruggedly handsome soldiers, who open fire into the elevator.

Jin'Kai.

I instinctively curl up into a defensive position, one arm draped across my father—the closest person I can reach—to draw him in safe. But as it turns out, the maneuver is unnecessary. The Jin'Kai aren't aiming at us. Instead, they very precisely gun down Alan and the rest of the Almiri—all save for Jørgen, whom Dr. Marsden has locked in a chokehold. There's a gap of about one meter between the elevator and the hovercraft, which seems to be tethered to the elevator at four points, though it sways unsteadily as we continue to ascend up the cable.

"Doctor," one of the Jin'Kai calls across the gap to Marsden. "Good to see you, brother."

"Good to see you, brother," Marsden replies in kind.

"We need to move," the Jin'Kai continues. "Another two minutes and we won't be able to match the elevator's speed as it passes the apex of the Earth's gravitational well."

"No reason to dawdle, then," Marsden says. He looks down at Jørgen, whose eyes are bulging out of his head. "Jørgen, was it? It's been a pleasure. But about your desire to escape Antarctica at any cost?" Marsden forces Jørgen's head down so that he's looking at the gap between the elevator and the ship. Then, without another word, Marsden pitches the helpless Jørgen down—and his scream is immediately cut off by the air whipping around us. Marsden doesn't waste a second, scooping Bok Choy up by the arm. At first the kid resists him, turning to me and making a plaintive mewing noise. But before I can so much as scream in protest, Marsden easily and roughly tosses the boy across the gap into the waiting arms of the Jin'Kai.

Marsden then turns back to us.

"Time to go!" he shouts over the whirling winds.

"Where are you taking us?" I ask, crouching next to Dad.

"Sorry, Elvie," Marsden says, a genial smile on his face that belies the steel in his eyes. "Not you."

My mother stands up, still carrying Olivia, and makes her way to Marsden at the edge. My eyes go wide.

"What's going on?" I shriek. And as soon as I do, there are immediately three Jin'Kai weapons pointed at my face. One twitch, I realize, and I'm toast. My bones have very quickly turned to jelly.

Mom looks at me sternly. "You were right, Elvie, about needing help. Our people need help now. And I'll do whatever must be done to make sure they get it."

And that's when I notice the papoose, still strapped uselessly to my chest, despite the fact that there is no baby inside it. There is a steady, blinking blue light emerging from the bottom.

Bernard's book of maps.

My mother—my own *mother*—triggered a homing beacon. I reach for my baby, blissfully unaware in my mother's arms, but the gunmen only cock their weapons higher. I lower my hands. My chest is bursting with all I cannot do to stop the scene that's unraveling before me. "You called them here!" I spit at my mother. She and Marsden planned this together, I realize. Either while we were on the *Echidna* or on the way back—I dunno, but somewhere along the way they agreed to deceive me. I've been played. I am *useless*.

"Those with mutual enemies make for good allies," Zee says. My baby grabs for a lock of hair at the base of my mother's neck, and my heart pounds. "Someday you'll understand."

"You're going to trust *him*?" I shriek in disbelief. "The guy who just tossed someone to his death in cold blood?"

"Tossed an Almiri," she says. "I'll make sure Livvie's safe. Take care of your father."

And as she turns toward the hovercraft, preparing for the jump, I make a dash for my baby. Fuck the gunmen. But Marsden, of course, is too fast. With one quick flick of his arm he knocks me down on my ass. The soldiers across the way lock their weapons on me again, but Marsden raises his hands.

"No!" he hollers at them. "No need for that." He places his hands on Zee, sheltering Olivia from the wind and guiding my traitor mother as she makes the jump across to the hovercraft.

With what is probably the last of the strength he can muster, Dad inches across the floor and takes me into his arms. And I curl up in his lap, like the powerless child I am, and begin to weep. Marsden looks down at our pitiful little scene, that goddamn smile plastered on his face like he just gave us a great deal on a car lease.

"I'm truly sorry, Elvie," he tells me. "I'd take you with us, but we both know that our objectives are in conflict."

I look past him at Olivia. She's crying in my mother's arms, but I can't hear it, thanks to the wind.

"My problem is, I always put my faith in the wrong people," I say.

Marsden smirks at that. "Perhaps, given the opportunity, we could have come to an understanding," he tells me. "But there's no time for that now. They're coming. And we need to be prepared."

"Hey, Dr. Marsden?" I say. He lifts his eyebrows. "I'll be seeing you again. Real soon."

"Please, Elvie," he says, still smiling. "It's Ken."

Marsden leaps easily across to the hovercraft, which is starting to tremble and shake as it struggles to maintain a matching speed with the accelerating elevator. Then he turns and gives me a wave as the hovercraft's door closes and obscures my view of Olivia.

The ship—and my daughter—pull away from us. Tears are streaming down my cheeks, but I don't even have the energy to sob. I've never felt so hollow in my entire life. So enraged and yet so helpless.

"No, *don't!*" Dad shouts in my ear. I don't know what he thinks I could be doing from my place on the floor, but quickly I realize that it's not me he's yelling at.

Alan—bleeding out but not dead—has dragged himself on his stomach toward the door and is aiming his blaster at the hovercraft. But he's a split second too late. As the hovercraft tethers disengage from the elevator, whatever overrides our Jin'Kai attackers had in place go offline, and the elevator door slams shut.

Just in time for Alan's shot to blast it right off its hinges.

The explosion is loud—leaving a large gaping opening out into what is quickly going to be space. The Jin'Kai hovercraft must have been using some sort of pressure regulating field while it was attached, and with it gone, the instant pressure drop immediately sucks Alan out of the elevator, without so much as a peep.

No sooner do I witness Alan's quick and silent death than I begin skittering across the floor myself, but Dad grabs me with a fierce grip and pulls me in. He's braced himself along the wall. The dead Almiri, who do not have quick-thinking fathers on board, fly out the hole in the side of the elevator right after Alan. I watch them float on the air like macabre kites without strings as my father clutches me tighter to him. The air is incredibly thin, and I'm getting light-headed.

"I can't breathe!" I shout.

"We need to get out," Dad hollers back. "We're about to cross into the atmosphere and get pulled up into space!" His hold on me still brace-tight, he motions with his elbow to the wall above our heads, where the red emergency sign is blinking. Directly beneath it sits the release lever.

God, I hope the Almiri keep this thing up to code.

With Dad bracing me, I lift myself up the meter and a half or so toward the lever. It takes every ounce of strength I have, but at last I've got a grip on the lever. It sticks when I try to pull it, so I reach up with my other hand, and using all of my weight, I yank it down hard. The emergency panel pops off, revealing a bright yellow package behind it. The Velcro *riiiiiiiiiips* as I tear the package from the wall, clutching it to my chest against the pull from the opening behind me.

It's the funniest-looking parachute I've ever seen. On closer examination I realize that's because it's not a parachute at all — it's an air raft, essentially a large inflatable cube. I've seen vids of them, of course, but usually on the same kind of sites where you go to watch idiots trying to ride their bikes down a handrail and breaking their faces in the process. I did *not* know the things were used as emergency escape devices.

Velcroed to the wall behind the raft are at least twelve smaller packages, presumably jumpsuits. I rip two down and hand one to Dad before tearing open the flimsy package. It's not a jumpsuit.

It's a flipping gliding cape.

Good thing Ducky's not here.

"There's no way these things will work this high up!" I cry.

"It's just a precaution," Dad assures me weakly, already slipping the half jacket/harness on awkwardly with his free hand. He pulls the hood and goggles down over his head. "In case something happens with the raft."

Like I'm so sure *that* thing will work either.

But there's no time to argue. The elevator is still climbing higher and higher, and it's getting more and more difficult to struggle against the pull from the opening, and the blast marks around where the door blew off the hinges are fizzling dangerously. Braced firmly against the wall, I toss off the papoose with the goddamn book of maps and pull one arm, then the other, through the sleeves and zip up the front, the long nylon drapes flapping out toward the gap.

"Ready?" I ask Dad, positioning my hand over the pull string on the side of the raft.

"As I'll ever be!" he shouts back.

I give a sharp tug. Something pops, and the raft starts to inflate. Only problem is, I neglected to unfasten the bindings holding the folded-up contraption together.

Note to self: always read the instructions.

Dad and I wrestle to pull the bindings off the swelling raft, which pinches and rips at our fingers as it expands beyond our control. One binding does pop off, due less to our efforts than to the sheer pressure of the rapidly inflating raft. But it's unfortunately no cause for celebration—the force of the popped binding sends the raft shooting away from us, across the elevator floor, where it is promptly sucked out the window.

Shit.

Looking out the opening, I can see the raft below us, which is—rather infuriatingly—inflating just fine now that it is several dozen meters away.

"Aim for the raft!" I hear Dad cry, and before I can even turn back to look at him, my *hypothermic father* lets go of the wall and is sucked out into the open air.

"Dad!" I screech after him as I clutch tighter to the bench—the only thing between the certain death of the void of space and . . . well, certain death. The elevator is rocking violently side to side now.

I don't have a choice.

I jump.

I'm not sure exactly what I thought the sensation of flying out into near space would be like, and I'm still not sure, because for the first few seconds I'm pretty certain I'm passed out. As soon as I come to, I'm hurtling downward at terrifying speed. My nylon cape is flapping behind me, seemingly doing nothing. I look around frantically, the wind brutally fierce against my neck, before spotting the raft below. Sure enough, the giant contraption is fully inflated, more spherical than cube-shaped. A few seconds more of searching and I lay eyes on Dad, whizzing nearby. He's soaring like a flipping bird, arms outstretched, his cape filling and falling as the sensors in the material adjust automatically. It's hard to hear much of anything, but it definitely sounds like the noise he makes as he goes past me is *"Wheeeeeeeeeeeeeeeeee!"*

Trying to follow suit, I extend my arms, and the nylon under them catches the air—which has the effect of violently jolting me backward, as if I were attached to something above by a string. It takes a little getting used to, but soon I find myself flying in slowly descending circles. Too slowly. The air is incredibly thin, and I'm still way too high up—much, much higher than Dad has managed to get. I'm not sure why I haven't passed out again, but perhaps it has something to do with the time I spent in the zero-grav hangar bay on the *Echidna*. Could it be possible that my hybrid physiology took the opportunity to adapt to low-oxygen environments?

Well, if I have rapid adaptation on my side, my father has sheer ingenuity—and at the moment, his seems to be the greater gift. Still struggling with my own stupid suit, I watch as, farther and farther below me, Dad flattens his arms against his sides and shoots toward the raft with uncanny speed, until an instant later he penetrates the surface through one of the collapsible side openings and disappears.

So Dad's safe. That much is a relief.

But I'm not safe yet. Mimicking my father's body positioning, I straighten out and aim myself as best I can at the raft. And all at once I'm zipping downward, air roaring in my ears as I cut through it like a goggle-wearing knife through butter. I'm focused on that raft, nothing else even entering my thoughts, until I hear the boom, so loud it resonates through my entire body. I feel a tremendous push from behind me, as though the very air is attempting to escape from something.

The elevator has exploded.

Right on the cable. A glance above tells me as much. The damage must have been more serious than it seemed. The spray of debris spans wide above me, but that's not the scary part. The scary part is the large, thick cable, which has been severed and is snapping down so fast that I barely have time to roll out of the way. My roll sends me spinning out of control, and even when I extend my arms again, I'm rolling too fast for the materials sensors to determine which way is up. The fabric tenses and relaxes erratically, sending me flipping end over end. As I am bounced around in the air, I watch in dizzy horror as the cable comes down and slices right through the air raft.

Dad . . .

The raft immediately deflates, two halves flapping flaccidly down toward the ever-approaching ground. The cable whistles past me, crashing into the train depot far below, creating a dozen more explosions that pop one after the other in rapid succession. I focus my attention on one half of the deflated raft. The half that seems considerably chunkier than the other.

I pull my arms in, a human arrow once more, and soon I'm righted and heading toward my father. What I *hope* is still my father. I speed down until I'm just above the tattered raft, and reach out to grab it. Doing so causes my cape to reengage, pulling me up and away from the raft, so I clamp my arms down again until I crash right into it, and I make hard contact with what is pretty clearly my father's gut. Now the raft, my father, and I are spiraling down to the Earth as one, so quickly and loopily, I'm surprised I haven't pulled a Ducky and spray-barfed everywhere, but I manage to gather my senses enough to pull at the folds of the raft until I find my father. He is half-conscious, but as far as I can tell, still alive.

I would cry with sheer relief, if I weren't, you know, otherwise occupied.

Using my last reserve of strength, I yank the folds of the raft away from my father, and soon we're both in freefall. I'm clutching Dad between my knees, like he's a flipping pony, and my cape is struggling against the weight of two people.

"Come on, Dad, wake *up!*" I shout into the wind. But the words are only flung back into my face. I kick my father in the side, and—I'm not sure I've ever been so happy—I feel him stir. He lifts his head, looks around, and then seems to sense that I'm holding on to him. With one reassuring squeeze of my leg he wiggles free from my grip and extends his own arms.

Crisis averted. Now all we have to worry about is smashing to itty-bitty bits on the ice.

As we near the surface, I'm keenly aware that even with my cape, I have too much velocity. I have to either create more drag or—if I can't lessen the speed of my impact—try to find a way to level out my trajectory, and land as close to parallel with the ground as possible. I lift my arms out and slightly over my head and pray that the sensors don't bug out again.

Thankfully, they don't, and I reach about thirty or forty meters above the ground before I level out. Beneath me the train depot is gone. The cable has smashed it to smithereens, and fires are scattered around the ruins.

Fire in the snow.

I circle down, closer and closer. Soon I'm only a few meters above the surface, but I'm still traveling so quickly, I know that I'll break every bone in my body if I touch down. I arc instead toward one of the larger fires. The heat has melted a good deal of snow, creating a slushy surface. My feet touch down and scrape along the ground before I drop completely, hitting the mush hard and plowing through it like, well, like a plow.

I come to a stop, breathless, and it's several minutes before I can convince myself to move. I'm afraid I might be in shock and not even aware that I'm now a cripple for life. But as I lift one trembling arm, then the other, and push myself up, I realize to my very great relief that I am, in fact, still in one piece. I probably have the world's worst case of snowburn, but hell, considering that I just *flew down from space*, I think I did all right.

I can't quite muster the strength to stand. My legs feel a bit like wet spaghetti. So I merely sit in the snow, looking around me. I spot Dad, walking toward me from a short distance away. For a dude who nearly bit it numerous times in the past twenty-four hours, he's looking pretty good.

He's even smiling.

"Landed in the slush, right?" he asks, as if we were discussing our preferred shortcuts to the mall. "Used the softened surface to your advantage?" I nod rapidly, smiling back like a loon. Too much adrenaline. My dad is okay. I'm okay. My whole body is vibrating.

"Smart thinking," Dad says as he reaches me. "You are your father's daughter." Then he gets a weird look on his face and turns his gaze skyward, where tiny bits of debris still trickle down like burning sleet. "Huh," is all he says. And he collapses into the snow, unconscious.

After checking to make sure that he's still alive and well, and finding the answer to be yes on both counts, I push myself up onto my knees and try to get a lay of the land. The train depot was a several-hour dogsled ride to the camp, but there are no sleds remaining in the wreckage strewn around us, so we're not getting to shelter that way. I shiver suddenly, and I realize that the skin on my face is covered in ice crystals. Not from when I landed but from the way down.

And it's getting colder.

I might be able to survive the dropping temp for a while, but I don't know if I can make it all the way to the camp, and that's if I even knew which direction the camp *was*. And Dad, in his state, definitely won't make it. There's no shelter anywhere—the best we can do to offer us any protection against the chill is to stay close to one of the fires until it burns out, which probably won't take very long. But I won't die. I will *not*.

I have a little girl who's counting on me.

"Elvie?" Dad's voice calls out weakly from beside me in the snow.

"You still with me, Dad?" I ask, trying to sound cheery. My voice, though, is incredibly hoarse. No doubt a result of all the screaming I did on the way down.

"I fear I have concussed myself," he tells me.

I try to laugh, but nothing comes. I feel completely empty. All I can muster is a cynical exhalation. Dad, still lying on his back in the snow, reaches out and pats my knee reassuringly.

"It's okay," he says. "We're okay, Elvie."

"I know, Dad," I reply. But I *don't* know. Literally the only thing we've got going for us right now is that we're alive. And when you add up everything that's against us, it really doesn't seem like much at all.

"Maybe that penguin is coming to help us," Dad says wistfully.

I look at my dad. His head is turned to the horizon, a dazed smile on his face. His ruddy windblown cheeks offset the slight-blue tinge that still remains on his lips.

"Unless the penguin has a sled, Dad," I say, choosing to humor him just for the moment, "I don't think it'll be much good to us." I stroke his face gently. It's starting to snow, but the heat from the fires is causing some of it to melt on the way down, and the drizzle blurs my tears. *This is it,* I think. *This is where I'm going to lose him.*

"Elvan Sabeth Nara, I did not raise you to be a quitter," my father replies stubbornly. "Did I?"

*Stay brave, Elvie. Stay brave.* "No, sir," I say, and I even manage a smile. "I'm not giving up." I squeeze his hand tighter. "Not ever."

"Good, then." He focuses past me into the distance again. "Because it appears that the penguin *does* have a sled."

Um, zuh?

Sure enough, there is a single black speck on the horizon, waddling toward us.

No, not waddling. *Mushing.*

I stand up, my legs unsteady underneath me, and wave my hands over my head. "Over here!" I screech. "Over here!" I don't care who this person is—friend, foe, Almiri, Jin'Kai, human, hybrid, or Jehovah's Witness. I just care that they see me. "Over *here!*" In this moment I could not care less about the genetic race war between warring alien factions. I am not concerned with the potential invasion from some even scarier force that Marsden seemed so freaked about. An armada of those Devastator chumps? Get in line.

I'm getting my goddamn baby back.

"Over here!" I continue, shouting like a maniac against the wind as the sled looms ever closer. "We're alive! Here!"

"Ahoy!" comes the call back, and I stop waving my arms, stunned. Perhaps, like my father, I too have suffered a concussion. Or a stroke.

Yes, I'm definitely having a stroke.

The sled swooshes up in front of us and comes to a halt. The dogs are yammering excitedly at the chaos around them, but the driver of the sled barks sharply at them to heel, and immediately they all fall silent and sit in place, looking up at him obediently. He's wearing a long scarf wrapped around his head, but I don't need to wait for him to finish unfurling it to recognize who it is underneath. I rush him, leap atop the sled with my wobbly legs, and give him the most gigantic hug in my repertoire.

"I thought you got eaten by killer whales," I tell him.

"Whales?" Oates says with a dismissive laugh. "Me? That seems unlikely."

I'm sobbing into his coat now, full-on shuddering sobs. The first good news in days, and it makes me bawl like an infant. I don't know how he survived. Maybe the whale swallowed him and he punched his way out, like Jonah reincarnated. I'm just glad he's here. The rush of emotion has allowed the pain to gush out, and it gushes all over Captain Oates's chest. He holds me tightly.

"It's all right, child," he says as I blubber.

"They took her," I gulp out between sobs. "Olivia. They

took her. Marsden and . . . and my mom. They're gone."

And he doesn't even bother to ask how Marsden is still alive, or where he and my mother have gone off to. He just straightens up and replies coolly: "Well, then, I think we'd better go find them."

I look up at Oates, tears streaking my face. He's gazing down at me with a kind, loving expression, but it's hard, too. This is a dude who wrestled with a killer whale under the ice and came back without so much as a scratch on him. If you had to go track down a bunch of asshole Jin'Kai who had kidnapped your daughter, this is the mofo you'd want on your team.

"Yeah," I sniffle. "We'd better go find them."

Oates helps me lift Dad out of the snow. Dad, for his part, doesn't seem surprised in the slightest that Oates is alive, although he's disappointed that there are no actual penguins on the sled.

"We'll need to get Cole and the others from the camp," I say as I settle myself next to Dad on the sled. "Cole, Ducky, the Almiri, the hybrids. All of them. And then we're finding a way out of here. If Bernard can walk all the way to Cape Crozier from the coast, we can find a way back out. Together."

"I see," Oates says. Then, slowly: "There are many Almiri still at the camp who want nothing to do with you and your new friends."

"They can remain here if they want," I say matter-of-factly. "Or they can come with. But they sure as hell better stay out of my way."

Oates looks at my superserious face and nods. He slides effortlessly into his seat on the sled. The dogs sit with their heads turned, watching him anxiously, tails wagging, eager to get running again.

"All right, then, my dear," he says, giving me a small nod. "What are we waiting for?"